LIGHT
ON A
DARK SECRET

BY
GLYNNIS HAYWARD

Light on a Dark Secret

Published in England
by
Abela Publishing Ltd.
Sandhurst, Berkshire, England

Email: Glynnis@AbelaPublishing.com

Website:
www.AbelaPublishing.com/GlynnisHayward.html

ISBN 13: 978-1-909302-10-5

First Edition, 2012

An invisible red thread connects those who are destined to meet, regardless of time, place, or circumstance. The thread may stretch or tangle, but it will never break.

- An ancient Chinese belief

GLYNNIS HAYWARD

ACKNOWLEDGEMENTS

I am grateful to former President Nelson Mandela and publishers Little, Brown Book Group, for giving permission to quote from his autobiography, *LONG WALK TO FREEDOM*.
(Copyright © 1994 Nelson Mandela)

I am profoundly thankful to my friend, actress and writer, Penny Bunton. She reviewed my work with insight and honesty. Penny also shared her story with me as she searched many years, on multiple continents, to find her birth mother. I was honoured to be part of the search party; it was her quest that sowed the seed for *LIGHT ON A DARK SECRET*. Other friends, who are adoptive mothers, enabled me to see the story from their different perspectives. My thanks go to them as well.

I am also thankful to Ken Andrew for sharing his experience and knowledge of South African politics during the apartheid era.

Thanks to Kristin Campbell Hart for describing her experiences as an American student, studying abroad in South Africa. Her observations were illuminating.

My family has been patient and supportive. Writing can be solitary, but Brian listened, critiqued and encouraged; Graham and Kate's design advice was invaluable; artwork on the cover is from an original pastel by my daughter, Lindsay Rothwell. Thanks to all of you.

Last, but not least, thanks to John Halsted of Abela Publishing, for his guidance and patience.

4

FOREWORD

"Apartheid not only discriminated politically and economically against people who weren't white, it also dictated how everyone conducted their private lives, from conception to the grave. The Immorality and Mixed Marriages Acts were two of the laws that caused widespread angst and misery. As an opposition MP, I was asked to assist people who wanted to change their race classification so that they could marry someone they loved, but who was classified in a different racial group. It was distressing to witness what personal pain and suffering was caused by those Acts that outlawed intimate relations and marriage between races.

As the impracticality of apartheid became obvious and unmanageable, adjustments were made and some Acts were repealed. But through the 1980s, the apartheid government was determined to maintain an iron-fisted grip on the situation; bannings, detentions without trial and hit squads remained regular occurrences."

- Ken Andrew.

Ken Andrew was an opposition Member of the South African Parliament from 1981 to 2004. He was heavily involved in the constitutional negotiations from 1992 to 1996 that brought about longed-for change to the new, democratic South Africa with Nelson Mandela as president. Mr. Andrew has long been an advocate of human rights and an important voice in South African politics.

The Immorality Act and Mixed Marriages Act
were both repealed in 1985.

All characters and events in
LIGHT ON A DARK SECRET
are fictional.

PART 1

VALERIE SPENCER

Injustice never rules forever.

- *SENECA*

GLYNNIS HAYWARD

Chapter 1

When I think back, it's hard to know which was greater: happiness, because I was in love – or fear, because I was in love. Whatever my feelings were, despite the obvious dangers of our love affair, I was in denial that we might be caught. I was young, after all.

Johan Barnard came into my life at a student conference when I was eighteen years old. He caught my eye immediately I entered Student Union Hall; he was standing on a raised dais, engrossed in conversation with the Student Council President. The room was teeming with so many people that their voices reverberated around the brick walls and high ceiling, making it sound like a crowded bazaar. It was my first year at University and the freedom of new ideas and people was exhilarating. This conference was a novel experience for me; we were combining forces with students from the medical school, situated on a different campus. They were not on a different campus because they were medical students, but because we were white and they were not. Ours was a whites-only campus, by government decree.

It was August, the beginning of second semester, and although it was winter, the days were warm and sunny. Returning from July vacation, many of us had been congregating at our usual meeting place on the steps leading down into the Student Union. That's where I heard that somebody in one of the men's residences had obtained the banned Pink Floyd tape, *Another Brick in the Wall*.

Supposedly it was top secret that he had it, but it was fairly common knowledge. News like that spread fast. Who cared that the government deemed it subversive? We were elated that somebody, returning from a controversial cricket tour to England, had smuggled a copy into the country. Protestors had boycotted their matches wherever the team had travelled abroad, so their only real success was getting hold of contraband. It not only satisfied our curiosity to see what we were being denied, but it was also an act of defiance; we didn't want to be cut off from the outside world because of a government we despised. Customs officials rigorously searched luggage of returning overseas passengers, so it was a miracle to outsmart them. This smuggler had sewn the tape recording into a cricket pad. Banned books and magazines were confiscated from the rest of the team, but the tape went undetected – a small victory in the battle of students versus government. Buoyed by this win, I entered the Student Union Hall with plans to hear the music later.

That was the moment when I saw Johan. I couldn't stop staring at him; he was so good-looking that I was surprised not to have seen him on campus before. I'd been there a full six months already; there weren't so many people that somebody like that would go unnoticed for long. He stood out from the crowd; tall, dark-haired, with a self-confident presence. Eager to see his name tag and try to wangle a meeting, I pressed forward – and then I saw his visitor's sticker. I froze in my tracks. He was a coloured student from the medical school.

I'd been brought up not to notice blacks and coloureds, except as hired help who worked for white people. There was nothing menial about this man. Despite the shock of realizing he was coloured, I couldn't take my eyes off him – and I was close enough to see that he had noticed me too. When I moved away, his eyes followed me. As I was wearing platform shoes that made me taller than usual, it wasn't easy to slip out of sight. Attention from a coloured man made me nervous and uncomfortable, even if I found him attractive.

The noise quieted as organizers requested that everyone take a seat. By then, despite my tactics to avoid him, he had disengaged from the president and maneuvered close enough that he could speak to me. Before I could obey my instinct to walk away, he introduced himself and I discovered that his deep voice was as magnetic as his looks. "Hi, I'm Johan Barnard." His eyes twinkled as he put out his hand to me, showing no concern that we were from different racial groups.

The year was 1980 and I had never before shaken a hand that wasn't white. My childhood had been spent with a Zulu nanny, Goodness, looking after me. I played with her two children, but on reaching puberty, I was sent away to a whites-only boarding school and our contact ended. Goodness remained in my parents' employ, working as a cook, but her children disappeared from my life. I never really touched a black person again, although Goodness would still hug me sometimes if nobody else was looking.

My hand was trembling as I reached out to shake his hand; admiring him from afar was one thing, but having contact with him was drastic. In a voice barely audible, I said, "I'm Valerie Spencer."

I was attending the conference as a Zulu translator because I spoke the language fluently. It was a skill learned growing up on a farm in Ixopo, a small village in the heartland of Natal Province, South Africa. Although I wasn't much interested in politics, my language skills were useful for NUSAS, the whites-only students association at racially divided South African universities. Johan was a delegate representing the black campus of our University; he'd been on the council of SASO, a black students' organization that had been banned three years earlier.

The South African government of the day had an elaborate system of classifying people according to their colour; Johan was 'coloured' because he was of mixed race (which included anybody who wasn't totally white, whatever the mix). He was swarthy and Mediterranean looking – his genetic mix could have included many nationalities. Peter Naidoo, a friend seated on the other side of him, was 'Indian.' His forbears had come from the Indian subcontinent over a hundred years ago, to work on sugar plantations. Johan and Peter were both 'non-white' by government classification. They could fraternize together. I, however, was 'white;' this group was to be kept separate from 'non-whites.' Relationships between races were made extremely difficult by laws put in place to keep us apart – and as for sexual relations across the colour bar, they were absolutely forbidden. We hated the terms by which the government classified us, but that's what we were; I was 'white' and Johan was 'coloured.'

I sat next to him, acutely aware that I had never sat next to a coloured man before. It was a reflex action to put my head down and study the floor. After a few deep breaths to compose myself, I looked up and saw people staring at me. Johan leaned over and whispered, "Don't worry. You aren't breaking the law." I was embarrassed that he had noticed my discomfort, but his confidence made me feel more at ease. I tried to concentrate on the speakers, who were taking their seats on the dais.

The conference opened with the President's address. He observed that for every step forward we made in the struggle against government policies, we seemed to go backwards two steps. He spoke of the announcement by the Dutch Reformed Church of South Africa, which – in its interpretation of the Bible – had helped devise apartheid. But now, after many years and much introspection, they had declared their opposition to the *Immorality Act* and the *Mixed Marriages Act.* These laws were the backbone of apartheid; they prohibited sexual relations and marriage between the races. It was an inconceivable breakthrough the church had made. But then came the backward step; the government, as if in retaliation, immediately sentenced nine people to prison for undergoing guerilla training abroad and recruiting others to do the same.

"Don't be cowed by them," he urged students. "We must show solidarity with fellow students of all races. It is not enough that coloured schools and universities are the only ones to boycott classes. We should do the same."

There were roars of agreement, but also much heckling. Someone leapt up shouting, "What good will that do? We'll be arrested like those coloured school kids in Johannesburg who confronted the police. They squelch us at every turn with the *Riotous Assemblies Act.*" Others shouted, "I'm not going to jail for them," and "I can't afford to pay for classes I don't attend. I need to get my degree."

There was loud reaction to this and retorts of, "You take advantage of the colour of your skin – shame on you." Arguments were drowning out any discussion.

Amidst the turmoil, Johan stood up and walked to the dais. His stride was purposeful and his poise was commanding. All eyes turned to him as he took the microphone and began to speak.

"We are at war; all of these things are skirmishes and battles. Some we win and some we lose, but believe me, ultimately we will win. You see, it is not a war of black against white; it is a war of darkness fighting the light of justice and democracy. The government, with its police and army, are the dark forces. They can ban us, imprison us, hang us, whatever they find to do, but no matter what – *right* will one day beat *might*, and they know it. They fear us as much as we fear them. We fear their army, but they fear our cause."

He paused and looked around at the now rapt audience, before continuing. "Just two months ago, Thozamile Botha escaped his banning order from under their noses and made it to neighbouring Lesotho. They couldn't get him there, so the government retaliated with a show of force; their army attacked cities in our neighbour, Angola. They think that they frighten us – and our neighbours – by doing this. They claim they are destroying our allies and training camps. They say they'll beat us into the ground. But fellow students of South Africa, please believe me; we have the world on our side. One day we will win; good will triumph over evil. One day, not too long from now when I qualify as a doctor, I hope to treat my fellow citizens in any hospital in South Africa – not in segregated hospitals. All children will be free to attend any school in the country and have the same quality education. That will be their right – not an unequal, second rate education tossed out for those who are not white. And trust me, we know we are making strides when the Dutch Reformed Church sees the injustice of government policy; now *there* is a window that has opened to let in the light, so don't be downhearted." His face was glowing with perspiration and passion, and as I looked around, it was evident that the entire audience was as entranced as I was.

"I speak as a student whom the government has labeled 'coloured.' We don't ask you, whom they label 'white,' to boycott classes," he continued. "But we do ask you to cry out about injustice. Demonstrations and protest marches get attention without wasting educational opportunities. It will fall to us and our generation to make changes, and we need our leaders to be educated. It is a duty for all of us to get the best education we can. Thank you for your solidarity; we are in this together because we are all South Africans. We are the light of reason fighting the forces of darkness."

As he returned to his seat next to me, I shivered, despite the warmth of the day. Amidst all the applause, he looked at me and said, "And in this war, Valerie, the enemy is right among us in our camp. Of that I have no doubt." My eyes widened in surprise that he should use my first name so freely; I was accustomed to being addressed as "M'am" by people of other races. Unabashed, he continued, "Look around; there are plain clothes policemen in here and plenty of informers – we just don't know who they are. Don't smile at me if you're afraid of them. They'll be watching." He winked at me and I couldn't help it; I smiled. Of all the people in this hall, he had chosen to sit next to me. I was very conscious of the warmth of his body next to me and I could feel his heat, even though we weren't touching.

Yet a sense of self preservation made me try to ignore his undeniable attraction. The following day I chose a seat somewhere else, but after I was called on to translate for a Zulu delegate, Johan saw where I was and sought me out at lunch. "Quite the linguist," he said. "I'm impressed." I thanked him and turned away, but he stood in front of me, barring my way. "There's an empty chair next to me. I saved it for you." I bit my lip and looked down. When I looked up at him, his smile had gone. He looked intently and said, "Is it because you don't like what I said yesterday, or because you're afraid? Or maybe you just don't like me."

Speaking very softly I said, "Johan, I can't say whether I like you or not because I don't really know you, but this is pointless. Please understand; it's not you, it's – you know… I'm white and you're coloured. It's not possible for us to have a friendship after this week."

"No, I don't understand," he said. "I thought you might be brave enough to befriend someone of a different colour. I guess I was wrong." He shrugged and then said, "I'm sorry you feel that way. It's giving in to them; but I do understand fear, Valerie. I've had to live with it all my life. Except now I refuse to accept their control over me anymore. Enough is enough. But that's me. I can't expect everyone to feel the same way."

Immediately I caved in. He was right; I was being a coward. In truth I really wanted to get to know him and was honored that he had sought me out – so I summoned my courage and returned to sit at his side. I was conscious of eyes watching me all around the hall, but suddenly I didn't care whether they watched out of curiosity, admiration, or disapproval. I was sitting next to a brilliant orator who wanted to sit next to me, and I didn't need anybody's permission to do so.

The conference lasted a week and we were seated next to one another most of the time. Medical school delegates had special dispensation to be on our campus that week, so that made it easy. We talked endlessly and laughed even more. Nobody seemed to care about colour in that environment, even if we knew there were informers in our midst. We were cocooned from reality. A girlfriend commented on the good-looking guy I was with all the time and I didn't feel alarmed, but rather flattered. It seemed perfectly natural, after just a short while, to seek out one another every moment that we could. I knew – as well as anyone – the strict racial laws of the country and I questioned myself: Was I trying to prove a point because I wanted to be a white liberal? Was it the excitement of forbidden fruit that was tempting me – an act of defiance, like smuggling a banned book? I didn't think so. I went out with white guys all the time and had fun with them, but none of it meant anything to me. The attraction I was feeling for Johan was different. He was so self-assured it was hard to believe that anyone in their right mind could view him as a second class citizen. The government might do so, but he certainly didn't view himself that way. You could tell from the way he walked – tall and upright, as well as the way he spoke, looking very directly at you. He was unexpectedly funny too; Johan saw humor where others saw the mundane. And he was extraordinarily good-looking. His dark eyes, when they weren't twinkling with laughter, looked penetratingly and approvingly at me. Each morning I found myself racing to the conference, looking out for him. I was eighteen – and breathless with excitement.

But the week came to an end all too soon. We alone lingered, as everyone else began to make their way out of the hall at the close of the conference. Neither of us knew what to say because we didn't want to part. Slowly, and in silence, we walked up the stairs to the mezzanine floor where we stopped in unison. I turned to look at him and murmured, "I suppose this is goodbye then."

He was staring at me intently. "I want to see you again, Valerie," he said simply. I nodded; my heart was pounding. If he had been white I would have given him my phone number and said, "Give me a call." But he wasn't white.

I was trying to figure out what to say when he blurted out, "Hey, could you be a bit clearer than nodding your head, please? Does it mean – you know I want to see you? Or does it mean – you want to see me too?" His eyes were twinkling again.

"I want to see you too," I replied.

"Good, I was hoping you'd say that. And before you tell me that it's impossible, I'll tell you that I have a plan. Meet me tomorrow, outside the main entrance to Woolworths in West Street, at 4.55 p.m. Can you be there? It'll be almost closing time, so there'll be lots of people rushing around; nobody will notice us. We can make another plan when we're there."

Not daring to be so bold myself, I smiled with relief at his courage. It was catching. "I'll be there," I said with confidence I'd never felt before.

But the next day my stomach was in a knot. What was I doing? This was madness. As I brushed my teeth, I considered forgetting the idea and not showing up. That would put an end to it because he would have no way of contacting me. I was terrified, as if I were on the edge of a huge precipice and losing my balance. Yet at the same time I was drawn to him, and the thought of never seeing him again was unbearable. So I rinsed the toothpaste from my mouth, stared at myself in the mirror for a few seconds, and made my decision – to follow my heart.

I chose my clothes carefully, wanting to look my best. The lime green mini skirt that I'd made recently was what I really wanted to wear, but I decided against it for fear of standing out from the crowd too much. Instead I chose a grey sweatshirt and blue jeans – and when I checked in the mirror, I smiled. Thirty minutes later, when I saw him outside Woolworths, the look on his face was one of such pleasure that I knew my decision was right; I couldn't reach him fast enough. He was also dressed in jeans and a sweatshirt, looking more handsome than ever. I was a teenager; his good looks were a huge part of the attraction I felt for him. My impulse was to reach out and hold his hand, but of course I couldn't do that; we had to keep apart by at least twelve inches at all times. That first introductory handshake was the only contact we were allowed.

"I'm really glad you came," he said. "I was afraid you might change your mind." My face reddened uncomfortably.

We walked up and down West Street that day – not the most exciting venue for a first date, but all we could think of at the time. We were able to talk quite freely, as the streets were crowded with everyone in a hurry to catch buses or get to cars. We even brushed against each other at times as we were jostled along, and I felt his arm rub against my back for just a moment. My spine tingled with the contact.

Our meetings continued in a variety of places after that, always changing the location to keep suspicion from arising as there were government informers everywhere. At first we met only occasionally, but every success made us bolder. I found myself growing more and more fascinated by him. My head told me to stop doing this as it would only lead to trouble, but I didn't heed my own warnings. Not only was he good-looking, he was also very funny – and instead of stopping the relationship, I wanted to speed it up instead. Soon we were meeting more frequently and before long, it was as often as possible. Each time we met, we would set the time and place for the next meeting – in some public place where we could try to be anonymous. Attempting to be somewhere private was out of the question; it was too risky. He lived with others and I was housed in a dorm. Johan's friend at Medical School, Peter Naidoo, suspected that we were seeing one another. He cautioned us, reminding us of the dangers we faced, but we ignored him and denied that there was anything going on.

Weeks went by and our relationship grew stronger. We became more confident, but it was mightily frustrating that we were unable to touch after that initial handshake – apart from the occasional, fleeting contact as we brushed against each other. Whites and coloureds were not even allowed to ride in a car together, unless one sat in the back and the other in the front. Movies and restaurants were not possible because they were segregated, as were most parks and beaches. Our choices were limited, but we were always on the lookout for new ideas.

The government might have decreed strict segregation and put enormous obstacles in our way, but no matter what they did, they couldn't stop us falling in love. One day we were walking along the Embankment in the middle of a storm, watching boats blowing around at the Yacht Harbor. We stopped after a while and leaned against a palm tree to rest. The wind was so strong it was hard to hold onto our umbrella or hear above the gale. Johan lowered the umbrella so that it was facing into the wind, to stop it blowing inside out. It was an unexpected boon; although the rain poured down on us from above, we were out of sight behind the umbrella's large dome, while behind us we were partially hidden by the palm tree. It was the most private we had ever been. Laughing, I heard him say, "Well what do you know? Do you dare to kiss me now?" When I looked up at him, the rain was streaming down his face, his hair was hanging over his forehead in wet strands, and he was smiling. I giggled, looked around furtively, and nodded. My heart was beating faster as I lifted my face to his.

His lips were almost touching mine, when suddenly we heard a car screech to a halt and a door slam. Instinctively we took off in different directions. I heard footsteps behind me and started to run; by now my heart was pounding as I imagined what might happen. Someone was following me and I had to get away. I didn't know who was after me, but they couldn't be allowed to catch me. I managed to dash across the street, between cars, before the traffic light changed. In this way I made my escape, never looking back in case my face might be recognized. I spent a sleepless night, agonizing over what had happened to Johan, but I didn't dare call to find out. If he had been caught, the security police would be bugging his phone by now. They would be trying to catch the white girl who had been with him.

We had already planned to meet the next day outside the Botanical Gardens. The day dawned bright and I kept to the plan, praying he would show up. It was a huge relief to see him at last, sauntering towards me. He walked right past, seemingly without a care in the world. As he drew level with me however, he raised his sunglasses a moment and gave a surreptitious wink. I waited a few moments more and then began to walk behind him. He turned and pretended to look over my shoulder for someone, while I pretended to look in a book describing the local flora. With my head down, I said, "Did anyone follow you yesterday?"

"Yeah, but I managed to get away very quickly and shake them off. How about you?"

"I think somebody came after me, but I didn't stop to look. Thank heavens I made it across the street and got away."

"I'm sorry I didn't get to kiss you," he said, "but I'm really glad you got away."

"Can I take a rain check on the kiss?" I asked.

"Man, it was so close," he said. "We almost made it. Maybe we'll have better luck next time. Let's pray for rain!"

I looked at him, longing to ignore all danger and fling my arms around him. Instead I said, "I'm counting on it."

We walked over to an information board and stood in front of it a while. I watched his reflection in the glass and he was watching me as he talked. It was such a novelty to be looking directly at him, even if it was only a reflection. After a while he stopped speaking and said, "You haven't heard a word I said." I shook my head and although I wanted to reply, I couldn't get the words out. We stared at each other's reflections for a long while after that, both fighting back our tears. They were tears of frustration and they were tears of defiance. But it was defiance that made us proud; how dare a government tell us we couldn't fall in love with one another because we had different colour skins? I loved his olive skin that was about the same colour as my father's. Have you ever seen a farmer without dark skin in Africa?

We were still standing there when Johan said, "We're not supposed to find each other attractive, but we've just proven the government wrong again. They're a bunch of narrow-minded old bigots who don't know what love is. They probably only have sex once a year to procreate – and they pray before they do it each time." I laughed at him as he hopped onto his knees to mimic the scene with his hands together, licking his lips lasciviously. Although I was laughing, I felt myself blushing too. The words "sex" and "love" were ringing in my ears.

I didn't know how it would work in the long term, but I blindly believed somehow we would figure it out by trusting the universe. My belief in the universe seemed justified when an opportunity presented itself to move out of the women's residence. I jumped at the opportunity and couldn't wait to tell Johan. Living on my own would at last provide privacy and a short-term solution to our problem; the long-term solution could wait.

When our next meeting took place however, it was clear something was eating him. He usually bounced with life, but on this day, his demeanour was downcast. I was filled with foreboding as he sat on his haunches, as if planning not to stay long, and spoke haltingly. "Valerie, we can't do this anymore. I can't go on like this – it's sheer, bloody torture not being able to be together. That kiss that we never had is about as much as we'll ever get – and I want so much more. But if we try to change anything and get caught, we'll both go to jail." He looked away and swallowed. "I'm going to walk away from you now, not because I want to, but because I have to." Then he turned and looked at me and there were tears in his eyes. "I've fallen in love with you – it's crazy, but I have. It should be the happiest thing in my life, but it's tearing me apart instead. If I didn't love you so much, I'd take a chance and say screw the government. But I do love you, with all my heart." I opened my mouth to speak, but he shook his head and continued, "No, don't say anything. It would hurt even more if you said you love me too. We can have no future together. You know that. This is forbidden love. It's impossible to go on like this."

Despite the news that I was so eager to give him, the shock of his words made me cry. He couldn't put his arms out to comfort me. We were in Farewell Square outside Durban City Hall, one of the few open spaces in the city with lots of people around of all race groups. Here we could melt into the crowd, watched only by a statue of Queen Victoria on top of her plinth. Unable to sit on a bench together because they were for whites only, I was sitting alone, with bags and parcels spread across the bench so that nobody else could sit there. He was crouched on the grass a short distance away.

"I'm not going to let you walk away from me," I replied. "I've never been rebellious, Johan. I've always obeyed the rules, but they were rules that made sense. This is nonsense. I ask you, who has the right to forbid love?" I was trying hard to stifle my sobs and had to look away for a few minutes. When I turned around again, he had got up and was turning his back on me to walk away. Without thinking, I jumped up and ran next to him. "I will not let this happen," I said, still without touching him. "I love you too. There, we've both said it. That's all that matters. We could live to be ninety and never feel this way about anyone again. I refuse to bow down to inhumane laws. If you're afraid for yourself, well that's your business, but please don't be afraid for me." He looked at me out the corner of his eye and my heart skipped a beat. I so badly wanted to grab hold of him and feel him next to me, but a sideways glance was all we dared.

Looking straight ahead, he said, "So how do you propose we go about this, Valerie? I can't even touch you in public."

"The thing is," I replied, "I don't care about touching in public – that's not the way I want to touch you. And I have a plan."

He stopped and turned, took a deep breath and then burst out laughing. It was a great deep laugh that made people turn and stare at us for a moment, before they went on their way. When he stopped laughing, it was to say, "You little hussy. My brown skin has gone pink – you make a man blush!"

An elderly couple had not gone away, however. They stood firmly planted, staring at us, while shaking their heads and whispering to one another. The woman began pointing at my parcels and bag on the bench, saying to me, "Be careful, dear. Somebody will steal your things." The man, prodded by his wife, approached and asked if I was having trouble with this coloured boy pestering me. Speechless, I shook my head.

Johan stopped and frowned. A look came over his face that I had never seen before. His eyes flashed and then narrowed, as he glared at the man. "You know sir," he responded, "at my age that's an insult. You can hear that my voice has broken and I assure you my testicles are fully developed. I'm long past puberty; I'm a man. Perhaps at your age if someone called you a boy, you might take it as a compliment, but I find it offensive."

Despite the tension, I giggled nervously and this time it was the elderly couple who were momentarily speechless. When they found words, it was to curse. "You cheeky bastard! How dare you speak to me like that? I've a good mind to report you," the man shouted, as his wife tugged at his sleeve to pull him away. "It's indecent. What is this country coming to? The cheek of it! There's absolutely no respect anymore."

She was muttering at him, "You're too old to try and fight now. That coloured boy could knock you down too easily."

"Just let him try. I'm going to find a policeman and report him right now." He glared at Johan before shaking his fist and saying, "You leave our white women alone. Do you hear me?"

Johan opened his mouth to respond but I intervened as best I could, without drawing any further attention to ourselves. "Don't say anything more, please. Let it go." As the couple moved away, I stood firmly in front of Johan and pleaded with him quietly. "Forget about them. Stop and listen to me. I have something important to tell you."

He shook his head and said, "Don't make this harder than it already is, Valerie. You've just seen what we're up against. And that's only the tip of the iceberg."

"Listen to me, will you? You're right; I know only too well how hard it is. But it's our business, not theirs. There is a solution, Johan, and I've already got it figured out – if you would just give me a chance to tell you. I'm moving into a flat on my own. We can be together, alone and unseen."

He pushed the hair out of his eyes and frowned. "Oh yeah! And how is 'a coloured boy' going to get into a flat in your 'white area?' Do you think the neighbours won't see me? There are eyes in walls, Val."

"Well, I'm sub-letting from a friend who is moving away. I'm taking her place, next Monday; I told my parents there was too much noise in the residence and I can't study. It's done already, Johan – *fait accompli*. So, how you get there is up to you, but I promise – if you come, I'll open the door and let you in."

I gave him the address which he repeated a few times, and then he stopped and stared at me. "You really are serious," he said, "but what if someone else is there when I arrive? Have you thought of that?" he asked. "It's not so simple."

I considered this a moment. "I'll say that I didn't order a pizza, it must be another flat they're looking for…. so do your best to look like a delivery boy."

"I have to hand it to you, you're a crafty woman," he laughed. As he stared at me, I could see his dark mood lifting. "Make sure nobody else is there Monday night. I'll see you then." We smiled at one another and then he said quickly, "Now let's get the hell out of here before that old fart returns with half the police force in tow."

****

The days dragged until then, even though I was madly busy moving. It was hard to think of anything but Johan and being together. My studio flat was close to campus in a purpose-built block; lots of students lived in the area, but also middle class, white families. We would have to be careful.

When Monday evening came and I heard the knock on my door, I flew to open it with a pounding heart. However, as soon as I closed the door behind him and locked it, a strange feeling of

28

awkwardness overcame both of us. This was the first time that we could have held each other; instead, we stood staring nervously, saying nothing. Feeling like Eve, considering the bite of an apple, I took his hands in mine and ran my fingers over his palms. They were the same colour as mine and soft to the touch. When I looked at his face, there were tears in his eyes. He began to run his fingers through my hair and then he traced around my eyes, nose and mouth with his fingertips. There were no words that could express the wonder we felt in those moments. All Johan said was, "I love you, Valerie." I was too choked up to reply.

When he drew me into his arms for the first time and kissed me, I knew only the happiness of love. Nothing else mattered.

Chapter 2

We were soon to know the fear that came with our love. Would we have done anything differently, had we known what was to come? I think not. We loved each other and that was all we cared about for the moment.

Johan managed to get a postman's uniform from his brother Roelof, who asked no questions, but handed over his uniform and announced to the post office that it had been stolen from his washing line. Johan came and went dressed in this, without rousing any suspicions from neighbours. We were almost carefree and it was exhilarating to believe that we had beaten the system. For the most part we felt safe and happy inside our nest, like any other couple in love. Johan loved to dance. He moved with such rhythm that sometimes I would stop, just to watch him. He taught me to cook Cape Malay dishes from his hometown of Cape Town, and he spoke a lot about his mother, Greta. He assured me that she would love me when we met.

"Holy Smoke! You really want me to meet her?" I asked. "I wouldn't dare introduce you to my parents."

"Sure, I want you to meet her. You're the two most important women in my life and it's important for me that you know each other. You'll love her too. My Dad – now I'm not so sure about him. He carries a grudge against all white people. He had his house confiscated when the government claimed it for a white area. It was nasty; his financial compensation was a pittance and he could do nothing to appeal. There was no public hearing or discussion; the government decided what they wanted and deemed fair, and that was that. That's apartheid for you. He won't forgive and forget." The look that crossed Johan's face suggested that he felt similarly, but it was only a moment and then he said, "My Mom wouldn't care what colour you are. If I love you, she'll love you. That's the way she is."

We had a terrifying scare one day when the door bell rang several times on a Saturday afternoon, while we were lying in bed. It was easy to ignore the persistent ringing until I heard a voice calling my name. My eyes opened wide and I mouthed to Johan, "It's my Mom." My heart was beating so loudly I was sure she'd be able to hear it on the other side of the door. A neighbour then called out, "I haven't seen her go out today, but she might have done. I can give her a message later if you like. I'll watch out for her to come back."

We froze. For a few agonizing minutes we barely breathed, but lay staring at one another panic-stricken. My mind was racing, trying to figure out what to do. Fear had paralyzed us both. I opened my mouth to speak, but very quickly Johan put a finger on my lips and shook his head. After what seemed an eternity, a note was pushed under the door and we heard her footsteps going away down the passage. Just to be sure, we remained motionless for some time after that, until finally I crept over and picked up the note. It read: *I'm in Durban for the day to see a client and hoped to catch you for a cup of coffee. Sorry I missed you. I also really want to see your new flat. Unfortunately, I'm flying back to*

Johannesburg this afternoon. Better luck next time.... Love, Mom.

Our nest suddenly felt like a cage; Johan would have to stay until Monday morning because no postman would be walking around in uniform on a Sunday. We were trapped. We couldn't risk the neighbour seeing him. Even though we were together, the day had been sullied.

Our happiness was clouded by that narrow escape and for a while we were much more cautious, making plans for such eventualities if they should happen again. Word got out that the police were going to crack down on student dissenters, and so we made plans that could be put into action if anything happened to either of us. Communication would be a problem, because Johan's phone could be tapped and his mail screened, if he were put under house arrest. I wouldn't be able to visit any of the limited places where he could go, and his moves would be constantly monitored by the special branch of the police.

"You could write to me as John Brown, c/o Peter Naidoo, but don't put your name to anything. I'll warn him; he can try and pass letters on to me. But if he gets imprisoned, or put under house arrest, we're stuck. Then our only hope is to send letters to South Africa House in London."   Johan shook his head as he said this. "It's crazy to think this way, but we have to. It'll be our last resort; send letters to me there, addressed to Mr. John Brown. That way, my identity remains secret."

For about a year we kept up this cat and mouse game. We were happy mice, creeping quietly and stealthily to our nest, eluding the predatory cat that could pounce any moment. We were still foolish to dream that we had a future together, even planning a trip to Cape Town to meet his mother. How crazy was that? We were young and hadn't lost our sense of invulnerability, so the shock was even greater when disaster finally struck. And when it hit us, it came as a double blow.

As had been rumored many months earlier, the government went ahead and cracked down on student dissension. They were dark days. Several student leaders from NUSAS around the country were banned and put under house arrest. Non-white students were also targeted. They could attend lectures, but were not allowed to be in other public places, nor in groups of more than two people. In addition, they were confined to their houses and allowed only one visitor at a time. Everyone knew that the security police monitored all their activities and their houses, and additionally their phones were bugged. House arrest was ordered under the *Suppression of Communism Act* and lasted either ninety, or a hundred and eighty days. It was feared that "white" NUSAS would soon be banned, just as "black" SASO had been a few years before.

I was terrified. When Johan didn't show up at my flat the next day, I knew something was wrong. As a very outspoken opponent of the government, he was one of the student leaders they wanted to silence. I didn't dare phone him – or Peter for that matter. In desperation, I went to the NUSAS office to find any information I could, and sure enough, there was a list of names on a bulletin board of all those in the latest round of banning. I was shaking as I stood in front of it. Names were listed according to university and my eyes raced to find the University of Natal. I stared in horror; Johan Barnard, ninety days.

The office was buzzing with enraged people planning demonstrations, but none of them knew just how much this affected me personally. No protest would do anything to help. I wept uncontrollably. I don't remember how I got home that day. I don't remember much about anything for a few days after that, either. I was so anxious that I felt ill and couldn't get out of bed. I didn't want to eat, so it didn't matter that I had no food in the flat. I forced myself to drink water so that I wouldn't dehydrate, but even that made me feel ill and throw up violently. I wanted to die.

This was when the second blow struck home. I had a lot more to be anxious about; my period was late. The nausea I felt was morning sickness. Fear swept over me like an icy Atlantic wave. I was on my own, unable to contact Johan, and carrying our child.

This baby would be classified coloured when it was born. Our affair would be out in the open and made into something dirty, fit only for the back page of the *Sunday Times*. I could protect Johan, by refusing to say who the father was; I could say that I was raped; but I couldn't protect our child from a lifetime as a second class citizen. There would be no white schools and home for this child of ours; I wouldn't even be able to live with it. What would become of our baby?

I was afraid and vulnerable. And all the time I was considering the plight of my child, it was growing relentlessly inside me. I needed to figure out what to do. Nothing could stop what had happened except an abortion, but that was illegal and posed great difficulties. Besides – I didn't want to take that route. This child was part of me and the man I loved. I couldn't think straight.

Every avenue I explored led to some probable disaster. In desperation, I did the only thing I could think of; go home to my parents for help.

I drove back to the farm without telling them I was coming, stopping frequently to throw up at the side of the road. It was a relief to finally see the familiar gateposts guarding the entrance to the farm; *The Oaks* written on one, and *Spencer* written on the other. Although anxious about facing my parents, as I drove up the long, unpaved driveway, I was comforted by the familiarity of home. Looking around, I could see that life here had gone on as usual with its seasonal cycle. The bare rose bushes had been pruned; the azaleas were in bud; the lawns were as green as ever – winter or summer; the huge oak trees had lost their leaves, their bald shape even more beautiful than their summery coif; the vegetable field was strewn with compost and manure, ready for planting. This was where I had grown up and where I belonged; it was my refuge.

As I climbed out the car, the dogs raced to greet me, barking and wagging their tails. They followed me all the way to the bathroom, where they stood whining outside the closed door. When I emerged, their excited barks brought Goodness, the cook and my erstwhile nanny, running to see what was happening. She threw her hands up to her face with pleasure and flung her arms around me. I sobbed quietly in her arms and she patted my head, like she did when I was a child, asking no questions. She just gave me a damp cloth to wipe my face – I suppose I didn't smell too fresh after so many wayside stops. I knew then that my parents were not home. She would only have given a verbal greeting in their presence, not a warm embrace.

The house was very quiet. Goodness insisted on making tea for me as I walked from room to room, remembering moments from my childhood that had been so happy. I stupidly began to dream of bringing my baby up here, sequestered on the farm. Nobody in the outside world need know. Such beguiling tranquility permeated the place that I was lulled into believing all would be well, especially as I stood in the living room and looked at old family photos placed on the piano. There were so many framed photos of the three of us, Mom, Dad and me, at different stages of my life. Our smiles reflected our happiness. I think that they wished there had been more children – but I didn't really care not having a sibling; I had them to myself. Besides, there were always others to play with on the farm and my cousin, John, came to stay during vacations. He was like a brother to me. Then when I went away to boarding school, it didn't matter that I had no siblings; I had lots of good friends. Perhaps I should have called John and told him what had happened, but it was too late now and anyway, it would put him in a difficult position. There wasn't much he could do.

The grandfather clock was ticking in the background and I heard it gearing up to strike two o'clock. The hour struck with a crescendo that, by contrast, made the soft ticking of minutes afterwards sound incongruous. The steady rhythm was hypnotic. I lay on the sofa with my eyes closed and was calmed. Sleep must have overtaken my weary body; it was a shock to wake hearing the clock strike four. My tea was cold and someone had put a rug over me. It must have been Goodness. The dogs were asleep on the floor next to me and I smiled for the first time in weeks – until I needed to dash to the bathroom again. I was there, throwing up, when I heard my parents' car arriving. They both rushed inside calling my name, as they had seen my car parked outside. They looked concerned when I emerged from the toilet, looking ill, and I suddenly panicked. My courage was gone. I wasn't sure of them any longer. How was I going to tell them that I was pregnant? And then, when they'd recovered from that shock, how would I tell them that the baby's father was coloured? They would be having a coloured grandchild. My trust of a few hours earlier was suddenly not so strong and I wished I hadn't come home after all. I should have gone to my cousin, John.

My mother quickly guessed my condition and, as it turned out, was strangely supportive at first. I was relieved that she had guessed and I didn't have to spell it out to her. She was a little excited I think – until I told her the second part of the news. Then she froze. My father's response, by contrast, was instantaneous and terrifying. He erupted like a volcano. It was like a horror movie. The loving man I had watched growing up, who had taught me right from wrong, and who had always treated everybody with fairness, disappeared in an instant. He struck me across the face with a resounding smack; I could feel it burning long after the sound of his shouts had dimmed, but the sting of his words has never faded. He ordered me out of the house, screaming abusively, "Go and live on the Cape Flats – and take your bastard child with you. That's where you belong now, not here. Get out of my house."

I had never seen him lose his temper before and could not believe what I was witnessing. His violence and bigotry were terrifying. In an instant he had become a stranger, totally detached from me. He would have thrown me out on the street and left me to perish if it weren't for my mother's intervention, of that I'm certain. I filled him with disgust.

She was more reasonable and went into practical mode, coming up with a solution. Thank goodness she was American by birth, because I was able to leave and go with her to California. She'd had the foresight to get me an American passport as a child, so I needed no visa.

I never saw my father again. I don't know where he went for the next few days; he couldn't have stayed in his study all that time, so perhaps he went to the Ixopo Hotel and drowned his sorrows at the bar. It was a favorite meeting place for the local farmers, but I doubt that he went there as he would not have wanted anybody asking questions. It's a mystery where he went, but I never saw him again. It was as if I didn't exist for him from that moment onwards.

I suppose I should be thankful that he and my mother paid to get me out of the country, in addition to all my medical expenses. I don't know what I would have done without their financial support. I could have used more emotional support though; they had always given it to me before, no matter what. But such was the power of bigotry that a new life, which should have heralded the continuation of our family, drove a wedge between us, signaling the end of it instead.

Did I care? Yes, of course I did. I was devastated because I had always loved my parents; but I felt anger, as well as pain of rejection. They gave me no chance to explain anything; all they heard was the word "coloured". It didn't matter that I loved Johan, that he was a wonderful man, or that he was going to be a doctor. The colour of his skin was what mattered. They saw themselves as the injured party, whereas Johan and I were actually the victims of their prejudice – as was our innocent, unborn child.

We made preparations to leave with great haste. My mother booked our tickets and made plans for me to stay with her sister in California, while my father was notably absent. I was still feeling ill, but worse than the misery of morning sickness was the constant fear that gnawed in my gut. I fretted about how to let Johan know my plight without getting him into even more trouble. The police had powers with which they could ban him repeatedly under the *Suppression of Communism Act,* even without evidence of transgression. Suspicion was enough to do that. But if they discovered that he had fathered a child with a white woman, it would be proof he had contravened the *Immorality Act.* That was an even greater crime in their eyes. If we were found out, the force of the law would come down on us with all its might. We had managed to operate under the radar and were fortunate not to have had police barging into my flat in the middle of the night, trying to catch us in the act, or checking the sheets for telltale signs of love-making. But there is no greater proof of sexual relations than a pregnancy. A baby of colour, born to a white woman, would start a witch hunt that would only end when the father was found – and both parents incarcerated. If we were lucky, the baby would be given to Johan's coloured family, but they might choose to put it into an orphanage. I might not be able to bring up my own child.

The day of departure dawned and I still had no solution. In desperation, I decided to take a chance. I would do as we had planned and write to Johan, via Peter Naidoo. Our plan of sending letters to South Africa House in London was almost useless. It was one thing saying he would escape and go into exile, but Johan was stuck in his house in Durban, with his every move watched by the security police at all times. Escape was unlikely. If it were possible, Peter would get my letter to him.

There wasn't much time, but I quickly wrote a note without mentioning my name, explaining that I was pregnant and going to have the baby in America. I gave him my aunt's address so that he could write to me. My hope was that he could get political asylum and join me there when his banning was over; we would be able to live normal lives together there.

I remember that I left the note in an open envelope on the hall table, before running to find a photo of myself that I could enclose. It took a few moments. When I returned, there was just enough time to pop the picture into the envelope, seal it and stamp it, and then we had to leave. I kissed the envelope as I put it safely in my bag, ready to post at the airport. Little did I know how dearly I would pay for those few unguarded moments.

****

The journey to California was interminable. It began with an overnight flight to London, during which I slept very little as I was so distraught. When the plane lifted off from Johannesburg and I saw the brown veld of the Transvaal disappear, I knew I was leaving Africa behind and my heart was breaking. Somewhere back there was Johan; every mile I flew was taking me further away from him. I was leaving everything I knew, for better or worse, and going to the unknown. This was the first time I had ever left South Africa and, although I had always dreamed about travelling, there was no joy in this, my first trip abroad. I was afraid. Despite feeling grateful that they were taking me in, I had never met my American relations and I was apprehensive about spending the next several months with strangers. Additionally, I was filled with anxiety about being pregnant and unmarried.

When we arrived at Heathrow Airport at six o'clock in the morning, all I wanted to do was lie down on a bed and sleep. This was not possible. There were seven hours to kill before our next flight to San Francisco, stuck in a transit lounge that was very difficult to find. We seemed to walk for miles, travelling on moving passages and following arrows, with people all around us going in every direction. It was hard to believe that so many people could be travelling and Heathrow was very bewildering. Everybody spoke English; this was convenient, but it was strange to hear no Afrikaans, Zulu or much of anything else. Even the black people here spoke with an English accent, which was odd. And it was even stranger to see a white woman mopping the floors, as well as black and white men working side by side, doing manual labor; I'd never seen that before. I stared at workers through a glass wall as we passed by, loading and unloading baggage onto trucks; there was no white foreman overseeing the black workers. Everyone was busy doing the job. When we lined up to use the restroom, every colour and creed were in the same line, using the same toilets. It was a revelation.

When we finally arrived in the transit lounge, it seemed as if we had travelled for miles, weighted down with our carry-on luggage. I was exhausted. My mother was equally tired. We stretched out on benches to rest and I watched her lying opposite me, slumbering fitfully and uncomfortably. The gulf between us was strained and I longed for her to say, "Valerie, everything will be fine. I'll stay in America and help you with this." But I knew that wouldn't happen. Instead, through half-closed eye lids, I saw her watching me with a frown at times. I know she found it inconceivable that I could love a coloured man, and there was no way she was going to accept a coloured grandchild. It was the only thing that almost made me smile; thinking of my parents' shock that there was going to be a coloured Spencer. Their plan, however, was that there definitely would not be a coloured Spencer; it would be handed over for adoption and left behind in America, far away from their comfortable existence, without anybody at home being any the wiser.

Although the thought of another long haul flight was unpleasant, it was a relief to commence the second leg of the journey, a daylight flight to San Francisco. But my heart sank as we climbed into yet another claustrophobic cabin and found our seats. My mother and I didn't talk much on the journey; we both read books and I was sick several times. It was caused by a combination of turbulence, exhaustion and pregnancy – not a good combination for anyone. Travelling westward with the sun, the day never ended, but exhaustion made us both sleep on and off, despite the cramped space. When we finally landed ten hours later, the sun was still shining and it was early afternoon in California; I was happy to get off that plane and breathe fresh air. No more airports, transit lounges or airplanes with their stale, recycled air. Aunt Lorna was there to meet us as we emerged from the immigration hall, and she immediately put her arms around me, hugging me tight. Other than a hug from Goodness, it was the first warmth I had felt from another human being since the nightmare began. It felt so good. She seemed genuinely pleased to meet me; her bright smile was a contrast to my mother's strained looks.

I fell in love with California immediately. As we headed south down a valley on Highway 280, the inland hills on the left were golden in the summer sunshine and dotted with dark oaks. The cloudless sky was vivid blue, like an African sky. By contrast, fog capped the coastal hills on our right, like a shroud on the dark green foliage beneath. Despite my exhaustion, I was fascinated by everything I saw – none of it was what I had imagined California would be. I had expected neon lights and huge billboards, but there was none of that. It was beautiful and tranquil, with cows grazing in fields. If it weren't for the vast satellite dish on top of a hill, and the busy, multi-lane highway we were travelling on, it would have been as bucolic as the road to Ixopo. I didn't even realize that this was the famous Silicon Valley.

Aunt Lorna was a haven in a storm and I will always be grateful for the kindness she showed me, both then and for years afterwards. My mother left in a hurry, after only four days, so that people wouldn't be suspicious; I was supposed to be studying abroad. She was extremely concerned to keep up this pretense so that the family name would not be sullied. It was like a knife wound hearing her say, "The Spencer's name has always been respected, Valerie. It's not going to be dragged through the mud now. The baby will have a good home here, you aunt will see to that, and we can then forget all about this. I wish it could be otherwise, but it can't. You must accept that and start again.

Nobody need ever know. It will be best for the baby and best for you. I don't know what you were thinking, but what's done is done. We must make the best of things and move on. This will be water under the bridge."

Water under the bridge! I said nothing. There was no point arguing any longer about the evils of apartheid, or saying that I loved Johan. I had no intention of doing as she wished, but I pretended to agree with her in order to keep her quiet. I truly believed that by the time our baby was born, Johan and I would be living together with our child. He would get my letter and come to me – and we would start again, turning our backs on damnable apartheid.

Despite the hurt I felt, it was devastating when my mother left so soon. I felt very unsure of myself afterwards. She had been my security in this foreign place, but her hasty departure seemed to indicate that she couldn't bear the sight of me; she cared more for the family reputation than her own daughter. Abandoned by her, as well as my father, I felt cast aside.

My aunt was supportive and kind; she asked no questions and made no judgments. Instead she looked after me, driving me to doctor's appointments and making sure that I ate properly. I grew to love the little town of Los Gatos in California, where she lived. It was a caring community that reminded me of my happy childhood, a time when I felt loved and secure. But Los Gatos was no sleepy village. I loved walking down the main street which was full of countless shops and restaurants – nothing like Ixopo, with its simple farming community's needs. Aunt Lorna often treated me to lunch downtown and I grew to love Mexican food.

The cuisine was new to me; fajitas, burritos and tortillas soon became my favorite fare. I even began learning a bit of Spanish to pass the time; it sounded beautiful. I babysat my young cousins and joined the local library. It was an inviting place that was bright and spacious, very different from the one-roomed Ixopo library. I managed to get a temporary job there for a few months, re-shelving books.

I had never lived anywhere so free of prejudice; children of all ethnicities played together and their parents were equally tolerant of each other. South Africa and my parents had made me feel ashamed; California and Aunt Lorna made me feel worthwhile again.

As I settled into life in Los Gatos, my fear abated and I grew tender towards the baby growing inside me. I looked forward to its arrival and longed to hold it in my arms, with Johan by my side. I was sure he would come. I daydreamed about what our baby would look like, mixing up Johan's features and mine in my imagination. His darker genes would be dominant, I was sure, but would it be a boy or a girl? Would it be my shape or his? I dreamed the happy dreams of any expectant mother, while playing along with arrangements made by Aunt Lorna. She busied herself organizing my baby's adoption.

I wrote often to Mr. John Brown, South Africa House, London, and waited hopefully for a letter in return. Nothing came. Right to the end of the pregnancy, I lived in hope that he would contact me and we would ignore all promises made to my parents. As the months passed, however, with no contact from Johan, my fears returned. As the due date approached, I was filled with utter dread. I feared something even more terrible had happened to him; maybe he was in prison - maybe even sent to dreaded Robben Island, where political prisoners went for life.

And sometimes during sleepless nights, I feared the unthinkable. Perhaps he was scared off by my letter. Perhaps the thought of being encumbered by a child at this stage of his life had stopped him replying. Maybe he didn't want me anymore.

In the end, I had no choice but to give in to pressure. I was penniless, single, far from home - and I didn't know whether Johan was alive or dead.

****

Childbirth was traumatic. As I was rushed into the Labour Ward, its cold sterility made me shiver and I couldn't get warm, despite the exertion of labour. I sweated and shivered and screamed with pain; it was not only physical pain, it was anguish. I felt as if I was being ripped apart as I strove to push my baby into the world - and my heart was breaking at the same time. The moment of birth would be the moment of our separation. I knew there were hands waiting to take my child away, waiting outside the delivery room like vultures. I screamed in despair.

After the baby was born, I almost went insane. All I wanted was to keep my child; I was even more desperate to renege on the promises to my parents, angry that they had made me agree to such an inhuman act as giving up my own flesh and blood. Bright lights were shining and my feet were up in stirrups, when I heard a male voice arguing with my aunt. I couldn't hear what they were saying because I was concentrating on the small body to which I had just given birth. I heard the nurses say, "It's a girl," as they took her to be weighed and measured. Someone else asked, "Have you chosen a name?"

I was crying as I replied, "Yes, she is Greta."

With tears streaming down my face, I was vaguely aware of Aunt Lorna leaving the room. The tears were a mixture of joy, relief and anguish. I called loudly for someone to give Greta to me. Dr. Smith, always so kind, gestured to the nurses and I enjoyed a brief moment holding her in my arms, drinking in her beautiful face. A nurse took a Polaroid photo of Greta for me and then, all too soon, announced she needed to take the infant away. As they tried to remove her, I clung to my baby, weeping. "Please, no. Don't take her. Please no…"

But nobody listened. The nurses pulled her from my arms. That was the last I ever saw of my child.

Grief washed over me in waves and I wanted to die. The pain has never diminished – if anything it has grown worse. Those moments are the only memory I have of my child; one single memory to last a lifetime. Every year on her birthday, I buy flowers to remember that sweet baby girl – and I wonder what she's like. Twenty years and twenty bunches of flowers; an annual ritual is all that I have.

I have paid a steep price for love. Now as I trudge through life without him, I feel neither happiness nor fear – only the pain of loving Johan Barnard.

PART 2

FRANCESCA

To be ignorant of what occurred before you were born is to remain always a child.

– *CICERO*

GLYNNIS HAYWARD

Chapter 1

My name is Francesca Walker and it's been sixteen years since my parents told me that I was adopted. It was one of those defining moments in life that changes everything; I was four years old at the time.

The day had started much like any other, until the moment when the phone rang. I remember that my Mom and I were busy baking brownies; I was anxious for her to pour the mixture from the bowl into the baking tray so that I could scrape the dregs with my finger. 'Licking the dish,' we called it; I could almost taste the chocolate as I watched her and my mouth was watering with anticipation. Then the phone interrupted us. I groaned as Mom dusted her hands on a towel and ran to get the call, but I wasn't paying much attention to her. I was deliberating whether to risk sticking my finger into the brownie mixture for a little taste, or whether that would jeopardize my licking rights later. When I suddenly heard my Mom scream, I got such a fright that I almost knocked the bowl over. Then she started running around in circles, shrieking. I'd never seen her behave like that before; I'd never seen *anybody* behave like that. I watched for a moment and saw her quickly make another phone call, crying and laughing at the same time. Now that I'm older, I understand that it was hysterical behavior, but then I was so young that it scared me. I forgot about the brownies and climbed under the table, clutching a doll. The big, pine table was my protection and I blocked my ears.

The next day they brought my baby brother home and told me this strange thing that was hard to understand; I was adopted. They hadn't made me, they had chosen me.

It was 1986. My happy world in Los Gatos was shaken – as if the San Andreas Fault that ran through our town had suddenly moved, like a precursor to the big earthquake that shook us a few years later. My trust faltered; everything that I'd thought secure, suddenly shifted. I was afraid to believe anything. It was confusing. It seemed as if they'd selected us like puppies. I don't think I ever stopped feeling that way. It was like I wasn't really theirs and that made me nervous they might want to return me. After all, my mother was always buying things and then taking them back again, because they weren't quite right. I cried when we returned a dog to its previous owners because it barked too much and dug up the lawn. Could they take me back too?

The confusing news prompted this exchange:
    - Where did you get me?
-We fetched you from the hospital the day after you were born.
    -How did you know I was there?

It became the same scripted conversation for years and my mother, Grace Walker, would always hug me as she explained:
    -We couldn't have a baby ourselves, so we went to an adoption agency. They matched us up with someone who had a baby that they couldn't look after.

Then she'd tell me the bit that I always loved to hear:
    -We waited a long time to get you, ages and ages. One day, out of the blue, the agency called to say we could fetch you. It was the

happiest day of my life; I saw you a few hours after you were born – you had a little pink face, with lots of dark hair and big dark eyes. I loved you immediately. We rushed out to buy all the baby things we needed and I told my boss that I couldn't work anymore, because I had a new job; I was going to be a mother – *your* mother.

I felt reassured and liked her to tell me that story; she always hugged me and got tears in her eyes. Once I asked, "Why are you smiling and crying? It's like the sun is shining while it's raining."

That made her laugh and she told me that they were 'happy tears.'

   -I'm happy because I have you for my daughter, Frannie. One day you'll know what happy tears are.

Life returned to normal and I was pleased to have a little brother. My favorite book was one by Dr. Seuss, *Are You My Mother?* I often read it to Billy, showing him the pictures and cheering when the baby bird finally found its mother. It had special meaning for me; Grace and Robert Walker were caring parents, but they weren't my "real" parents. The book seemed to say that if I looked hard enough, I could find my mother too. I would daydream, sometimes making secret plans to run away in search of my biological parents, other times fantasizing that my "real" mother returned to fetch me. One day a strange woman approached me in the park near our house; I was on a play structure under some giant redwood trees. She stopped and asked whether I had seen her white dog. With my heart pounding, I ran in terror to Grace Walker who was nearby, pushing my brother on a swing. I clung to her sobbing, afraid that the strange woman actually was my "real" mother, coming to take me away. I didn't want to go.

My fantasies simmered quietly on a back burner until I was twelve, at which point they erupted into a boil. I was thrown into a situation which reminded me, with painful clarity, that I was not Grace and Robert Walker's biological child. My best friend Josie's sixteen-year-old cousin got pregnant. Her name was Beth and she came to stay at Josie's house until the baby was born. Josie lived in the same street as me and we grew up together. We went to the same school and were in the same class; we did homework together and had sleepovers at one another's houses; we rode bikes up and down our cul de sac and discussed boys, make-up and clothes; we shared many secrets – but not all. Nobody outside my family, not even Josie, knew I was adopted.

When Beth arrived, I befriended her immediately. She was lonely and homesick, so I suppose she didn't mind hanging out with a twelve-year-old. I watched over her as she ran to the bathroom throwing up. Josie was grossed out by it, but I felt sorry for Beth. We became friends and sometimes she would walk down the road to my house; we would go upstairs to my bedroom and look at magazines and stuff. I think she liked getting away from Josie's family for a change of scene. Then one day, about two weeks before her baby was born, I was lying next to our swimming pool with her when she burst into tears and sat up suddenly, hugging her knees against her large belly. "I've changed my mind. I don't want to give up my baby anymore. It's *my* baby and I'm not giving it away," she announced between tears.

Not sure how to respond, at length I asked, "What will you do? Will the baby's father help?"

She grimaced. "He's a jerk. Do you know what he said? 'Have an abortion. It's your fault for not being on the pill.' If I keep the baby, he would have to help pay and it would serve him right." She sniffed loudly and added, "At first I didn't care, but now it's different." I wished I could think of something that would make her feel better, but I could only think to hand her a box of Kleenex. She blew her nose and wailed, "I don't know what to do. I've got no money and I don't know what my parents will say if I change my mind; they were so mad when I got pregnant. What would you do, Fran?" Sobbing, she took my hand and said, "Here, feel my baby moving." I had always wanted to do so, but it seemed an invasion of her space. Biting my lips, I put my hand on the spot she indicated. It was weird to think of a baby, just a few inches away, waiting to be born.

For a long time I sat still, keeping my hand there. I was transported, imagining myself floating in my mother's womb twelve years before. And then a terrible sadness came over me; it was the only time I'd had with her. She gave me life and then she went away. For just a moment, my past and the present came together and I felt sympathy for the woman who was my mother. Before I had known only curiosity or anger, but this was a new angle of perspective. I don't think her decision to give me up was taken lightly. Finally when I spoke, my voice came out in a whisper. "I think if I were you, I would keep the baby."

I'll never forget the agonized sound that escaped Beth. It was almost inhuman – a cry that seemed to start from deep down in her belly in a long, protracted moan.

****

My birth parents were never far from my mind after that, no matter what I did. I liked school as much as any preteen enjoys junior high, but I loved after-school activities – particularly cross-country running. This was when I could be in my own world, thinking my thoughts without interruptions. They were often thoughts about my birth parents. What was their situation? Were they young like Beth? Was my birth mother sad when she gave me up? Did they ever think about me now? What did they look like and where did they live? Were they still together? Did she want to have an abortion? Why did they give me away?

I had felt the sensation of a baby moving in its mother's womb and I wanted to know my own mother. Sometimes I would stare in the mirror and examine my features; thick, dark brown hair, a little wavy and hanging to my shoulders when it wasn't in a ponytail; olive skin and wide-set brown eyes; high cheekbones; my nose just a little bit too long. I longed to know – did she look like that too? Was she tall like me and did she run fast like I did? Was she afraid of the dark and whistle when she was scared? I wondered about my birth father too. What did he look like? Countless unasked and unanswered questions played through my mind.

I almost told Beth that I was adopted, but she seemed to have enough to think about and besides, I hadn't told anyone else. If I were going to say something about it, I would rather tell Josie. But what was the point? She might think differently about me, or ask questions that I couldn't answer. I didn't want that. I had no memories of my mother, only my thoughts and dreams. I didn't want to share those with anyone. I didn't want my dreams spoiled.

I was there on the morning that Beth was rushed to hospital, doubled up in pain. Josie and I watched until her Mom's silver Volvo drove out of sight. After that we couldn't concentrate on anything. We waited anxiously all day until the phone rang with the news that Beth had given birth to a healthy girl named Suzanne. We jumped up and down with excitement and wanted to see the baby immediately, but of course we were not allowed to do so.

Beth didn't keep the baby. She came home the next day, but didn't want visitors. Nobody even answered the phone when I rang. It seemed like Josie's house was suddenly off-limits. I didn't see Beth again before she left, but she returned the next few summers. The adoptive parents allowed Beth to meet with her daughter every year on the child's birthday. It was called an open adoption. It turned out that they didn't call the baby Suzanne after all; the new parents named her Elizabeth. Josie informed me that the child would be Suzanne Richards on her birth certificate; the name could be changed but it would always be Suzanne on her birth certificate, along with Beth's name as the mother. I had no reason not to believe her.

This information from Josie became a beacon of hope for me. It seemed my way forward; I had to find my birth certificate. I'd had no starting point for my search before, but now this document would provide tangible information I needed; the names of my birth parents. Finally I had focus. I felt too awkward to ask for it, so searched the house, upstairs and down. I also checked in the garage, garden shed, attic and basement, always waiting until my parents were out before digging around. It was a slow process and it was all to no avail.

About this time, I had my first period. Spots of blood appeared in my underwear and I was scared there was something wrong with me. My mother hadn't discussed periods, and even though Josie had started having hers, I didn't really know what happened. I knew an egg came away each month and it was icky, so you had to wear special stuff in your underwear, but I didn't know blood was involved. Josie told me all sorts of things, but she hadn't told me that. I thought it just made a mess, like when you drop an egg on the floor. When a second day produced even more spots of blood, I plucked up courage to tell my Mom. She blushed and then apologized that she hadn't prepared me for this event, taking painstaking care to explain what took place with menstruation. It was a shock to realize that I was old enough to have a baby of my own. My Mom reassured me that I was perfectly healthy, adding, "Now you are a woman, not a girl anymore. But I hope you will always feel you can talk to me about anything, Frannie."

I didn't feel like a woman. Although this was a perfect moment to ask about my birth mother, for reasons unknown, I opened my mouth and blurted out instead, "I don't want to be called Frannie anymore. It's stupid. You can call me Fran or Francesca." My Mom didn't flinch, but nodded as she stroked my hair. "And don't patronize me," I screamed. "I'm not a Barbie doll for you to play with." I felt bad when I saw my Mom biting her lip. Part of me felt I should apologize, but I couldn't; instead rage overcame me and I blurted out, "You never tell me anything. I hate living here." I couldn't believe that I'd said that and clearly my mother was equally shocked. "I didn't mean that," I sobbed and quickly buried my head in my hands. If only I had stopped myself earlier it wouldn't have been so bad, but my mouth seemed to take on a life of its own, independent of my brain. My Mom said nothing as she walked away; I felt a terrible gulf between us that I wished with all my heart could be bridged. I loved her because she was my Mom, but I hated her because she wasn't my Mom.

****

Three years later when we were fifteen, Josie announced that Beth was getting married and wouldn't be coming to visit Elizabeth any more. "Why not?" I asked. "Just because she's getting married doesn't stop Elizabeth being her daughter."

Josie shrugged her shoulders. "She doesn't want her husband to know she had a child."

I was furious. "But that's dishonest." Josie said nothing, so I continued with my tirade. "What you're saying is that Elizabeth will never see her Mom again?"

Josie shook her head. "Nope, never. She has an adoptive mother, what's the difference? She doesn't need two mothers. It's great for Beth; she's having a big wedding and she's asked me to be a bridesmaid – you should see the dress I'm going to wear."

I wasn't interested in the wedding, or Josie's dress. "But poor

Elizabeth," I persisted.

Josie waved her hand in the air as if she were chasing flies. "My Mom says it's much better this way; Beth can move on with her life."

I did not agree. They had dismissed that child, their own flesh and blood. I rushed home and slammed my bedroom door behind me, sobbing. When my Mom knocked softly and asked if I was all right, I ignored her. I didn't want to speak to anyone. I needed to be on my own, to think. Elizabeth would grow up feeling what I felt. Beth had abandoned her, just like my biological mother had abandoned me. We were embarrassments; we were inconveniences. I hated Beth – and I felt humiliated. If only I could be like my brother Billy, who didn't think about his birth mother at all. His only comment was, "I don't know and I don't care. She didn't want me and I don't want her either."

But I did care and I wanted to know.

Chapter 2

It was difficult for me to find information back in 1997. I needed my birth certificate; that was the key to my quest. Without it, I could find nothing. On a couple of occasions I came close to asking my parents for it, but then I couldn't find the words to do so. I felt like a traitor. There would be another two years before I had a reason to ask. Fast forward those two years; I was applying to college. As I began to fill in forms, the words 'Birth Certificate' leapt out at me from the page. I could hardly contain my excitement. I stared mesmerized and then, trying to feign nonchalance, remarked as casually as possible, "Um, I need my birth certificate for this college application, Mom." My voice didn't sound quite steady as I addressed her.

She nodded and left the room wordlessly. The world seemed to stand still for me and I felt lightheaded. My heart was pounding so loudly that I was sure my Dad could hear it on the other side of the room, where he sat reading the paper. The family room, in which I had spent every day of my life, suddenly seemed foreign and I had the sensation of observing it from afar. How had my Dad got old without me noticing? When did those holes appear in the sofa? Were the walls always green? I listened to the clock ticking, each sound bringing me closer to a revelation. Two squirrels were chasing each other around the trunk of an oak tree outside the window, going round and round several times before one gave up and scampered away. The victor scurried onto a branch and looked around in triumph, before gathering up his strength to leap onto the fence below him. As the minutes ticked by, I watched entranced by their speed and agility. The squirrels' lives were enviably uncomplicated – the only thing they had to search for was acorns. And still the clock ticked. Why was my Mom taking so long to find the document?

When she finally returned to the family room, her face gave no clue to her feelings. If she were anxious, she wasn't showing it. "We'll need to make a copy," she said very matter-of-factly. "That's the original, so don't lose it."

It was the moment I had been waiting for since I was twelve years old, when Josie told me about birth parents' names appearing on birth certificates. My hands were shaking as I took the paper from her and began to read:

Certificate of Live Birth, State of California.
Francesca Grace Walker, female, March 9th 1982, 9.25a.m at Good Samaritan Hospital, San Jose, Santa Clara County.
Father of Child: Robert James Walker: State of birth: California
Mother of Child: Grace Evelyn Walker: State of birth: California

I stared in disbelief and wailed, "No."

"What's the matter?" she asked.

"You aren't my parents. Why are your names on my birth certificate?" I didn't even realize that I was shouting as I flung the certificate across the table at her.

"Well…" my Mom began to say. Then she stopped speaking as she bit her bottom lip.

In the ensuing silence, my father rose from his chair and walked over to us, putting his hands firmly on my shoulders. "This is your amended birth certificate, Fran. Do you want to know who they were? Is that it?"

I spun around and looked at him. "Yes of course I do." I was shaking with barely suppressed rage and frustration. It didn't sound like my voice, but rather a high-pitched shriek. "What do you know about them? Did you ever meet them?" I wanted him to stop touching my shoulders as if I were a small child having a tantrum, so I shrugged him off and moved away. Looking out the window, I tried to get a grip on my feelings while inwardly cursing Josie; she had inadvertently given me false hope all these years. Stupid Josie knew no more about adoption and birth certificates than I did. What an idiot I'd been to listen to her.

His voice sounded sad when my Dad answered me, but while I regretted my outburst, I couldn't contain what I felt. "We never met them and we never saw pictures of them either, before you ask that question. Your original birth certificate is filed with the State Vital Records Department. That one has their names on it, but it was re-issued with our names when you were adopted. That's the one your mother just handed you." I opened my mouth to speak, but he continued to say, "All we know about your birth parents is that they were from South Africa."

"South Africa?" I gasped. "What the…"

He nodded. "Yes, it was surprising to us too, but apparently your birth mother had a relative who lived nearby. That's why she gave birth to you in San Jose. She stayed with the relative while she was pregnant."

"Whoa, wait a minute. She had a relative living nearby? I…"

"We don't know who that person is, Fran," he said.

"Just like Beth and her baby. That's weird. What were my parents' names? Did they call me Francesca?"

My Mom came over and stood next to me, taking my hand in hers. "She named you Greta Karin Spencer. We adopted you on September 25th 1982, and your name was then officially changed," she explained.

Greta! My name had been Greta Karin Spencer! It was surreal. I said it to myself a few times and it was strange; a nice enough name, but I preferred the sound of Francesca Grace Walker. I was used to that and it was me. When I looked around, my Mom was watching me with an anxious expression on her face, as if she wasn't breathing. I nodded my head and stared at her unseeingly. Eventually I sighed. "Can you tell me anything about them, anything at all?"

"I'll tell you what we know – it's not much, but it's the background we were given," my Dad said. "Your birth mother's name was Valerie Spencer. She was young and healthy, and she came from a city called Durban. She and your birth father were unmarried students at university there. His name was Johan

Matthys Barnard. When she got pregnant, she came to a relative here in California and gave birth to you at The Good Samaritan Hospital. After we adopted you, she returned to South Africa and we never heard any more."

"And so Billy wasn't her child?" I asked. My Dad shook his head and smiled. I was surprised by that; somehow I had always presumed that we had the same birth mother. Now he wasn't even my "real" brother. It annoyed me that my Dad smiled right then; it made me feel foolish. I frowned and said, "I thought you got me at the hospital after I was born."

"Yes we did. You were a day old. You know that – we've talked about it often," Mom replied.

"But you just said that you adopted me in September. Was I Greta Spencer until then?"

My Dad scratched his head, a habit he had when trying to think how to say something. He was a cautious man who measured his words carefully. "Technically," he said, "I suppose you were Greta. But we called you Francesca. You grew up hearing that name. However, according to the law, we had to wait six months before we could finally adopt you. Up until that time, your birth mother could have changed her mind at any time and taken you away from us. As soon as we could, we made you 100% ours."

I should have been more sensitive about their feelings, but my emotions were running wild and I thought only about myself.

"But I'm not 100% yours. Did you think if you kept quiet it would disappear and we could pretend I wasn't adopted? Why didn't you ever tell me this before? Why wait until I'm eighteen to say anything about it? Do you think I haven't wanted to know?" My outburst met with silence.

I turned my back on them and stared blankly at the floor, trying to absorb what I'd been told. My mother's name was Valerie, and for six months she could have taken me back, but she didn't; she returned to South Africa and never saw me again. I didn't know exactly where South Africa was, but presumed it was at the bottom of the African continent somewhere. It was often in the news and everybody talked about Nelson Mandela being a hero. I'd seen "Release Mandela" bumper stickers on lots of cars, and when he was released from prison after a very long time, the world went crazy. That much I knew, but I wasn't sure why he went there in the first place. Now, this distant place was suddenly part of me. It was too much to digest.

I got up and said I was going for a walk. My brain was in overdrive; Greta Spencer or Greta Barnard – South African, or Francesca Walker – American. Which one was I? It was a throw of the dice that had made me Fran. If Valerie had made a different choice, or if somebody else had adopted me, I would have been someone else. That made me angry. This was me being handed around after all. It was my life and my identity. Who was I?

And then I thought of Beth and her baby... Maybe Valerie had felt the same pain when she had to part with me – but what had happened to her after that? I wanted to find her and know what she was like. Had she made a new life for herself and found happiness, with no place in it for her past? Would I be an unwelcome embarrassment, like Elizabeth was for Beth?

It was a chance I felt compelled to take. I had to know.

Chapter 3

The new millennium brought exciting changes for me; I would be going to college in September and living away from home for the first time. It was the beginning of my future; it was also an opportunity to start discovering my past. I would have my own computer at last, with no need for furtive genealogy searches on my Dad's computer. All the knowledge on the internet would be at my fingertips.

My search thus far had produced a copy of my original birth certificate from the Vital Records Department, which didn't provide any more knowledge than I already possessed. I had searched a genealogy website, but there were so many Johan Matthys Barnards, dating back to 1700, that the information wasn't helpful. All I could glean was that I came from an old South African family on my biological father's side. There was nothing about Valerie Spencer at all; I supposed that by now she was Valerie something else. I hated to think of her married with other children and felt a rush of resentment and jealousy. But it was something that I needed to consider; perhaps she had kept my existence a secret and would not want me landing in her life, eighteen years later.

That summer, before going to college, I read everything I could about South Africa to prepare myself. First I read James Michener's novel, *The Covenant*, which gave some historical perspective about the country. This was followed by Nelson

Mandela's autobiography, which was disturbing yet inspirational; and then I read about Steve Biko, an activist during the apartheid era who was arrested, beaten, and tortured to death while in detention. The accounts of police brutality turned my stomach. Fortunately I read some positive things as well, like the story of Chris Barnard, an Afrikaner surgeon who performed the world's first heart transplant in Cape Town in 1967. Was Johan Barnard related to Chris Barnard? Was I related to the famous surgeon? Was Johan an Afrikaner?

The more I read, the more I discovered that it had been a strange society during apartheid days, enforcing strict separation of the races. I cried when I read about Sandra Laing, a girl born to white parents, but classified black because she looked different. How did that happen? It meant she couldn't attend the same school as her brothers, because they were classified white. There were separate schools for different races. It was bizarre that everybody had to be classified according to their colour, and the state legislated where you lived, worked and studied. Yet despite the regime's stranglehold, there was enough resistance to change it and South Africa finally held democratic elections in 1994. All the laws of 'apartheid' were repealed after that.

I read everything I could about "the struggle" against apartheid, wondering whether my parents had played a part in it, and I became more and more obsessed with finding out about these two people. There seemed to be so much more excitement about them than the dull lives led by the Walkers. I was thankful my gene pool was different; I loved my adoptive parents, but their lives were essentially dull. They had no desire to discover new places or try something new. Not for me though; no matter where the road took me, I was going to explore it. And I was going to find Valerie and Johan.

When September finally came, as my parents drove away, leaving me to begin my freshman year at the University of California, Los Angeles, I felt mixed emotions. It was sad seeing them leave, but I could hardly contain my excitement being on my own for the first time. Finally, I was independent. I was glad that Josie had chosen UCLA as well, thankful for the familiarity of a good friend. I already knew that I wanted to major in English, but I found that I could also study Afrikaans, Zulu or Xhosa – all languages from South Africa. Languages were my strength and I registered to learn Afrikaans, a Dutch derivative; it seemed another step along the way of uncovering my roots.

At the end of our freshman year, Josie and I had an argument that caused a temporary rift in our friendship. She had a boyfriend called Jake, whom I didn't like. He was a pothead and a bad influence on her. I could smell marijuana in our dorm room. They tried to cover up by spraying deodorant and room freshener everywhere, but the smell lingered on everything. One day, as I opened the door, I saw that Jake was in our room as usual and the two of them were laughing crazily. He stood in the middle of the room, but stopped what he was doing the moment I entered. I ignored him and stepped over all the clothing strewn across the floor, while heading for my desk. We ignored each other and he continued telling Josie, loudly enough for me to hear, that he was making plans to earn extra money as a sperm donor. I took a deep breath and pretended I hadn't heard. Soon he was guffawing as he began to fill in application forms, giving crude answers to make Josie giggle. Finally I lost it when I heard him say, "You could get big bucks for being an egg donor. Why don't you do it?"

I flew into a rage. "I can't believe the two of you," I said. "This isn't just about money. You'll have children running around with your genes and you won't even know it. And they won't know their real parents."

"Oh come on, Fran," Josie said. "Lighten up. You're such a prude. It's not a big deal. It isn't like they'll be street children. They'll have parents who really want them, but who need some help along the way. We'd be helping. It's altruistic." She looked at Jake as she said this, and again they giggled.

"Yeah," he said, rubbing his hand on his crotch, "it really is pure altruism." He roared with laughter once more and moved his hips suggestively.

"You are disgusting and you have no idea what you're talking about," I replied, turning my back on him and looking at Josie. "Think of the ramifications."

"Like what?"

"Like… you might have six children born before you actually give birth to one yourself."

"So?"

"Josie, what if two of your children end up marrying one another without knowing that they're brother and sister?"

"They'd only be half brother and sister, and I'm sure there are ways to prevent that happening."

I glared at her. "Would you do it for nothing?" I asked.

"Hell, no."

"Well then you aren't being altruistic – so don't tell me you're helping others. You're being totally mercenary."

Jake groaned as he muttered, "Jeez Josie, did you actually request to live with Frigid Fran? Get a life, girl!" He shivered mockingly and left, slamming the door behind him.

The atmosphere was tense for the last weeks of term and it was a relief when we headed home for the summer. Josie and I both had vacation jobs and saw nothing of each other for three months. Now I was alienated from my best friend and no closer to finding my birth parents.

What I needed was a plan of action, rather than making random stabs at things – and flying off the handle at people. It was frustrating to have names and nothing more; everything led to a dead end. My plan developed to study abroad in South Africa during my junior year, but meanwhile I needed to try and get more information closer to home. I couldn't just arrive in South Africa and hope to find them; I needed to go armed with something helpful as a starting point.

My thoughts turned to the relatives that had once lived in San Jose. Accordingly, I placed a notice in *The Mercury News* personal column for two weeks: "Will anyone with information about Valerie Spencer please reply to this phone number...." I gave my cell phone number. There was no response.

The next logical step seemed to be a visit to Good Samaritan Hospital, checking with the records department. Perhaps they kept records from 1982. I went there on the day before I started my summer job; it was a strange sensation to enter a building, knowing that my mother had given birth to me there. This is where my life had begun, just a few miles from where I had lived all my life. I stood for a while looking around the lobby, trying to imagine my mother here. With visuals of the place but no idea of what she looked like, there was an integral piece of the puzzle missing. I tried to convince myself that I could feel a connection to her, just being here, but in truth it was my imagination willing it; I felt nothing. The gulf between us seemed bigger than ever – I had to find that missing piece to complete the picture. I needed to find her. I needed to find my father too.

The entrance lobby was cheerful and a receptionist directed me to the right place, through a maze of corridors. However, finding the records department was easier than finding the records. I worked through bureaucratic hoops without success until eventually Bob, a student on a summer internship, offered to help me. He was kind of cute and took my number, saying he'd call if he found any information about my birth. The very next day he rang and suggested we meet at Starbucks down the road, as he had uncovered some stuff in a file that had been stuck behind an old cabinet. It was my first day at work, so I arranged to meet him at lunchtime. By the time I got there, he had selected two armchairs and ordered us each a latte. He looked too pleased with himself for my liking and suddenly seemed less cute than he'd been the day before. But there was a manila folder in his hand; he announced that he'd copied all the details from the file into it. I grabbed it from him hastily. This was my information, not his.

Very quickly, I turned aside and opened the folder. Sure enough, there it all was – my blood group and my mother's, as well as my weight and length. Then there was my first breakthrough; some handwritten notes from the doctor whose name appeared to be W. G. Smith, with offices on nearby Samaritan Drive.

My negative feelings about him were forgotten; *he* was forgotten. I leapt from the chair, thanked Bob and grabbed my latte as I raced out the door. I could hear him calling after me, "Let me know what you find out." I nodded and waved. There was not a moment more to lose after so many years of lost time. I drove to the address in nearby Samaritan Drive. It was a low, sprawling, Spanish-style building, with courtyards and pathways connecting the different wings. Eventually I found the building directory and quickly scanned the S section. "Please still be here," I prayed. "Don't let this be a dead end." There it was: Drs. Walter and Grant Smith. They were obstetricians in suite 303. Surely one of them had to be the right one?

The room was very hushed when I entered. Patients sat in an adjoining waiting area, watching me idly as I stood in reception. The receptionist was away from her desk and I felt conspicuously out of place. Doubts began to besiege me; what was I going to say? How would I begin to explain? Feeling beads of sweat on my forehead, I made for the door and was about to walk out when a voice said, "Can I help you?"

I turned nervously. The receptionist smiled and repeated her question.

All heads were turned my way. My mouth opened and shut and I swallowed hard. "I'm…I'm looking for Dr. Smith."

I felt really stupid when she laughed and said, "Well, we have two of them." Seeing my discomfort, she apologized and shrugged, adding, "It's confusing, I know."

Speaking in undertones, I said, "I don't know if you can help me, but I'm looking for the Dr. Smith who was present when I was born. He attended my… mother." It was exhilarating to make that statement. With much more confidence, I smiled and said it again. "I'm looking for the doctor who attended my mother. All I know is that he was W.G. Smith and I was born in 1982."

"I see," she replied. The smile had gone from her face and she looked at me inquisitively now. "I think Sue will be able to help you. She's been here a long time. Why don't you step into that office over there and she'll be with you in a moment." This was the first time I had made progress in my quest. I sat in the small office and examined the artwork – all paintings of babies and pregnant women. It was restful, despite the background sound of phones ringing and photocopiers humming. A woman with greying hair entered and introduced herself as Susan Briggs, asking how she could help. I began my story again, explaining that I had been adopted, but was trying to trace Valerie Spencer, my birth mother, whom I thought had been a patient here.

"Well in 1982, there was only one Dr. Smith in the practice. That was Walter G. Smith. Now his son, Grant, has joined him. I would have to go into the old records to find any information we might have, if Dr. Smith is agreeable of course. I was working here then, but it was a long time ago." She studied me carefully and frowned. "You know, we did have a patient back then – a young girl who gave her baby up for adoption. She was the only patient we ever had who did that. It's coming back to me. She was from some strange place; I'm trying to think of it. It was somewhere in Africa I think. Yes, that's right, I'm sure of it."

I went hot and cold and then hot again. "My mother was from South Africa," I said.

"Oh, well then...." She looked at me and shook her head. "Well, well..." I thought she was going to stand there all day saying "well," but finally she stopped and continued with her train of thought. "The practice was much smaller then. I used to help in reception, but I was really Dr. Smith's nurse. I had a chance to talk to patients. Now I think of it, I remember remarking to her once that I thought all people in Africa were black. Was that dumb of me or what? She laughed for a long time and I was glad that I made her laugh, even if it was at my own expense. She usually looked so sad." Now that she'd started talking, Susan Briggs was enjoying herself. Recalling the past, she was unstoppable. "I think that young woman left soon after the baby was born. I'm sure it was you, because we've never had another case like it." She patted me on the shoulder and said, "It might take some time, but I'll search records from 1982 and get back to you if I find anything. Leave me your email address. I'll need to check with the doctor, of course."

As I wrote the information down, I said, "You're the first person I've ever met who has seen my mother and talked to her – if it was her." When I looked up, my eyes were moist. "How old was she?"

"I couldn't say offhand, but she was young. If I can lay my hands on the file, that information will be there." She paused, and then added, "I'll speak to Dr. Smith and see if he can remember anything interesting. If I remember rightly, she spoke with an accent that sounded like she was from England. In fact I thought she was at first."

I was hungry for information. "Can you tell me what she looked like?"

Susan smiled and sat down. "Oh lawdy, it was a long time ago. Let me think about it … hmmm…. I'd say she was about my height – I'm 5 feet 6 inches. She was fair, I would say her hair was light brown; and she had a pretty smile – I remember that much. It was such a long time ago, though…" The older woman reached out and touched my hand. "It must have been difficult for her. I'm sure she did what she thought was best."

I nodded. "I want to find her."

Chapter 4

It was another week before Susan Briggs contacted me. My summer job at the library kept me busy, but I constantly checked emails whenever I had a chance. I didn't have time to open it when her message finally arrived, although I could see that the subject line read: *Valerie Spencer's records.* The day seemed interminable until I could actually read the message: *Valerie Spencer was a patient here in 1981/1982. She gave birth to a baby girl on March 9th. I have the file and Dr. Smith says that, under the circumstances, he will allow you to look at it, but you can't take it away. He also said he would like to see some documentation, if you have any, like your original birth certificate. If you come during lunch hour, I will sit with you in the office while you look at the file. Let me know when. Tomorrow would work for me.*

It was her. I had finally made a link with my mother. My fingers were trembling as I hit reply. *See you tomorrow at noon. Thanks very much.*

I couldn't bring myself to tell my adoptive parents what I had discovered. When my Mom said that someone named Bob had called for me and left a number, I felt myself blush. It would be difficult to explain a trip to Good Samaritan Hospital, so I quickly said, "Oh, he's a guy I was chatting to in Starbucks the other day. No big deal. I really don't want to see him; if he calls again, tell him I've gone back to LA."

I was a clock watcher at work the next day and took off as fast as I could for Dr. Smith's office. He was curious to meet me and was waiting with Sue Briggs when I arrived. "I don't often get to see the babies I bring into the world when they're grown up. I'm sorry about the formality of seeing your birth certificate, but I can't just show records to anyone who asks," he said. I must have looked puzzled, because he gave a cursory glance to check the names and dates on the documents, before explaining, "As you are mentioned in the file on record here, you have a right to see it. I hope you understand." I was relieved that I had the original document to prove my case if I needed to – perhaps I would need it in the future as well. He smiled at me and said, "Good luck with your search. I'll leave you with Susan to look at the records, but I must be on my way. Babies even arrive during lunch hour, you know. They show no consideration for my digestion."

I watched him walk away, feeling a strange sensation that this was the first person in the world to see me. On impulse I ran after him and called, "Dr. Smith, did my mother hold me after I was born?"

He turned and frowned, then laughed. "I'm an old man and my memory isn't what it used to be, young lady. I've seen so many births in my time, but funnily enough, your birth stands out and I do remember it. And yes, your mother did hold you. Another woman, a relative I think, was with her; there was a bit of an argument as I recall. I had to intervene and tell the relative that she was distressing my patient. I'd never had to do that before, which is the reason why your birth stands out in my memory. We had heated words and I made her leave the delivery room before we handed you to your mother." His face was kind and when he smiled, he looked more like a grandfather than a doctor. "Your Mom was very brave," he said.

I felt tears in my eyes. "Did she say anything? I know it was a long time ago, but can you remember?"

He laughed as he spoke. "You're asking a lot of an old man; I can hardly remember what I had for breakfast, let alone something that happened years ago. But actually, I do remember that moment. I was expecting her to say her baby was beautiful; that's what most new mothers say. Instead she stared at you and said that you were 'so fair.' It sounded old-fashioned and I wondered if it was a South African expression for beautiful." Pursing his lips, he said, "Strange, I hadn't thought about that for years until you asked the question. It's funny how things stick in your memory like that." He smiled again and said, "Now, I really must go."

As he turned, he suddenly added, "The nurses took a photo of you and gave it to your mother. She clutched that photo as if her life depended on it." He shook his head as he began to walk away. "I've never taken a case like that again – it was too emotional for me. I always refer them to someone else."

 Susan Briggs guided me gently to a chair and placed the file on a desk in front of me. "I'll sit here and eat my lunch. Take your time, Fran. You can make notes, by the way."

I hardly heard what she was saying as I opened the file and read;

Date: August 14ᵗʰ 1981
Name: Valerie Spencer
Address: 15640 Zinnia Lane, Los Gatos, California
DOB: 14ᵗʰ February 1962
Age: 19
Weight: 115 lbs.
Height: 5 feet 6 inches
Blood group: A positive
Allergies: none
First pregnancy
Next of kin: parents, Sharon and Tom Spencer, South Africa
Contact in case of emergency: Lorna Scott
Relationship: aunt
Address and phone number: 15640 Zinnia Lane, Los Gatos. (408)356-6897

I jotted down all the information I needed and continued reading. It appeared that my mother visited Dr. Smith once a month from that date onwards until the end of January 1982. Then she came once a week, every Thursday morning. By the time I was born, she had turned twenty and weighed 140 lbs. It was a trouble-free pregnancy, but a difficult delivery that lasted thirteen hours. An episiotomy had been performed on her. I wasn't sure what that was, but it sounded painful. Dr. Smith noted that against his medical advice, Valerie Spencer had chosen to make a lengthy flight of thirty hours, one week after giving birth. Attached to his note was a typed letter, signed by my mother. It read:

To whom it may concern:
I plan to return to South Africa on March 16th. I am aware of Dr. Smith's objections and I absolve him of all responsibility regarding my air travel.
Signed: Valerie Spencer

Another hand-written note was attached as well. It read:

Dear Dr. Smith,
Thank you very much for your kind attention during the past months. I apologize that I am acting against your advice, but I hope you understand how painful it is for me to remain here. Everything reminds me of what I've lost and I need to put my life together again. I'll never forget your kindness and support; holding my baby meant so much to me. It was the hardest thing I've ever done to let her go.
Sincerely,
Valerie Spencer

I couldn't contain my emotions as I read these words, written in my mother's own hand; it felt as if she was speaking to me. Susan Briggs looked up and cleared her throat as she spoke, "Would you like me to photo copy anything?"

I nodded. When I handed her the note written by my mother, she looked at it first, photocopied it at the machine next to her, then handed me the original. I hesitated, but she insisted. "It means more to you than it does to this file. Go on, keep it. I'll put the copy in the file."

I clutched the note in both hands against my chest. Once, a long time ago, my mother had held this very piece of paper and I could imagine how she wept as she wrote it. Now it was mine. I had a letter from my mother.

Chapter 5

Looking at my watch, I realized I was due back at work in five minutes. Telling a half truth, I phoned the library to say I'd been held up at the doctor's office and would be back as quickly as I could. Then, throwing caution to the wind, I went in search of 15640 Zinnia Lane. Would Lorna Scott still be living there?

I drove to a tidy, tree-lined part of Los Gatos with well-maintained, single-family homes. As I neared my destination, my eyes were already racing ahead; which house would it be? Numbers weren't clearly visible, so I drove slowly, peering at each door and mailbox, until at last I found what I was looking for; it was a neat, yellow home with a huge magnolia tree outside – and 15640 on the front door. There was a swing hanging from the magnolia branches that looked old and well-used, and children's bicycles were lying in the driveway. As I watched, a blue minivan pulled up and the garage door opened. A small boy jumped out of the car to grab the toys, moving them out of the way as he complained. "Why do I have to do this? I didn't put them all here. It's not fair."

The driver turned and stared at me curiously, then pulled into the garage. Now I felt conspicuous, like a stalker. Did I dare get out the car and ask questions? I stared vacantly, trying to decide what to do, when a young woman emerged and called to the boy. She looked at me uneasily and then beckoned the child, hurrying him in before the garage door closed.

I grabbed my cell phone and dialed 356-6897. After two rings a woman's voice answered.

I took a deep breath. "Is Lorna Scott there?" I asked.

"Who is this?"

"Fran Walker. I'm her niece."

There was a long silence. "Lorna died last year. This is her daughter. Lorna had no niece called Fran Walker, so whoever you are, give it up."

Afraid she was about to put the phone down, I said quickly, "I'm Valerie Spencer's daughter."

There was a long silence and I could hear her breathing on the other end. Finally she said, "Are you parked in a car outside my house right now?"

Almost choking, I said, "Yes."

"You'd better come in."

My hands were trembling and the strange words, "I'm Valerie Spencer's daughter," echoed in my head. There was much at stake, not the least losing my job if I didn't get back to work. That, however, was far from my thoughts. From the moment I entered that door, I had a different facet to my identity. Lorna's daughter opened the door for me, but we both remained motionless and silent, staring at one another. There was no unease in our awkwardness, simply disbelief. My arrival on her doorstep came from out of nowhere, and she was stunned as she tried to assimilate my announcement. For my part, this was the first time I had met anyone who was a blood relative, however distant. She was my mother's cousin. She looked young and athletic, dressed in a white T-shirt, khaki shorts and running shoes.

At length she broke the silence. "I'm Addie Scott Marshall. Did you say your name was Fran?"

"Yes," I said.

"You've taken me by surprise," she replied. "I'm at a loss for words."

"Me too. All I know is that this is the first time I've ever met a real family member." I felt a stab of guilt and hastily added, "I mean a family member that I'm actually related to by blood. I have my adoptive parents and brother, but this is different. I want to find my birth parents. I've only just discovered the link to Lorna Scott." I explained briefly how I had come by the information.

"I'm beginning to understand," Addie murmured. "Valerie was a lot older than me, so I don't remember her much. I have an older sister, Mary. She might know more. My mother would have been the one to answer all your questions. Why don't you come in, instead of standing in the doorway?"

I entered the living room, strewn with toys and art projects that children had been working on. Addie made no apologies, but simply pushed clutter aside for me to sit on the sofa next to her. "My mother had a sister called Sharon, who was Valerie's mother. Sharon married a South African; they had a farm I think. I know my Mom went to go and visit them once, before I was born, and Valerie came to stay with us when I was about six; Mary was seven. I don't remember much about her stay, but we never saw her again. My Mom kept contact with the family and my aunt came to visit. I was afraid of her; she always seemed angry. Mary and I kept out of her way," she laughed. Suddenly she frowned and apologized, "I'm sorry, that's rude of me. She's your grandmother after all."

"I don't mind. I want to know anything you can tell me, even if it's not flattering."

"Well that's about all I can tell you, but I'll look and see if I can find any photos amongst my mother's things. There are boxes of her stuff stored in the garage. And I'll phone Mary to see if she can help; she lives in New York." Suddenly Addie stopped talking and walked over to me. "This deserves a hug," she said. It was good to feel her warm acceptance and, as she put her arms around me, she laughed, "Are we first cousins once removed, or second cousins?"

****

The afternoon was a blur after that. Addie wanted to hear all about me and it was an hour before I thought about going back to work. There was a frosty reception as I apologized and the librarian grunted, "Hope it's nothing serious. We were worried you were in surgery you were gone so long."

I tried to come up with an explanation, but it was impossible to paraphrase the events of the past few hours. All I could do was apologize and say that it was difficult to explain. She looked at me suspiciously and muttered, "Don't let it happen again. You're being paid to assist me. Make doctor's appointments in your own time."

I didn't care about the reprimand. I was inching my way forward in the search for my birth parents – and I had found Addie. She was as excited and intrigued as I was, and promised to follow up with her sister. I didn't explain anything about all of this to my parents. They had kept secrets from me, and now this was my own secret. I told nobody.

GLYNNIS HAYWARD

Chapter 6

I was filled with hope and excitement. Despite the fact that Addie and Mary didn't know my mother or her whereabouts, they found photos that showed Sharon and Lorna together through the years, along with other people whose identities were a mystery. There were some marked on the back with the words, *South Africa 1962*. In them, Lorna was standing behind her sister, who was holding a small baby. I couldn't be sure, but it seemed logical that the infant was my mother, as she was born in 1962. There was another close-up of the baby and on the back was written, *V aged 3 months*. It was her, I was certain, but it was frustrating that there were no further photos of her. One baby looks much like another, I thought, but at least I had a glimpse of my mother and grandmother. Addie very kindly made copies for me to keep.

Mary had more success; she retrieved some old letters written by my grandmother. They had been tossed into a suitcase that was discovered in the attic, after her mother's death. She sent the letters and I read them over and over, absorbing and memorizing every word.

The Oaks
Ixopo
June 11th 1981

Dear Lorna,

Thank you so much. I wish we could take you up on your offer, but Tom is stubborn and difficult; he says he'll sort out his own problems. I think it would be a great solution to have her come and stay with you a while; living in California would take her mind off all these issues going on here. The country is in turmoil and the political scene is frightening. I wish she would be sensible and mind her own business, but she continues to defy us and doesn't seem able to see the danger all around. Ever since she went to university, she seems to feel that we're personally responsible for apartheid and that we treat our farm workers like slaves! I'm finding it very hard to be patient and, even though I worry about her being away from us, when she occasionally comes home, it always seems to end in a fight. I've tried to visit her in Durban a few times to keep communication open, but she is never available. The more I warn her that the police can make life difficult for her if she joins the protests, the more she seems to think it would be a badge of honor.

What happened to my sweet girl? Her nose was always in a book when she wasn't riding her horse or dancing. How she loved ballet! She spoke Zulu as much as she spoke English, playing with the African children on the farm. They were all friends together. Why does she think they're so badly treated now? She should know better than anyone how happy they are. It reminds me of the troubles in the South at home, when everything turned upside down. It's the same sort of troubled time as it was then, with civil unrest throughout the country. It will sort itself out though and there is no need for her to get into danger.

Thank you for being so understanding. I don't feel that we are able to talk to her anymore, and it's almost like Tom and I can't even speak to one another either. I wish you were closer. We are going back to Johannesburg next week, as Tom has some meetings to attend and of course, I have work to do as well.

I have a big design project starting for an embassy in Pretoria and I can't wait to get my teeth into it. Johannesburg is an exciting city and reminds me of being back in the States. There's energy everywhere, not like sleepy Ixopo. (There's more to life than how much milk the cows are producing daily and when the rains will come!) I always feel happy to be in our house there, even though most people say that Johannesburg is such a terrible city. I don't agree at all. I'm glad we have tight security; high walls topped by barbed wire, as well as an alarm and burglar bars on all the windows. We're very diligent about locking up at night and setting the alarm, so I feel quite safe. We have good friends there and I enjoy the social whirl. I try to like the farm, but it gets lonely and empty. Tom is always busy and time seems to hang heavily, giving me more time to worry about Valerie. He's always busy in Johannesburg too, but at least I have my business. The shop that I started when Valerie went to boarding school has grown a lot. Now I have someone running it for me so that I can do the designing.

Valerie has announced that she isn't coming home for the July break, but is going to Cape Town to visit a friend's family instead. I asked her how she was paying for it, and she said there was nothing to pay; she was getting a lift and staying with his family. I noticed the slip when she said "his" family. I asked who he was, but she said curtly – a friend! I asked whether he was a boyfriend, to which she said, "Well he's a boy and he's a friend, so I suppose he's a boyfriend". She finds it impossible to be civil, even when I'm trying simply to communicate. I asked where his family lived in Cape Town, in case I need to contact her, and her response was,

"District Six." This was a coloured township that was destroyed by the government years ago. Now it's just a wasteland, but it was supposed to become a very nice neighbourhood. Nobody will build in the area though, so she's clearly not staying there. Were we difficult like this, Lorna? Daddy would not have tolerated such behavior, would he?

I look forward to being back in Johannesburg. It'll take my mind off all this. Sorry you've had to listen to my moans.

Love,
Sharon

****

So my mother was a political activist, involved in the struggle. I was pleased; she was fiery and brave. She loved books, so we had something in common. My grandmother sounded like a whiner; maybe if she had been my mother, I would also have rebelled. Most important of all, I now knew the name of the farm where she grew up, and the unpronounceable name of the town. When I asked about that back at UCLA, the professor laughed and said it was an onomatopoeic Zulu name; the sound of a cow pulling its hoof out of the mud. He demonstrated with a loud click sound for the X in Ixopo.

There was another letter from my grandmother to her sister. This one was short and frantic.

The Oaks
Ixopo
July 31st 1981

Dear Lorna,

We arrived back from Johannesburg to find Valerie on the doorstep. She didn't go to Cape Town after all and looked terrible. In fact when we arrived home she was throwing up in the toilet. You might have guessed – she's pregnant. There was an almighty row with Tom not being very helpful at all. I can't really tell you about it in a letter, but we desperately need to get her away. Please can we take you up on your earlier offer? I feel terrible asking this of you; it is such a lot for you with two children of your own, but I don't know where else to turn. I am so angry with Valerie, and Tom is ready to disown her. We can't believe what she's done. I think it is better that I explain when I see you though. Nobody here must know that she's pregnant. That would be best.

Love,
Sharon

Another letter was stuffed in the same old envelope, dated a week later. It read simply:

Dearest Lorna,

It was a relief to hear your voice on the phone. I don't know how to thank you. We've booked our tickets and will fly British Airways, arriving San Francisco on August 10th on Flight 56 from London. I'll stay for a short while to get her settled if that's alright, and then I think it'll be better if I return. That way the story will hold up that she is studying abroad for a

95

year. I hope this is convenient for you. I'll explain everything when I see you. We didn't say much on the phone as one never knows who else is listening, especially here in Ixopo with the phone being a party line. I heard someone's clock chiming as we spoke and I don't think it was yours. Thank you for being so discreet.

Love,
Sharon

There was only one more letter, dated September 20th 1981. Sharon was obviously back in Johannesburg, after delivering my mother to California.

Dear Lorna,

I feel guilty not being with you to help, but I am thankful that Valerie is safely away from the turmoil she has left behind. It won't be easy for the father of the baby if the police catch him. Tom met him in Durban when he went to collect Valerie's belongings. The boy was under house arrest, with security police watching his house all the time from across the street; yet he managed to get away and enter Valerie's flat, trying to find her. After Tom rowed with him, the wretch managed to escape the police from right under their noses. Now he is on the wanted list. If they catch him, he won't see the outside of prison for a long, long time. I'm sure they will catch him soon. Road blocks have been set up all over the place.

I'm so thankful that Valerie is with you – please don't tell her about this. I hope this boy doesn't try to contact her; fortunately he has no way of knowing where she is. Tom read him the riot act, but he said the fellow was actually polite. He claimed to love Valerie very much and wanted to marry her if he could. A pity the two of them didn't consider the difficulties before they started the relationship.

Good news that Valerie has agreed to work with the adoption agency. At least she is being reasonable. I was afraid she would insist on keeping the baby and God knows how that would that have worked. She simply cannot keep it. I hope her resolve doesn't weaken. Please call me immediately if there is any hint of that happening and just say that Valerie is finding the workload very difficult. I'll understand what's happening and if I need to come back, I'll do so immediately. How can I ever thank you?

Love,
Sharon

My mind was in turmoil. What did all this mean? From what I had read about South Africa at that time, house arrest seemed to be a common penalty for political activists, particularly students. But why were my birth parents unable to marry? Was Johan already married? What happened to him after he escaped? Was he ever caught? And why was my grandmother so adamant that my mother couldn't keep me? It sounded unnatural and unfeeling. Immediately I didn't like her. She had clearly forced my mother to give me up.

I rushed to search online for information about Johan Barnard that now might make more sense; there was one entry that seemed as if it could refer to my father. *The Times* of London reported on July 5th 1985 that dignitaries had met with ANC exiles in Stockholm, to discuss economic sanctions against South Africa. Several names were listed and amongst them was Johan Barnard. Did that mean that he still lived abroad and had never returned to South Africa? Had he found my mother and were they together? Were they both members of the previously banned African National Congress that was now the ruling party?

Suddenly I had leads on two fronts and on two continents. The first logical step seemed to be that I write a letter to Valerie Spencer, c/o The Oaks, Ixopo, South Africa. I deliberated a long time about what to say and decided to keep it short. I wrote:

Dear Valerie,

My name is Fran Walker, but you knew me as Greta in 1982. I hope this reaches you. If it does, please contact me by email at <u>*frangrace1@comcast.net*</u>

Love,
Fran

My sixth sense told me that if she had another family at this point, my appearance could be embarrassing. It would be better to not mention our relationship. I debated signing as Greta, but that didn't seem right. I wasn't Greta; I didn't want to recreate myself. Holding the envelope close to my chest, I kissed it for luck before hiding it in my purse to put in the mail. Would my letter find her – and even more important, would she want to see me? And then that unbearable thought forced itself back into my head; maybe she wouldn't want me in her life. She didn't want me then, why would she want me now?

Once again I felt angry with her, although I couldn't understand why I should have such a reaction after desperately seeking her whereabouts for so long. I felt out of sorts and let down. She had given me away and deprived me of knowledge that was my right to know. For most people, the future is a question mark, but for me, my past was an unanswered question as well. My genetic past had been taken away from me and I'd been handed something flimsy in its place; I felt like a paper doll, wearing a strange outfit that didn't fit. Grace Walker was the one who had dressed the paper doll and I stormed home, ready to vent my anger.

My adoptive mother was taken by surprise when I flung the door open and burst into tears. This was followed by a torrent of venomous words that I remember with shame. "Why can't we be like other families?" I shouted. "I always feel a freak because everyone else knows their parents, but I don't. I know two strangers. You have no idea what's going on in my head and you never even try. If you were a real mother, you would know what to do. You'd know that I'm unhappy and you'd do something about it. But you've never tried. You think that you did me such a favour when you adopted me, but you don't realize how hard it is for me, not knowing anything." As she started to speak, I cut her off. "Why didn't you at least find out some information about my parents? Didn't you care? All you thought about was yourself; you didn't care about me. You can't buy a baby, you know. There's more to being a mother than feeding me."

I stopped to draw breath and Grace said very calmly, "Yes, there's a lot more to being a mother than that. And there's also a lot more to being a mother than giving birth. I wasn't able to do that for you, but I have done everything else I could. If it wasn't enough for you, I'm sorry." I opened my mouth to reply, but she stood up and walked to the door, pausing for a moment to add, "I'm truly sorry I couldn't supply that missing link. I had no idea it distressed you all this time, so you're right, I have failed you for not being able to help you through this." I wanted to run after her immediately and apologize, but my legs wouldn't move. I was still angry, but I realized in that moment that I wasn't mad at Grace; I felt lost.

It was Addie who calmed me down. She placated me by listening to my ranting and saying that if I wanted to stop the search, then I needn't mail the letter. The choice was mine. "What's done is done," she added. "You have the means now to try and follow a lead and find out the whole story, or you can ignore it and never have a chance of finding out. There's no point in being mad at Valerie or Grace – especially not Grace. Think about it, she also had sadness to deal with; she wasn't able to bring a child into this world. She could have felt life was unfair and become bitter like you're being at the moment, but she made the choice to accept the facts and do something productive. You have everything to thank her for. It's not just all about you, Fran." As I began to cry, she put her arms around me and apologized, saying, "I didn't mean to be so harsh. I have no way of knowing how you're feeling, because I've never walked in your shoes. I'm sorry, Fran."

When I recovered my composure, I mumbled, "I suppose you're right. I deserved it. You put things in perspective, Addie."

On my way home I mailed the letter, using my dorm as the sender's address. It was a shot in the dark; I knew it was unlikely that my mother still lived there, nearly two decades after those letters were written by her mother. It was the only lead I had to work on, however. I found myself staring at the mailbox for a few minutes, after the letter dropped through the slot; it was on its way to Africa. Who knew what it would find?

I stopped and bought a bunch of flowers for my Mom, who cried when I gave them to her. She hugged me and said, "I will always love you Fran, no matter what." As she began putting the flowers in water, she said, "But I want to tell you something; you might not always have a forgiving audience, you know." Wiping away tears with her sleeve while her back was turned, she added, "Your thoughts and feelings are your property and nobody can stop you having them; but the moment you say or do something, other people are affected. Then there are consequences. Think before you speak – or act."

I wished I could hit the rewind button and erase what I'd said to her. All I could do was say, "I'm sorry Mom. I didn't mean it."

It all came to naught anyway. When I returned to university two weeks later, the letter was waiting for me with RETURN TO SENDER stamped in red, as well as hand-written. The address had been crossed out and below was an inked stamp with multiple, possible reasons for the return. The one checked was: *not at this address.*

I scrunched it up and tossed the letter in the trash. In a way I wasn't surprised; I hadn't expected my search to end that easily. But the reason given for the return gave me a ray of hope; another unchecked option read *deceased.* At least it wasn't that.

When we returned for our sophomore year, Josie announced that she had broken up with Jake during the summer. I was pleased – although it was some months before we discussed the egg donor topic again. I thought about explaining how difficult it was for me, not to know my biological parents; I almost described my search. But once again I didn't want to divulge my secret. It was a relief when she told me that she had decided against the stupid idea of donating her eggs.

Things were never quite the same between us again, but I was pleased to have my friend back and the rest of sophomore year was uneventful. She made plans for a study program in Sweden the following year, and I was accepted for the South African study abroad program. We would both be away from UCLA for six months – the first time in our lives that we'd be apart for so long. In a strange way, we were both ready for it.

Chapter 7

If my adoptive parents realized that I was on a quest for my birth parents, they said nothing. They expressed concern about the crime rate in South Africa and were reluctant for me to go there, suggesting instead programs offered in Europe. They were keen for me to go to Sweden with Josie, but my mind was made up. Finally they agreed – and decided to plan a family vacation in South Africa, before I began my studies at the University of KwaZulu-Natal in Durban.

Our arrival on the African continent was unforgettable. We flew overnight from London on a direct flight to Cape Town, awaking with Africa beneath us. I could hardly contain my excitement as I peered out the jumbo jet and saw vast plains below. There were dry river beds, brown hills, footpaths, and a few dirt roads that snaked through the landscape, but little sign of habitation. Occasionally I noted a cluster of dwellings, but they were too distant to see their shape or inhabitants. These were the only signs of life until we were flying over South Africa itself. Then changes began to appear and I could see paved roads, with cars moving on them like ants. We flew over dams with big expanses of water, and then over a mountain range. As we neared our destination, the earth beneath changed to vivid green. The captain announced that we were flying over the winelands and soon we would see the back of Table Mountain. It was like a picture post card, with rows of neatly cultivated grape vines. We approached the airport flying over the city. Cape Town is nestled between the foot of the flat-topped mountain and the sea. I smiled; Barnards had lived hereabouts for nearly four hundred years and I felt that I belonged. It was like a homecoming.

We did the usual sightseeing stops, trying to see as much as possible in the shortest amount of time. I vowed to return so that I might have more time in this old city, steeped in colourful history. The day trip to Robben Island was particularly memorable, not just because a rough crossing from the Waterfront caused every passenger to be seasick. The island had been a top security prison for political prisoners; Nelson Mandela spent nearly a quarter of a century locked up here. We saw his cell and the limestone caves where he was forced to work. The tour was led by a former inmate who described his own incarceration with passion; he had reverence for the leaders, who emerged honed by fire. Robben Island was known as "the university" he told us – and they were all the graduates. There was pride on his face as he remarked that men like Mandela showed no bitterness, but had a vision of what South Africa should and could be.

I wanted to ask if there was a registry of former inmates, longing to know whether Johan Barnard had been caught after his escape and sent to Robben Island. But I couldn't find my voice to do so in front of my family and there was no opportunity to ask in private.

We continued our vacation with a trip to a game reserve in the Eastern Cape. It was awesome. Seeing a herd of elephants, padding through the bush and flapping their ears at us in a mock charge, was both exciting and terrifying. In this unspoiled place, everything was as it had been at the beginning of time; I was a visitor in the animals' world. Cocooned in a green Land Rover, I became an observer of their world as I put my own on hold. We saw herds of impala, kudu and water buck, as well as giraffe and a variety of bird life. The moment when we spied a pride of lions lazing under a tree, was most thrilling. They were escaping the heat of the blazing sun and the male lion lay very still, with only an occasional flick of his tail. Three lionesses lay nearby, watching us and their young, unblinkingly; the four cubs were tumbling and wrestling one another, like domestic kittens. We gazed in silence and felt the peace of the bush; a peace that could shatter at any moment when these creatures needed to eat again. The following day we came across the pride again, eating the remains of a giraffe they had killed during the night. Once again the male was asleep, having satisfied his appetite. The lionesses were taking their turns eating, and the cubs were grabbing what morsels they could.

On our last day, we were privileged to see a creature rarely observed; it is nocturnal, solitary, and camouflaged in trees during the days. Our first indication that there was something amiss was when we spotted a group of impala moving away, leaving behind a newly-born lamb. It faced away from the herd, looking forlorn as it stood on its wobbly, blood-splattered legs. We watched from afar, but it was oblivious of us as it stood immobile, staring into the distance. Our guide, Ollie, said, "Something's wrong. Where's its mother? Maybe she's been taken by a hyena or a jackal. Giving birth is a dangerous thing in the bush, but usually it's the baby that's taken. Sometimes the mother is killed, but not often. It happens if she is weak, or gets in the way while trying to defend her young." He watched for some time through his binoculars and said, "No, the baby keeps looking at that tree over there. Maybe it's a leopard." He and Billy trained their binoculars onto a huge tree, in hopes of finding something; I couldn't stop watching the young impala. It was defenseless against predators and fearful as it stood there, lost and abandoned by the herd. I wanted to protect it.

Suddenly Ollie said in a loud whisper, "There she is. I've got her in my sights." He pointed to a fork in the tree and talked us through which way to look. Sure enough, there – camouflaged so well that you would never have found her without some clue to her whereabouts – was a leopard. She rested along a branch, watching us as she guarded a dead impala. It was hanging just below her on an underlying branch. I cried out involuntarily and Ollie whispered, "It's O.K. Fran. The leopard has to eat too. She's watching in case other predators come, attracted by smells and alarm calls from monkeys. Listen! You can hear them chattering because they're afraid of this cat nearby. They live in the trees too. She has to hang her food high enough that nothing can reach it from below. If lions come, she'll move quickly and leave the kill behind, because she doesn't want to be trapped up there. Lions can climb, but not as high or as quickly as a leopard. They'd wait her out if she stayed – and then she'd be in trouble. That's why she's watching carefully. She doesn't like us here, but in the vehicle we're safe and no threat to her." He looked back at the baby impala and added, "Today that lamb was born, and for sure it's going to die today as well. The predators will be here soon."

"Can't we save it, Ollie? We could take it back to camp with us."

He shook his head. "We can't interfere – nature must take its course. In the wild you have to eat, or be eaten. It's all about survival. Survival of the fittest."

His reply was callous and I stiffened. Billy reached over and said, "It's OK, Fran. Wild animals don't think about things. They respond when they're hungry or threatened, but they don't have emotions." I frowned and he added, "They don't. Emotions have no place in survival."

"That little impala looks afraid, if you ask me. Fear is an emotion," I hissed.

Ollie leaned over and whispered, "Please be quiet." He put his finger to his lips and pointed to the leopard, who was twitching her tail. I was reminded that we were visitors in her world. She was beautiful, staring at us from her high vantage point, and we watched in silence for some time. As we finally drove away, vultures were beginning to circle and I had to accept the outcome for what it was.

Billy was enthralled. He was about to start his senior year of high school; he asked intelligent questions, was always the first person up each day for the game drive, as well as the first to volunteer for a game walk. He confided to me that he planned a return to South Africa for his semester abroad, adding with a playful nudge, that he wished we had the same birth parents. He added conspiratorially, "Good luck, by the way. If you find them and they're any good, maybe I can adopt them too!"

We both laughed and I was happy to get his approval, but then I frowned and asked, "How did you know?"

He smiled. "Give me a break! Do you think I'm stupid? Why else would you make such a fuss about studying here?"

I stared at him. "Do Mom and Dad know?"

"Are you kidding? Of course they do."

I quickly looked away, feeling like a traitor. Then I turned and grabbed Billy's arm. "What did they say?"

He shrugged. "Not much. Dad asked me if I wanted to find my birth parents and I said not really. Mom didn't say anything." I felt a stab of irrational jealousy. Why did they feel comfortable talking to Billy about it, but not to me?

These notions were fleeting though, and as we drove away from the Game Reserve, I felt a sense of loss, leaving behind the dirt roads and returning to civilization. The east coast of the continent had a rugged coastline and unspoiled beaches that seemed endless. There was so much open space that we seldom saw anybody. It seemed we were far away from everywhere – until we drew closer to Durban, a few days later. There were crowds of vendors and pedestrians spilling into the streets from sidewalks. Congested traffic emitted a dull roar and shrill whistles, blown by rickshaws and policemen, added to the deafening cacophony. Buses and taxis seemed to own the road and cars didn't appear to stop for red lights. It was pandemonium.

We made our way, as best we could, to a beachfront hotel in a small coastal town just north of Durban. It was a relief to be out of the car and we enjoyed the prospect of spending our last few days together, relaxing on the beach and swimming in the Indian Ocean – even though it was mid-winter. My Mom stayed close and I often caught her staring at me; at these times she would open her mouth as if to say something, but then she would smile and look away. Finally I said, "What's the matter, Mom?"

She shook her head. "Nothing, nothing at all. I'm just looking at you while I can, so that I can store the picture for the next few months." She took my hands and added, "Good luck with everything, Fran."

Chapter 8

Some parents have a hard time letting go of their children – mine certainly did. I correct myself; my birth parents didn't seem to have a problem, just my adoptive parents. They seemed reassured however, when they saw where I would be living. It was a well-protected house near the campus, shared with three other foreign students. It had sturdy locks, burglar bars on all windows, and good lighting outside. My Dad checked all that carefully. They admonished me to be careful one more time; then we hugged and they were on their way. My Mom waved out the window until I could no longer see their car.

As I watched them drive away, it registered that I would be on a different continent and days of flight-time away from them, yet I was exhilarated. I would miss them, but I was free at last to find my birth parents and I had six months to do it.

The house I lived in was set back from a busy road. It was an old home that had been converted into two separate dwellings; I lived upstairs. High ceilings helped keep the house cool, for I was about to discover that even in August – the end of winter in the southern hemisphere – Durban was a hot city. Luckily for me, the overseas student advisor had set up a program whereby foreign students could buy used cars for the duration of their stay. On returning to our home countries, the program resold them to incoming foreign students, on our behalf. The system evolved because several students had been mugged in previous years, while waiting for public transport. In the interests of safety, we were advised to participate in the program.

Durban campus reminded me of UCLA because of its hills, humidity and vegetation. It was also busy, diverse and big. The university was built on a ridge overlooking the city, and dominated by two distinctive buildings which were the oldest on campus; domed Howard College and Memorial Tower Building. Orientation took place in the Students' Union Hall, a sixties style building with high, brick walls and lots of glass. I had the same strange feeling I'd experienced when I went to Good Samaritan Hospital; I knew somehow that my mother had been here before me, maybe my father too. It gave me shivers.

Local students welcomed us with invitations to join various clubs. An American graduate student, Lauren Marlowe, spoke about her aim to build orphanages throughout the country. It was staggering to discover how many children were orphaned in South Africa, because of Aids; some were brought up by grandparents, others brought themselves up as best they could, and many ended up as street children.

After listening to her address, I sat staring for a long time as she responded to questions. She was passionate about these orphans and I felt humbled; my eyes were opened to the needs of other children who had never known their parents either. Unlike me however, they did not have the luxury of trying to find them. Their parents were dead, killed by a terrible epidemic – and these innocents were born into a battle for survival. I signed up immediately to volunteer.

Back in our house, my roommates turned out to be fellow Americans. Two were English Literature students like me; Lizzie from New Jersey and Brent from Chicago, and then there was Joe, a chemical engineering student from Berkeley. Lizzie and Brent were good company, but I especially liked Joe. Apart from the fact that he was tall and good-looking, we were both Californian and had much in common. We laughed at the same things and enjoyed chatting when our paths crossed; I began to make sure that our paths crossed as often as possible.

On the first day of classes, Lizzie and I discovered we were in the same tutorial group. We watched other students enter the room and were pleased of each other's company. All the others knew one another, as they had been together the previous semester. The lecturer began the tutorial by welcoming the Americans and asking us to introduce ourselves. Things went smoothly until Lizzie began to speak, saying she came from New Jersey. She described how she had always longed to come to Africa.

Before she could say any more, a fellow student started shouting at her. "You African Americans come here to find your roots and your culture, and it makes me mad. You're not African – you're American. Forget it and stop trying to find your 'roots.' Look at those beads you're wearing! Stop trying to steal our culture."

There was a moment of stunned silence in the small room, before Lizzie responded; her ability to think on her feet was enviable. She fired back: "I did not come here to steal your culture – and as I look at you, let me tell you that you have stolen mine!" With this Lizzie started from the top of the woman's head and worked down to her shoes, proving her point. "Your hair," she began.

"You've relaxed it. Well that relaxer was developed by an American woman, an African American hair care entrepreneur, C.J. Walker. That shirt you're wearing – FUBU. That stands for 'For Us By Us.' It was designed by African Americans, targeting the African American population. Those shoes you have on – Nike. Where do you suppose those come from? So something tells me that you're stealing my culture here, but hey – feel free. I'm happy to share. You're right, we African Americans don't know our history because of slavery – we don't know where our ancestors came from in Africa. But we have a culture of our own that we've created – and it seems to appeal to you. I'm flattered."

Apart from Lizzie, there was silence in the room. The tutor waited for her to stop speaking and said, "Thank you Ms. Johnson. That was very illuminating." Not another word was said about the matter after that, but I felt proud of Lizzie. To tell you the truth, I hadn't really considered her as anything other than another American girl, and it was a shock that this South African student was categorizing her. I felt nervous as I introduced myself, but the girl who had attacked Lizzie kept her head down and ignored me. It was a relief; I wasn't sure what she might have said to me, or how I would have been categorized.

The first weeks were so busy getting organized that there was little time to start my search. Every weekend had some activity or assignment that took a lot of time, and I liked being around Joe. I made one trip to try and find Ixopo, managing to get lost and ending up on a dirt road leading to nowhere. There was no sign of current habitation, but there were some burnt out cars lying at the side of the road that looked as if they had been there for some time. I grew nervous and eventually back-tracked, returning to

Durban after dark. Joe showed concern when he heard what I'd done and reminded me that I wasn't back in California. It was a bit annoying; I told him that I already had a Dad. After that I lost courage to explore for a bit, but a few weeks later I made another attempt. This time I studied the map very carefully and set off early, but just outside a small town called Camperdown, I got a flat tyre. Fortunately, the town was only about half a mile away and I was able to walk that distance quickly. I found a gas station and requested help, but the repair shop was closed for the weekend and I would have to wait until Monday. In desperation I phoned Joe, who came and changed the tyre with the spare.

"What's the big idea, driving off on your own?" he asked, as he worked. "I'd be happy to come with you," he added, and then whistled as he tightened the wheel. "It would be much safer if you weren't alone."

"Don't start that again," I answered.

"I'm not starting anything. I'm just saying it would be safer and I'd like to come with you, but if you don't want me to – just call and I'll come and fetch you next time you break down or something."

I wanted to scream at him that sarcasm was the lowest form of wit, but instead I swallowed my words and mumbled, "I'm sorry."

As he worked he said, "That's OK. I'll follow you back to the house. You can't drive this car on your own until you've had that tyre repaired. If you get another flat, you'll really be up the creek without a paddle. Besides, this spare isn't a proper tyre. It's not meant to go forever." When he'd finished, he stood up and looked at me. "I don't get why you keep going off on your own like this." I didn't answer and we didn't speak about it again. When we got back to the house it was late and I was surprised how glad I felt, knowing that he was there. In the weeks that followed, I kept noticing him looking at me – and I was looking back at him.

Frustrated that time was marching on and I had achieved nothing, I made another attempt to find Ixopo. Everything was in order; I had maps and had memorized the route; I was setting out in good time and the car was in good working order. As I drove into the midlands of the province, the countryside changed. In the distance I could see mountains – I was sure they were the Drakensberg, a range of rugged mountains that make a swath across the country. There wasn't much traffic on the road, but I was overtaken frequently by minibuses, travelling at the speed of light and overfilled with passengers. Children played at the side of the road and waved happily when I drove by. The sun was high in the sky and my expectations were soaring, until I came around a corner and saw that the road was blocked by barricades. There was an arrow pointing to a dirt road, signposted as a detour. Cursing, and hesitant to travel dirt roads again, I wondered how long the detour was. As if in answer to my questions, a car approached from the other direction. The driver shouted out the window, "I wouldn't do it if I were you. It's like driving through the Kalahari Desert. I got stuck in sand and there are four other cars still stuck down there. Where are you going?"

"Ixopo," I replied.

"Forget it," he said. "This track goes on for about forty kilometers. It'll take you all day, if you make it." He waved cheerily and drove on, while I burst into tears and beat the steering wheel with my fists.

Disheartened by my aborted efforts to reach Ixopo, I decided that I would take Joe up on his offer to come with me, next time I tried. But the months were flying by and it was November already. Soon it would be exams, the semester would be over and it would be time to return home. I was getting desperate. I couldn't imagine having come this far and not even reaching first base, let alone hitting a home run. As luck would have it, Lizzie and I were reading *Cry the Beloved Country* in our literature class. Alan Paton's novel was my favorite book on the reading list, and furthermore it was set partly in Ixopo. It wasn't hard persuading all my roommates to join me for a weekend away; we were all eager to see the countryside for ourselves and get a break from the smoggy city, just before exams. Classes were over, so we had free time. Piling into my car, armed with a map, bottled water, and a bag of samoosas from the local Indian greengrocer store, we set off.

The weather was fine and sunny as we headed into the interior, leaving the coastal sugar cane fields and bananas trees behind. We made our way first to Pietermaritzburg, an hour away. Its city streets were lined with purple jacaranda blooms, and although it was hot, there was relief from the humidity of Durban. Beyond that, Kwazulu was a wide open space, with odd villages and small towns dotted around. As we drove through the Umzimkulu Valley, I remembered Alan Paton writing about the rolling hills. It was just as beautiful as he described. There were cows that wandered onto the road periodically, with small children alongside them, running naked and waving as we drove by. No adults seemed to be supervising, although the children were some distance from the nearest thatched huts.

Then, without warning, we came around a corner and the lush grazing pastures suddenly stopped; there it was – we were in Ixopo. This was the place I had been looking for. My heart was thudding so loudly I felt sure everyone else could hear it, but nobody seemed to notice my excitement. The town consisted of one main street, with a couple of trading stores, a butcher shop and two hotels, each with a well-frequented pub. On the outskirts was a school, the same one where Alan Paton had once taught. Trying to disguise my feelings when we stopped, I pleaded the need for a restroom and took off immediately. I disappeared before anyone could ask questions, and headed straight to the police station.

The Ixopo police station consisted of only one room, although I suppose there were lock-up facilities close by. It was a very stark room with white walls and small, uncurtained windows. Seated behind a desk was the duty officer, reading a book and making notes in the margins. He looked up when I entered and grinned. "Good afternoon. What can I do for you?" He spoke slowly and deliberately.

I smiled back. "I'm looking for a farm called *The Oaks*."

"Yes *Sisi* (sister), that farm is just down the road. If you carry on down there," he said pointing to the main road, "and go towards Richmond, you'll pass it on the left. You can't miss it."

"Do the Spencers still live there?" I asked, holding my breath.

He scratched his head and nodded, "Sometimes old Mrs. Spencer comes there. Her husband died and the old lady lives in Johannesburg now. She is old, you know, and they tell me she is going to sell the farm."

"Is she there now?" I asked.

"I don't know. But you can go and see. It's a guest farm."

My eyes opened wide in astonishment. "Is it expensive?"

He exploded with laughter. "*Hau!*" he exclaimed in the Zulu manner. "It is too much money."

I had to sit down as my legs felt weak. There was a bench outside the door and I made my way there, as quickly as I could. My thoughts were racing: Was my mother down the road at this farm? Why had my letter been returned to sender if the Spencers were still there? Maybe she had a different name now, a married name. What would I say and what would she reply? What if she wanted nothing to do with me? What if she had other children now? They would be my half brothers and sisters? Had she ever told them about me? Did I dare go down the road?

My thoughts were interrupted by Joe Richard's voice saying, "Hey you, what are you doing outside the police station? You look like you've seen a ghost. What's the matter?"

I was shaking and there was no way I could disguise my anxiety any longer. He sat down next to me, looking very concerned. "What's happened, Fran?"

Relief flooded through me to see his big frame and hear his familiar voice, but I couldn't find the words to answer and dropped my head into my hands. His arms were around me in a second; it felt very comforting to bury my head in his shoulder. Finally I said, "It's a long story. Have you got an hour or so?"

"I've got as long as it takes," he replied. As he brushed my hair with his hand and waited for me to compose myself, I felt I could trust him. My secret had become a burden; I told him the whole story, everything I knew, right up until a moment ago in the police station. Other than Addie, he was the first person I had ever spoken to about it. He was an excellent listener, never stopping me or asking questions, just watching me intently. When I finished my story, he stood up and pulled me with him. "So this is what all your solo trips have been for. I get it. So what are we waiting for?" he asked. "I'm going to *The Oaks*. Are you coming with me?"

I was grateful that he had taken charge for a moment. I had no intention of letting him become the protagonist in my own story, but just then it was a relief to have someone else in the driving seat. It had been a very lonely journey up until now. We walked to the car holding hands and it felt very comfortable; I suddenly wished the others weren't with us for the weekend. Fortunately Lizzie and Brent were happily passing the time of day by chatting to locals in the hotel bar.

The duty officer's directions were accurate. About three miles out of town, white gates appeared with *The Oaks* written on one post, *Spencer* on the other, and a B&B vacancy sign alongside. We drove through the gates in silence, continuing up the long drive, lined with azaleas and rhododendrons. As we came around a bend, nestled next to a grove of oak trees and an expansive lawn, was a sprawling, white farmhouse. It had a corrugated iron roof with gables at either end, fronted by a wisteria-covered verandah and an open front door, beckoning one to enter. We parked the car and were greeted by three dogs that came running out, barking wildly with their tails wagging. A Zulu woman came around the corner, with a baby tied in a blanket on her back. She had a bucket balanced on her head as she smiled and greeted us in Zulu: "*Saubona.*"

We smiled back and greeted her. "Are there any rooms available?" I asked.

She smiled again and pointed at the door, with a slight shrug of her shoulders. I marvelled at her amazing balance; the bucket didn't move and the baby didn't stir. She continued on her way and we made our way up the stairs to the door bell. Before we could press it however, a middle-aged woman emerged from the house, shouting at the dogs to be quiet, and asking if she could help us.

I was dumbstruck and stared at her unblinkingly. If this was my mother, she bore no resemblance to anything I might have imagined. She was short and plump, with greying hair that fell in her eyes. She wore an apron and dried her hands on it before pushing her glasses into place, saving them from sliding off her nose. Joe broke the silence by saying, "We were passing by and wondered whether you have any rooms available for the weekend?"

She pushed her thick hair out of her eyes and said, "How many rooms do you want?"

In unison, we replied, "Two."

She grimaced. "Normally that wouldn't be a problem, but at the moment I only have one room available, I'm afraid. We're busy doing renovations you see. I can show it to you. The rate is R500 per person, and that includes breakfast. If you're students, I'll give you a discount and make it R250 each."

Converted to dollars, the rate for the room was nothing. "Fran, you'll have to be my roommate for the weekend. The others looked happy at the hotel, so maybe they can stay there? What do you think? I'll call and see what they say about it."

I nodded, still staring at the stranger. She stared back at me and said, "Do you want to see the room?"

I swallowed hard and nodded again.

She led us into the house. It had old wooden floors that shone from years of polishing, and the white walls were adorned with old photos. We entered a large hall, with doors leading off it. A long passage led to the rear of the house. Looking around, I had a strange feeling and felt myself shiver. Finally I found my voice and asked, "Are these old family photos?"

She laughed and said, "Yes, they're pictures of my husband's relatives, but most of them are long dead. We like them though. His family has owned the farm for over a century."

So she wasn't my mother. She wasn't even a Spencer, except by marriage. Knowing this, I felt disappointment, but also found courage to speak again. "How long have you lived here?" I asked.

"Just a year," she replied.

By now we had reached the vacant room. It was spacious and airy, with high ceilings. The walls were freshly painted pale lavender; against the middle of the back wall was a queen sized bed, draped with a white, cotton comforter and a host of floral cushions. The windows had white shutters, which opened to reveal a rose garden outside. Joe looked at me inquiringly and I nodded enthusiastically. I would happily sleep on the floor and let him have the bed, but I wanted to stay here. "Let's take it," I said.

"I'll give you the key; let me know what time you'd like breakfast. My name is Louise Spencer, by the way. If there's anything I can get you, just shout."

My eyes had strayed to a corner of the room; there was a table with a bowl of lavender on it, as well a silver-framed photo of a young girl, sitting on a horse. I picked up the photo and said, "Is this you?"

She shook her head. "No, that's a Spencer cousin. I grew up in Johannesburg and didn't see a horse before I was twenty. I still don't ride. My husband's uncle lived here at *The Oaks* for many years, but he died last year and we've decided to try and buy the farm, rather than let it leave the family."

Louise Spencer liked to chat. I didn't want her to stop the flow of information, so I threw out a question. "Did your husband come here much as a child?"

"Oh yes," she replied. "There were two brothers; Tom Spencer was the older who inherited the farm, and my father-in-law, John Senior. My husband's family came here a lot – they were very close. Tom's wife has been very generous to us and we're renovating, you see. Times are hard for farmers, so we started out as a bed and breakfast inn to get some extra income, but we're in the process of doing extensive alterations to turn the place into a spa. That's lucrative now, especially with overseas visitors and people from Johannesburg – the place where all the money is in this country. Don't worry though; you won't be disturbed by noise over the weekend. The builders won't be back until Monday."

We went to the car to retrieve our bags and Louise Spencer went to get a key. My head was reeling. Why had they bought the farm to stop it going out of the family? Was my mother dead, or did she not like farming? They would know the answer. I needed to find the opportunity to ask and I was shaking with excitement.

Louise returned with the key and asked us to follow her to the kitchen, saying we were free to make tea or coffee at any time. She pointed out the dining room next door to the kitchen, adding that breakfast would be served there in the morning. We heard the sound of a chair scraping; she responded by calling through an adjacent door, "John, we have some visitors." Turning to us, and by way of explanation, she added, "My husband is in his office."

A tall, middle-aged man emerged and smiled at us. His face looked like one that had been in the sun a lot and, although he still had a head of thick, grey hair, it was receding at the temples. He pushed his glasses into the top pocket of his khaki shirt and, with an outstretched hand, said, "John Spencer."

Joe stepped forward to shake hands and introduced himself. I hesitated a moment, then said, "I'm Fran." I was tempted to say more, but it wasn't the right moment.

We were warmly welcomed and they made suggestions about what there was to do in the area, and where we could have dinner. It sounded like there wasn't much choice for the latter, but there were numerous hikes, a river where we could fish, and horses to ride. We returned to our room and while Joe phoned Lizzie to make a plan, I went straight to the photo in the corner and removed it from the frame. I turned it over and on the back was written, "Valerie, eighth birthday with Snowy." It was her. It was my mother. It was the first time that I'd seen what she looked like, other than baby pictures. I had always secretly hoped to look like her, but I didn't. It didn't matter though… at last I could form a mental picture of her. She had blond hair and a big smile.

Joe and I reached an agreement about sleeping arrangements; I would have the bed one night and he would have it the other. We flipped a coin and I chose to sleep on the floor first. Lizzie and Brent were annoyed initially, but didn't seem to care that we were staying somewhere else. On our way to the pub for dinner, I said to Joe, "Please don't tell them about all this."

"I wasn't planning to," he replied.

I bit my lip and mumbled, "It's private. I've never told anyone before."

Joe nodded. "Agreed," he said. "You don't have to explain." I realized he understood and that if I wanted to talk about it, he would listen; if I didn't, he would say nothing. Even when we found Brent in the bar and he made ribald suggestions about our absence, Joe kept quiet.

It was so smoky in the bar that my eyes smarted. Brent had been there, sampling every South African beer several times over, and had made friends with a farmer called Mac. They were propping each other up and telling jokes without punch lines, but laughing all the same. Mac was eager for Lizzie to be his friend as well. "This is the new South Africa," he told her. "If you want to come home with me, that's no problem Babe. You and me, we can....you know..." His hands were trying to hold onto his beer and reach out to her at the same time. All he managed to do was spill his drink and make Lizzie mad.

"Listen dude," she said, "you're drunk. Take yourself home and sober up. And keep your filthy hands away from me."

It was surprising that she hadn't given him more suggestions about what he could do; I remembered her fiery temper and sharp tongue on the first day of class. But she turned to me and almost

126

spat out the words, "Drunks are the same the world over. It's not worth wasting your breath on them."

She was happy that we were back and quickly joined us at a table in the dining room. I was very quiet all evening – Joe and Lizzie chatted, but I was pre-occupied and had little interest joining the conversation. I resolved to speak to John Spencer as soon as I could. He was my Mom's cousin, if I had worked out the family connections correctly, and there was no reason why anything should be kept secret from him. If my mother was dead, I would have to accept it. If she was alive, I wanted to know where she was.

I hardly ate anything and couldn't wait to get out of there; Lizzie pleaded a headache and made for bed when we left. There was a full moon; as we drove in silence, I tried to enjoy the spectacle but my nerves were on edge. The farmhouse was gleaming in moonlight, as if it were day. It seemed eerie to me. Far away from city lights, the stars shone brighter than I'd ever seen before, but the beauty and quiet of an African night belied the turmoil I felt inside.

It was cool and I could smell wood fires burning. On closer inspection, there was smoke coming from a chimney on the far side of the house, near the kitchen. "I think I'm going to make some rooibos tea," I said to Joe. "Would you like some?"

He shook his head. "No thanks. Never touch the stuff. I'm going to make the most of sleeping in that bed."

I smiled. "Enjoy it. Turn the light off if you want to. I'll take the flashlight from the room so that I won't disturb you when I come back."

"There's room for two if you change your mind," he said, patting the bed.

"You sound like Mac," I said.

"That's an insult. I'm quite sober, you know."

He smiled as he spoke, and even though I was filled with anxiety, his presence made me feel better. His playfulness was endearing and I took his hands in mine, holding them tight. "Thank you very much for listening to my story," I said. He said nothing, but kissed the top of my head.

Chapter 9

The door to the living room was open and there was light coming from inside. I clattered around in the kitchen making tea, hoping someone would come out, but that didn't happen. After a while I plucked up courage to knock on the door and peer inside. John and Louise were on a sofa, reading. They looked up at me with a start; their faces were friendly, but questioning. "Can I help you?" asked Louise.

I sighed. "Could I speak to you, please?"

John Spencer rose like a gentleman, and beckoned me into the room. "Take a seat here near the fire," he said. The days were hot, but at night there was a chill in the air, so the fire was welcoming. "Is everything all right?" He looked concerned as he sat down again.

I nodded and said, "I want to show you something."As they watched me, surprised by this intrusion, I produced a piece of paper from my pocket where I had been keeping it safely; a copy of my original birth certificate. John Spencer looked at it and frowned, then handed it to his wife.

"What is this?" he asked.

"My birth certificate."

He scratched his head and frowned again. "I thought you said you were Fran."

I nodded again. "Yes, I am. But when I was born, I was Greta Spencer. My mother was your cousin, Valerie. She came to America to have me and I was adopted. My adoptive parents changed my name."

"Good God," he exclaimed, staring at the piece of paper and then at me. "Valerie had a child? I can't believe it! It's not possible."

"It's true," I replied. "She stayed with her mother's sister, and when I was born, she gave me up for adoption. I never knew her. I've only recently found all this out." I handed him another piece of paper to look at, the letter from my mother to Dr. Smith.

"My godfathers, I'm at a loss for words!" He shook his head in disbelief. "Are you sure?" he said, looking at me with a frown on his face.

"I'm quite sure," I replied. "I want to find her," I said simply.

I watched as he rose and walked slowly to a table in the corner of the room. Here he stood silently for a moment, before pouring himself some whisky from a decanter, placed on a silver tray. He closed his eyes as he took a sip and then, as an afterthought, turned to me and asked, "Can I offer you anything?"

I shook my head. "No thanks. I just want to know about my mother. I want to find her."

"What a dark horse," he muttered, before gulping the contents of the glass and walking over to stand in front of the fire. He stared at it for a while, then turned and looked at me over spectacles that were perched on the end of his nose. "Fran," he said, "Valerie never came back from America." He continued looking at me intently and seemed to be struggling with his emotions.

"No, that's not true. I know she returned. That letter she wrote to the doctor after I was born. She said she was flying against his medical advice. I have it in black and white."

John shook his head. "I don't doubt what you are saying, Fran, but she never returned to South Africa. Nobody knew what happened to her and she's missing, presumed dead."

Tears of frustration and despair welled in my eyes. This was not the answer I wanted to hear.

"I'm sorry Fran," he said, as Louise rushed to my side and held my hand. She had been sitting quietly, listening and watching. "I had no idea she'd had a baby. This is tragic. I'm so sorry. I don't know what to say."

John Spencer stared at me, not unkindly, while I sobbed. He was thinking what to do. Finally he said, "I think I should take you to Johannesburg to meet your grandmother. Will you come with me? I'm sure she would like to meet you."

"No," I shouted. "I never want to meet her. I hate her. She made my mother do it, I know she did. She wouldn't let my mother keep me."

Louise squeezed my hand sympathetically, but John stood firm. "How do you know that? If what you say is true, she might have influenced your mother, but ultimately it was your mother's choice. You can't blame your grandmother for your mother's actions – at least not without meeting her and hearing her side of the story. You can't be the prosecutor and the judge."

I stared at him in shock. "It wasn't my mother's fault."

He sighed and turned back to stare at the fire. At length he poured another drink for himself, clearing his throat as he took a sip of whiskey. When he finally spoke, he said, "I am stunned. I had no idea about any of this – and I can tell you, you're not the only one who feels angry. They deceived me, damn it all. I never even knew she was pregnant. I just can't believe that all this happened without them saying a word." He thumped the table with his fist and whiskey splashed out of his glass. He didn't seem to notice the wet patch on his shirt as he took another sip and thumped the table again. He was having difficulty controlling his agitation. At length he slammed the glass down and turned to me. "I think we should have your grandmother answer some questions." I remained stubbornly silent as he stared at me. "You're Valerie's child – our flesh and blood." Grunting slightly, he urged me again. "Come with me next weekend; I'll pick you up and we'll fly to Johannesburg. She's an old lady, Fran, and she lost her only child. Give her a chance to find the granddaughter she never knew. Maybe she can explain what happened."

"I'll think about it," I said, standing up and wiping my eyes. "It's kind of you, but this is a shock. I need time to think it over. I knew there was a possibility that I wouldn't find my mother, but I never thought she might be dead. I feel doubly cheated. It's not fair." I could feel myself wanting to cry again and excused myself hurriedly from the living room. I made my way slowly back to the bedroom, taking time to examine all the old photographs of family members – my relations. My excitement had ebbed, however. It wasn't relations I wanted; it was my mother and father.

I hoped that Joe would be asleep, but he was lying in bed reading. He looked at my teary eyes, making no comment as he put his book down. As I sat next to him, he put his arms around me; I found myself sobbing with my head buried in his chest, while he quietly stroked my hair. It was comforting to be held close. When I whispered, "My mother is dead," he said nothing, but kissed me gently on the forehead.

We stayed like that for some time, until I ran out of tears. At length he said, "Your phone's been ringing over and over. I checked the number in case it was Lizzie, but it wasn't. It's an out of area number."

I picked up my phone and listened to the messages. They were all from my Mom, Grace Walker. "Darling," she said, "Where are you? I've been trying to reach you all day on the landline. When you get this, please call me, no matter what time of day." There were three more messages that repeated the request. I knew that my cell phone had no capability to call internationally. I could only do that from a landline.

"Shit," I said with vehemence.

"What?" asked Joe.

"My Mom needs me to call urgently. I'll have to ask if I can use their phone. Shit," I said again. The last thing in the world I wanted to do was go back into the living room, but it was my only choice. My Mom sounded panicked.

As I approached the kitchen, I heard John Spencer on the phone. I stood silently and listened. "It's true Aunt Sharon. I saw the birth certificate."

He listened to a voice I could hear dully, and replied, "No, she doesn't look at all like Val. She's taller and darker, but I assure you, she is Valerie's daughter. I think you should meet her."

There was another silence as he listened, then he said, "Aunt Sharon, you owe it to Valerie and your granddaughter. She's your own flesh and blood. I'm going to try and persuade her to come with me next weekend. Whatever anger you are harbouring against Valerie, has nothing to do with this young woman. Be reasonable; she is the innocent here." After more words on the other end of the line, he said, "Well, I hope she'll agree to come with me. I'll try my best and let you know what happens."

I waited a while after I heard the receiver replaced, before knocking on the door. When I entered, John was staring at a photograph of himself next to a girl, who stood chest high next to him. They had their arms linked as they smiled at the camera. "We went to university at the same time, except that I went to Rhodes; this was taken just before we left. It's your mother. She was a beauty."

134

I stared at her image and felt an emptiness engulf me. I would never know more than this – and what people told me about her. Out of curiosity alone, I said, "I'll come with you to Johannesburg."

He hugged me without comment. As we drew apart, he said, "Welcome to the family. Sometimes families have to soldier through difficult times. I'm sorry I wasn't more welcoming, but I was in total shock."

It was an opportune moment to ask if I could use the phone. "I also have family back in California and there seems to be an emergency," I explained.

My Mom's voice was breathless when she answered the phone. She'd clearly been running. "Fran, is that you darling? Oh thank goodness you've called. What a relief," she gasped.

Alarmed, I asked what was going on. "Haven't you heard?" she cried. "That American girl you met, Lauren Marlowe; she's been kidnapped. Oh Fran, I've been so worried about you. I needed to hear your voice. It's been on all the news stations that she was abducted yesterday. Her poor mother is flying out to South Africa."

"What!" I exclaimed. "Oh my God, Mom, that's terrible. I haven't heard anything about it. I'm away for the weekend with some friends. Oh my God..." Lauren had made a deep impression on me with her noble work among orphans; this was dreadful news.

But I needed to calm my Mom. "I know everything seems worse when you're far away, Mom, but honestly I'm fine. It's terrible news about Lauren, but I'm fine. Stop worrying about me. I'm quite safe and not in any danger. She lives in Cape Town. Do you remember how far away Cape Town is from Durban?"

"I know, but I can just imagine how her mother must be feeling. I couldn't bear it if anything happened to you, Frannie." I heard her voice falter. "I'm sorry I alarmed you, darling."

I felt a rush of warmth and comfort. She hadn't called me Frannie since I was about twelve years old, when I rudely told her to stop doing so. It was good to be loved.

****

The week dragged. Exams were looming and I couldn't really afford the time to go to Johannesburg, but I wanted to get it over with. John Spencer promised that we could make it a day trip on Sunday and be on the last flight back to Durban. It was hard to concentrate with mixed emotions churning inside me and an overload of preparation for final exams. The atmosphere at the Aids clinic, where I volunteered, was subdued; we were all consumed with anxiety about Lauren. It was not an easy time. The day when the news broke that she had been found was a huge relief, but it was shocking to think what had happened to her in those days when she was missing. Rumours were flying that she'd been gang-raped.

Joe was even busier than the rest of us that week, with an engineering project he was working on; I barely caught sight of him and I missed him. We'd been close over the weekend, ending up sleeping in the same bed, but carefully avoiding the touch of each other's bodies. In the morning he'd teased and said I'd been talking in my sleep, calling his name over and over. His humour was a relief from stress and I wished I could see him again before the weekend trip to meet my grandmother.

John Spencer and I flew to Johannesburg that Sunday on the 6 a.m. flight. We rented a car and drove thirty minutes, on busy freeways, to a retirement community. Here we had to identify ourselves at the gate. An elderly security guard informed us we needed to wait for confirmation that Mrs. Spencer was expecting us. He wore a blue uniform with an air of authority, but his dark hands were unsteady as he handed us a registration form to fill in. Neither John nor I spoke; the only sound was the car idling. There was no going back and although I still felt embittered towards her, my heart was pounding with anticipation as I waited to meet my grandmother. After a few minutes, we were told that we could proceed. The guard lifted the boom for us to enter the estate and saluted us. "Thanks, Chief," John said through the open window, prompting the old man to grin as he waved us on.

The homes were small and neat, with tiny gardens and vine-shaded verandahs. I was struck by the apparent tranquility behind the gates, compared to the pounding pace of the city. We drove through a maze of quiet streets and stopped outside a house with a green door. Neighbours all around were sitting on their verandahs; some smiled with a polite "Good morning," others were engrossed in the Sunday papers. A sudden movement in the window before me caught my eyes; my grandmother had the advantage of seeing me first and, as I imagined her scrutinizing me, I felt an urge to run away. Sensing my anxiety, John took my arm and gave it an encouraging squeeze. As we walked towards the house, my heart was pounding and my knees were unsteady. It felt as if everything was happening in slow motion as I watched John pressing the doorbell.

By contrast, the door quickly opened wide at the first ring and there she was; my grandmother stood before me. She was small, neat and grey-haired. I had expected an ogre, not a warm smile that greeted me without reservation. "You are so beautiful," she said as she put her hands out to me.

Despite my prior reservations, I fell into her arms and cried.

PART 3

SHARON

People only see what they are prepared to see.

– *RALPH WALDO EMERSON*

Chapter 1

They warned me that I was being hasty when I announced my engagement to Tom Spencer. My parents begged me to visit South Africa first, meet his family and see the country for myself – not through his eyes. He made it sound exciting and romantic; they said it was a country with racial problems that would erupt one day. But he had swept me off my feet and I did not heed their admonitions. I can still hear their voices saying, "It's a long way away, Sharon. Family counts for a lot in life, and we will be on the other side of the world if you live over there. We can't come running – you'll have to fend for yourself in times of trouble. You'll be all alone."

Their words were prophetic, but I dismissed them. I said that Tom and our future children would be my family. Well, here I am, forty years later. My family is torn apart by racial problems, Tom is dead, our marriage failed, and Valerie – our only child – is alienated from me. My parents were right about everything. John Spencer is the closest I have to a relative, but he is Tom's nephew, not mine. As if it were a curse from my dead parents – I am all alone.

It was late when a call came from the farm. John Spencer was on the line. I'd been dozing in front of the television and when I heard his voice, I felt confused. It sounded like my late husband and took me a few moments to get my thoughts together. Tom had been dead over a year and this sudden reminder was a shock; my heart was pounding. John apologized for calling so late and I soon understood why he had done so.

As you might imagine, I couldn't sleep after he told me about the appearance of a young woman on the farm, claiming to be Valerie's daughter. I had been nervous that this might happen. A letter for Valerie arrived on the farm a while back and I was afraid that there was trouble around the corner. I took care of things though and, as time passed and nothing happened, I thought trouble had been averted.

There was a lot of explaining to do and I could sense John's anger. He never knew that Valerie was pregnant when she went to America; it was a secret known to few. I wanted to keep it that way, even when she disappeared. John and Valerie had been good friends as children and he clearly felt betrayed. To placate him on the phone, I told him as much as I thought he should know. But I simply couldn't tell him all, even though apartheid was a thing of the past. Attitudes don't change overnight.

I went to bed as usual and read a few chapters, until I felt drowsy. But the moment I turned the light out, my mind raced and I lay thinking about Tom and Valerie. They were the two people whom I had loved most in the world – and the two whom I had lost. My sadness felt new and raw again. Even my sister, Lorna, who had been so good to me in my time of need, was gone. She was dead; it should have been me who got cancer, not her. She had so much to live for; I have nothing. Life is not fair, but there's nothing we can do about it.

My mind wandered back to when I met my husband in San Francisco. He was studying in California for three months before returning to South Africa. It sounded exotic when he told me about the farm where he grew up, and I imagined him living in darkest Africa. He laughed as he explained that he didn't live in a mud hut with lions roaming outside. Our courtship was quick and our wedding was a small affair in my parents' garden. Despite their concern, I thought I was the luckiest person alive as we set out on our adventure – our marriage.

At first we lived in Johannesburg. Tom was a businessman and we made a happy life for ourselves, with a group of close friends. I soon realized that my husband came from a very privileged family; there were many who told me what a "catch" he was. His parents lived on the farm and they welcomed me into the family. But after only three years in Johannesburg, during which time Valerie was born, they died in a car crash. He was the older of two brothers and inherited the farm, so we uprooted from the city, moving permanently to Ixopo. He changed after the move; I don't know whether it was because of his parents' death, or because he felt that he had a different role to play back on the farm. He never seemed to laugh anymore.

Living in a remote place was a challenge for me. I tried joining women's groups, but felt like an alien who couldn't relate to their interests. I loved flowers – but I didn't want to enter into competitions to arrange them, and I didn't like making jams and cakes for bake sales. I felt uncomfortable with the role I was expected to play as a farmer's wife, especially having a staff of cooks, cleaners and gardeners whom I was supposed to oversee. It was always a point of strife between Tom and me; he couldn't understand how distasteful I found it. In the end, I capitulated and did the best I could to be a good farmer's wife, but I felt stifled. Motherhood helped, but it was a great sadness that I had two miscarriages after Valerie's birth and was never able to have more children.

When she left for boarding school, I was bereft. I argued against it and wanted her to go to the local state high school. It was a family tradition, however, for Spencer children to go to prestigious boarding schools. Valerie seemed happy to go, so I accepted it. But once again, I felt empty and stifled. Soon after that, I decided to save my sanity by starting a business in Johannesburg. I opened a shop in Rosebank, an affluent, northern suburb with fancy boutiques. Mine was an interior design store that initially carried Italian fabrics, as well as *objets d'art* from all over the world. Within a couple of years, I had a reputation that gained me entrée to the wealthiest homes in Johannesburg. I could hardly keep up with the demand for my work. Initially Tom was proud of my success, but then he seemed to grow resentful. He wanted me back on the farm; I wasn't prepared to give up my life in Johannesburg. I visited him from time to time – and he came to the city for meetings – but our lives grew apart. Valerie was what held us together.

I suspected that he had returned to a former lover. He tried to hide it, but it became obvious. I vainly hoped he would end the affair and that everything would be as it was before. I wasn't unfaithful to him – though I almost had an affair with a client, a surgeon, who plied me with gifts and lunches. I felt I was in control, until one afternoon we went to check on the progress of the project in his new suite of offices. He was divorced and on the prowl; I was lonely. Before I knew it, he was undressing me in the middle of his consulting room and I wasn't resisting. All reason disappeared and my thoughts were of nothing but desire, when the sound of a door banging stopped us in our tracks. We fumbled to get our clothes on again as we heard footsteps approaching. I'm sure I looked flustered and guilty when his assistant walked through the door. She seemed surprised to see me there, but thank goodness she arrived when she did for it would have been a regrettable act. I was a married woman, albeit estranged. Despite everything, I still loved Tom and would have forgiven him his transgressions if he had come back to me. But his affair continued right until his death. Divorce was out of the question because 'Spencers never got divorced.' It was such hypocrisy....why did I allow it?

Had he been the younger son, we might have stayed together in Johannesburg and remained happily married, but he felt compelled to take over the farm. It was expected of him. I was the immoveable object and he was the irresistible force, I suppose. Yet I *had* moved; I was the one who followed him from my country to his. He expected me to make all the sacrifices and I was no longer prepared to do so. I could not be a farmer's wife.

At some point during the night I must have drifted off to sleep, but I awoke in the morning with a headache and a buzzing sound near the window. I ignored it for a while, but sleep was dispelled. I got up and pulled the blind; there was a trapped beetle, attracted by the morning light, trying in vain to escape. I could open the window and set it free, or I could leave it suffocating. It was strange how long I stood staring, doing nothing. Eventually I went and made myself some coffee. When I returned, it had stopped fluttering and was lying still on the window ledge. Immediately I regretted my paltriness. The day was getting warmer and the glass was hot; the insect was beginning to roast. With haste I opened the window and touched the beetle with a gentle tap; it was still alive. After a few seconds it flew away.

As I waited for the weekend, I had internal conversations, warning my vulnerable self that much could go wrong. This young woman was going to ask questions that would open up old wounds, and seeing her would be a difficult reminder of the past. What would she look like? John had given no indication when he described her, but he did say she was darker than Valerie. Was that a hint of what was to come? Things could get very difficult.

I sat in my living room, looking around, imagining what she would think when she walked in the door. It was neat and tidy – I'm a person who even cuts my sandwiches exactly and precisely. I like order. The furniture from our Johannesburg house, and the farm, was too big for this downsizing, so I'd ended up giving most of it to John and Louise for the spa that they're building. I'd kept a comfortable chair, and a small table my parents had sent from America as a wedding present. Everything else in the room was new, with smaller proportions. It was the newness that made it look like a furniture showroom, rather than a home. It had the Sharon Spencer stamp, but I didn't love it. There were a few family photos on display, but I seldom looked at them; they brought back painful memories that I tried to avoid. There were always fresh flowers in the room; these were my one indulgence. I looked at the bowl of white Iceberg roses on a shelf and my eyes wandered to the painting next to it, an old oil painting of a Californian seascape that I'd inherited from my parents. It pained me that I would have nobody in turn to leave it to, other than nieces in America whom I barely knew. Perhaps Fran, my Californian granddaughter, might inherit it one day. What would she be like? What would she look like? Was Valerie's dalliance with a coloured man going to be very apparent?

Finally Sunday arrived. I was up earlier than usual, dressed and waiting at the window an hour before their arrival. My heart beat faster every time I heard a car; I hadn't realized how many people were up and about early on a Sunday morning. They must be churchgoers, I decided. I hadn't seen the inside of a church in twenty years after Valerie left. Tom wanted me to keep attending the little Anglican Church in Ixopo with him; he was a pillar of the church and it was the only place where I think he found solace. It was a farce to me. I refused to go, even at Christmas and Easter, but I did have to suffer through Tom's memorial service in that suffocating stone-walled church. All the eulogies made me want to scream, "You don't know what he was really like." But instead I sat like a grieving widow, formerly a dutiful wife, trying to look the part.

After the church-goers had gone on their way, a car pulled up outside the house. Although my stomach was in a knot, a smile lifted the corners of my mouth. I felt an involuntary twitch, as if I wanted to smile broadly but was afraid to do so. I could hardly breathe as I waited for the moment to see what Valerie's daughter would look like.

The car doors opened and out she stepped. Oh my goodness, she was beautiful; a tall young woman, dressed in the ubiquitous denims and T shirt of the young. She wore her dark brown hair hanging loosely to her shoulders and strode with determination, although her steps seemed to falter as she drew nearer to my front door. I stared in amazement; she looked like a feminine version of Tom as a young man – Tom whom I had fallen in love with so long ago. She didn't look at all like her mother. Looking around inquisitively, she pushed her dark hair out of her eyes. My nephew took her arm and gave her an encouraging smile; John was just as protective towards her as he once was towards Valerie.

As I watched my approaching granddaughter, my emotions ran riot. Excitement clashed with pain. It was not only the pain of my failed marriage; it was the collapse of my family as well. The laws of this strange land had damaged us beyond repair, and even though those laws no longer existed, the damage had been done. I had lost what was most precious to me – my daughter. My daughter had in turn lost her daughter. Perhaps her daughter was our phoenix.

This beautiful young woman's mixed heritage was living evidence of the bizarre laws by which we had been indoctrinated. She was freshness and innocence, not a second class citizen. She was the hope of the future; the hope for my future. She was my flesh and blood.

Her name was Francesca Walker I'd been told, and she lived near San Jose – the same town where I had grown up. I had never wished for anything as much as I prayed now, that she would accept me into her life. John had indicated on the phone that she was reluctant to meet me. It was her mother that she wanted and I was not a substitute. I opened the door and as I hugged her, she returned my gesture by putting her arms around me. The warmth I felt at that moment had nothing to do with the outside temperature. It was a long time since I had been embraced. Neither of us knew what to do next and it was only when we heard the door close, that we drew apart. John Spencer waved through the window at us. "I'll be back," he mouthed. Fran and I were left alone.

"Thank you for coming," I said. My voice sounded shaky and I was unsure what to do next. "Come in," I added hastily, beckoning her to sit on the sofa. But she remained standing, staring at me. It was more awkward than I'd imagined. "We have so much to talk about… How much time have we got before John comes back?" I asked.

"We've got all day." She continued to stare at me and then blurted out, "The main thing I want to know is why she gave me up? I don't understand. She was old enough to keep me, wasn't she?" The urgency in her voice made me realize that I had underestimated her anxiety through the years. It boiled inside her and the lid had just blown off. "Why did she give me away? Why didn't you help her to keep me?"

"Oh my dear," I whispered softly and sank down onto the sofa. "Will you sit here next to me and let me try to explain?"

She was so forthright that I was caught off guard. I listened to her accent and felt a warm bond of familiarity, despite the veiled hostility on her part. I thought with longing of the golden Californian hills that turned bright green with the first winter rain. The oaks were as majestic as the big oaks on the farm in

Ixopo. I remembered, too, the cherry blossoms in spring that made the Santa Clara Valley turn pink. That was all gone now, I knew that, but in my mind it would always stay as it was in my childhood. So much had changed for the worse.

"It's a hard tale to tell, but I'll do my best. Please don't judge us too harshly, Fran. We did what we thought was best at the time; best for your parents and for you. Let me explain." I pointed to a portrait that had been taken of Valerie when she turned eighteen, just before the nightmare started. "That is your mother," I said. We stared at it in silence. Fran was not going to make this easy for me by offering any platitudes. She wanted the facts and she wanted to get straight to the matter without any niceties. I felt like I was on trial, which I suppose I was.

"That picture was taken when your mother finished high school, just before she went to university. You can see how beautiful she was." Fran was staring at the photo intently. "She was tiny and looked fragile, but she was actually very strong," I continued. "Did you know that is what Valerie means? – Strong one.

"Growing up on a farm, she loved the countryside in a way that I never did. She learned that from her father; she was always at his side when she was home from school. She went to boarding school at the age of twelve, you see." My granddaughter shifted in her seat and I sensed she was getting restless. "I'm sorry," I said, "I'm rambling on. Can I get you anything to drink or eat?"

"No thanks. We ate on the plane," she replied. "I'm very interested to know about her, but please answer my question. Why didn't she keep me?"

150

I took a deep breath and sighed. "It was during the tough apartheid era in South Africa, Fran. For someone like you who grew up in California, where people are tolerant and diverse, it's hard to understand. I grew up there too, but I had lived here for two decades by the time you were born and I knew what to expect. It's not to say that I agreed with it, but the laws of the land enforced separation. That's what apartheid means – separateness."

Fran frowned. "I know what apartheid was – I've studied history and I've read a lot about it. But I still don't see what that has to do with my mother not keeping me."

I sighed. "When Valerie went to university, she became active in an organization that the security police kept close tabs on. That's where she met your father; I never met him and didn't even know about the relationship until it was too late. You see, according to the laws of the land, they were not allowed to be together."

She frowned and I hesitated, nervous to continue. Finally I said, "Your father was coloured."

She was still frowning. I allowed a moment for this to sink in before saying, "Do you begin to understand?" She sighed and looked away. I added, "That doesn't mean the same thing here as it does back home in the States. Here it means someone of mixed race. I'm not sure if they use the term at all anymore in America, but it used to mean a black person."

Her frown cleared and Fran showed no shock at this news, as I had expected her to do. Perhaps she already knew that her father was coloured. "Was that why you didn't want me?" she asked.

I looked away and closed my eyes, remembering the shock of that distant day. I had realized immediately that Valerie was pregnant as she emerged from the bathroom, throwing up. Tom, who never saw anything, asked if she'd eaten something that had made her sick! I confronted her and she burst into tears, confessing the truth. My heart sank, but I also felt a glimmer of hope. She could get married, leave university and all the trouble it had brought about – and I would be a grandmother.

I'll never forget Tom's reaction though. At first he said nothing; then his face went bright red and I thought he might be having a heart attack. He began yelling at her, shouting that she was a disgrace. After she ran from the room crying, I tried to pacify him. "It's the start of a new life," I'd said. "What's done is done. Let's make arrangements for them to marry. Let's welcome her husband and baby into our family."

I thought he would explode again. "Welcome him into my family? That'll be the day. I'll horse whip the bastard, that's what I'll do. What the hell does he think he's doing with my daughter? I'll castrate the bastard."

I found Valerie coming out of the bathroom again and put my arms around her. At least my pregnancy had been a welcome affair and I'd been able to suffer the nausea, knowing my world was secure. Valerie was in trouble and I wanted to make it better for her.

"Do you love the father, darling? Who is he?" I asked her. She nodded and burst into tears again.

"His name is Johan Barnard and he's a medical student. He comes from Cape Town – I was going to meet his parents, but then things happened and, and… I felt too sick to travel. I love him more than anything and he loves me, Mom. I know he does. It's not just a casual thing; we've been together for a year."

It was encouraging that he was to become a doctor, but I tried unsuccessfully to hide the hurt in my voice. "Why didn't you bring him home?" I asked, puzzled. "You were going to Cape Town, twelve hours away, to meet his family – but you didn't bring him two hours down the road to meet us?"

Her face crumpled and she began to shake, as her chest heaved. Finally she managed to say, "I couldn't."

My antennae were picking up danger signals. "Is he married?"

She shook her head. "No, he's not." She lifted her head and squeezed her eyes tightly shut.

"I don't understand, then. Johan Barnard did you say his name was? Is he Afrikaans? What difference would that make? We are quite open-minded; you know that," I said.

She snorted with derisive laughter and shouted, "Yes, he's Afrikaans. And he's coloured. Now just how open-minded are you?"

A chill ran through my body and I remember falling. I must have fainted, because the next thing I knew, I was lying on a bed with Tom sitting by my side, looking ashen. He had heard the exchange between us and quickly carried me to the bedroom. What happened next haunts me... Valerie was standing behind her father, concerned about me; he swung around and struck her in the face. I heard the smack and saw the red imprint on her cheek, as he bellowed, "Get out of my sight and take your coloured bastard with you. You're no child of mine any longer, damn you. Go and live on the Cape Flats where you belong now. Get out."

Tom and I never slept in the same bed again; I was repulsed by his actions that day. When he came to me that night, we began to argue. I pleaded with him to have compassion, to which he yelled that he never wanted to hear her name again. "But she's your daughter, Tom," I gasped.

His rage was uncontrollable. "I said you were not to mention her again."

I tried to stand my ground and replied, "She grew inside me and I gave birth to her. She is, and always will be, my daughter. I will always look out for her, no matter what."

"You are my wife and I'm telling you one last time; I want nothing more to do with her. We have no child anymore."

I closed my eyes, as if that would shut out reality. "Well I'm telling you," I said, "I may not always be your wife, but I will always be her mother."

"Let me tell you," he warned, "We will never get divorced. Spencers do not get divorced."

I gave a hollow laugh. "Oh, I get it. The Spencers are the royal family of Ixopo. What hypocrisy; you won't get divorced, but you'll throw your daughter out. We can't have a black sheep remain in the family, can we? You can divorce Valerie…"

"Dammit woman – I don't have a daughter anymore," he bellowed. I had my back to him when he grabbed me and pushed me onto the bed. The man I'd married disappeared and a monster forced itself on me. There was no love in the act; it was about power and rage, and I felt violated. For a long time afterward I lay still in bed, too afraid to move or cry. Finally, as I heard the clock strike three, I could tell that he was asleep; I crept out and tried to settle myself on the couch. The next morning he left for Johannesburg. His only words were, "Take care of the problem before I get back."

Deep-seated prejudice had blinded his reason. His position in society meant more to him than his love for our daughter. Tom never saw Valerie again. Although he seemed quite normal to everyone else, I knew otherwise. She didn't exist for him. His shame was so great that he insisted we tell people she had gone to America to study. He paid for me to take her to Lorna and get the problem out of his sight. I could never forgive him, but far greater than his shame was mine for allowing it. I wanted to leave him and stay in California with Valerie, but I didn't have the courage.

Thankfully, I intercepted a letter from my daughter to her lover when I saw it lying on the hall table. They were using an alias,

John Brown. I glimpsed inside the envelope and removed the note, replacing it with a blank page. Just as I thought, she was giving him her contact information in California. I pocketed it and destroyed the letter later, flushing the pieces down the toilet. It was a desperate act on my part; she could have noticed what I'd done. But we were pressed for time and she sealed the envelope without looking inside. The last thing in the world I wanted was for Johan to find her. Who knows what they would have done and the scandal would have been too much to bear. I was desperate to keep them apart – it was for the best.

A voice disturbed my reverie. "Your silence is telling. I asked you a question which you're not answering, but I get the message anyway; you didn't want me because my father was coloured."

I felt my cheeks redden. "No, Fran. That's not it. I'm sorry; I was lost in thought for a moment. You see, it was a situation with no happy outcome. We were all victims of apartheid. Firstly, your parents had broken the law – let me be blunt – by having sexual relations. Under a law called the *Immorality Act*, sex between people of different races was forbidden. They would have both faced prison for breaking that law.

"Secondly, the laws of the country classified every citizen by race on identity documents. You would have been classified coloured. You wouldn't have been allowed to live with your mother; the only possibility was that she left the country, or managed to get herself re-classified as coloured. So you see it wasn't an easy choice for her. She was fortunate that she had an American passport and my sister took her in. It seemed the best solution. If you'd been brought up in South Africa, your life would have been

156

hard. You wouldn't have had the freedom and advantages you take for granted in California. Please understand." I grasped her hand and said, "She gave you up for your own good. Your life here would have been unhappy." She made no response to what I'd said. "Did you grow up in a happy family, Fran?"

She nodded and grunted, "Yes."

"Thank goodness. At least some part of the story is happy then. The irony is that as I look at you now, I doubt anybody would have questioned your race. You look like one of us," I said.

There was an awkward silence as she glared at me, before firing a salvo. "My God, you still talk about 'us and them,' after all that's happened to your family. I can see, no matter what you would like me to think, you were ashamed to have a coloured in the family." Her voice was like a machine gun and echoed her mother's words, spoken many years before.

"No, Fran," I parried, "no. You're my flesh and blood. I couldn't care if you were orange with purple stripes, you would still be my granddaughter; and I hope that now we have found each other, we can learn to love each other. South Africa has changed and all those laws are gone. Anything is possible now, please believe me."

Her words still fired rapidly and relentlessly. "The laws might have changed, but have you? How could you say that I look like one of you? That's so condescending. Do you think I want to look like you? My parents – the Walkers – didn't care whether I was Italian, Iranian or Iroquois. They wanted me, for me. They either didn't know or care about my ethnicity, because it was never discussed. In fact I never gave it a thought until you made that remark just now. I felt different from them because they weren't my real parents, but not because I looked a bit different."

"It was a silly thing to say and I didn't mean it like that," I apologized. "You're beautiful, Fran. You actually look as if you could be Italian."

"There you go again," she shouted. "Don't you understand? Who cares what I look like? Only you do – nobody else. I am who I am because of me, not because of the colour of my skin. How can you be so narrow-minded?"

I tried to still her anger. "I didn't make the rules here, Fran, but I had to live by them. You grew up in a society that accepts differences. Be thankful for that – it wouldn't have been like that here." It was impossible for her to grasp how difficult those times were. Everything seemed simple in her eyes, but it wasn't.

Trying to diffuse the situation, I began to explain by using a different tack. "Your anger is understandable and I can see how hurt you are, but instead of arguing, let me show you something." I pointed to the seascape, hanging on the wall. "Look at that picture. Do you see how that painting shows waves breaking on sand? From here you can see it all; the movement in the water, the wetness on the sand, the white of the foam, and even the transparency of the water. It's the sea – easy to recognize, isn't it?" She nodded. "But come and stand right in front of it with me." Frowning, she followed me to a point very close to the painting. "Look now. All you see are little blobs of paint that don't come together to reveal anything. All you see are lines and smudges of colour." She looked at me with irritation and I swallowed hard. "What I'm trying to show you is this; you're standing too close to all that happened, examining pieces of the story. Step back. Try and see the whole picture, not just bits of it."

She had a very strong jaw line, which was emphasized as she gritted her teeth. With a shrug of her shoulders, she said, "Your nephew told me that Valerie never came back to South Africa. That's not true. I saw a letter she wrote to her doctor, saying that she was coming back immediately after I was born. What happened? Where did she go?"

I got up and walked to the window, looking out at nothing in particular. I wished I could spare this young woman the pain she would feel if she knew what had happened. I could lie and plead ignorance, but my sense of fairness wouldn't allow that. She was tortured by not knowing her mother's story; I was tortured because I knew it – or part of it. I knew as much as I was told by private detectives.

The room suddenly seemed oppressive; I needed to get out. "We have beautiful gardens here you know, and it would be nice to get some fresh air," I suggested. "There's a bench where we can sit and talk – it's quite private – and maybe we can get some lunch together afterwards. Will you join me?"

I locked the door behind me and we walked in silence for a while. I could feel a wall of anger building up around her and I didn't know quite how to deal with it. I feared that she would be angrier before the day was over, and hoped she wouldn't want to kill the messenger. It was a helpless feeling, as if I were holding a precious porcelain figurine that was slipping out of my hands in slow motion. I knew it was going to drop and I couldn't stop it. Would it break when it hit the ground, or would the fall be broken by a soft landing? If it broke, could it be restored?

The manicured gardens were full of scented roses and neatly trimmed boxwood hedges. As we walked along a path, neither of us spoke. I longed to hold her hand but knew that she probably would not welcome the gesture. Instead, I walked with an aching heart, watching her out the corner of my eyes. Slender and lithe, she would have been a graceful ballerina like her mother, until she got too tall. Although she had a slightly long nose, her features were neatly formed and her skin was flawless, with very little make-up that I could see. Her eyes were her most stunning feature however; almond shaped and dark brown. She was a beauty. I felt such pride and wished that Tom and Valerie could have seen her too. How different things could have been.

When we reached the bench, she waited for me to sit, before taking her place next to me. Thumping her fists on her knees with exasperation, she then said, "Could you please tell me what you know? I can't wait any longer – I've been waiting my whole life. Whatever it is, just tell me. What happened to my mother? I have a right to know."

I nodded. "Yes, you do. And I'll tell you everything I know, Fran." Settling back on the bench, I crossed my legs to get comfortable, before beginning to speak. "I spoke to Valerie on the phone after you were born and she said she needed to get away from everything. She was very tearful, and I think she was tempted to change her mind and keep you. But of course she knew all the difficulties that doing so would cause. My sister also felt that it would be better if Valerie left immediately because of this. So, ten days after you were born, she left California and flew to London. That's where she was to change planes for a flight to Johannesburg. We know that she arrived there, but she never took off on the next flight.

"I regret that I didn't fly to America to help her, when you were born. How different it all might have been, Fran. If I could undo things, I would, but I had no way of knowing the future, did I? Your mother needed support and I wasn't there to give it to her when she needed it most. I dream about her catching that plane, leaving you behind forever to be somebody else's child. It must have torn her apart."

"Why didn't you go?" Fran asked.

"Hindsight is easy, but I was looking blindly into the future. It was expensive. We spent a lot for her to fly there, support her financially while she stayed with my sister, plus all the medical expenses. It was a lot of money."

Fran nodded in understanding. "So what did you do when she didn't return?"

"We – actually I – contacted the police, who contacted the authorities in Britain. There was proof that she had landed and we were able to deduce that she had cleared immigration, instead of going to the transit lounge for her next flight. We contacted the South African Embassy in London, because she was obviously in

Britain – there was no record of her leaving again from any port or airport. The police weren't very helpful as she wasn't a missing person in their eyes – there was nothing to indicate foul play. I couldn't leave it at that, though. She was my daughter and I was determined to find her. I bought a ticket to Heathrow and went to stay with a friend in West London. Officials at the South African Embassy were sympathetic, but there wasn't much they could do other than suggest I hire a private detective. I did that. Beside myself with worry, because I couldn't believe that Valerie wouldn't contact us, I was convinced something terrible had happened to her, or that she was sick somewhere. It was so soon after giving birth that she could have been suffering from any number of post natal traumas."

"Why didn't your husband go with you to London?" she asked. Fran had a way of seeing to the core of an issue immediately.

I hesitated a moment too long. "Well, as I said before, it was a question of money, Fran."

"It was more than that with him, wasn't it?" she said.

I nodded and tears welled in my eyes. She reached out and held my hand, as tears made their way down my cheeks. In that moment I knew that I loved her with all my heart. As she searched in her pocket for a Kleenex, I let go of her hand to wipe my eyes. "Thank you," I said, and smiled weakly. "He never came to terms with it and… oh dear… I think I would rather not talk about that. It broke my heart. He was locked in a terrible place that was torture for him too. He loved your mother so much, but he couldn't accept what she had done. I tried to tell him that when you love someone, it should be unconditional, regardless of mistakes they make."

"Did my Mom love my Dad?" Once again, Fran went to the heart of the matter.

"Yes, I believe she did."

"Well, then it wasn't a mistake, was it? I wasn't a mistake."

"No, you weren't," I agreed. "You were unplanned, but you're not a mistake – far from it. It was the wretched system, Fran. Your parents tried to fight it, but it destroyed them. And for that reason, I am thankful that you were not part of this whole ugly mess. You grew up free of all the bigotry that abounded here. Your mother gave you that gift, even though it broke her heart."

For the first time she smiled at me, as understanding seemed to dawn on her. "So, did you find her in London?" she asked.

I nodded. "I was there two months when we got our lead. We'd tried hospitals and morgues, all the usual time-consuming efforts, with no results. Then one day I went into the South African Embassy again, covering the same terrain with little hope of success, but at least I felt I was doing something. This time I was greeted by a voice that said, 'Mrs. Spencer, I've got something to show you. Come with me.' I followed the clerk to the mail room, where he waved an envelope at me with a look of triumph on his face. 'Look what we found, buried under a pile of old letters. Someone must have misplaced this and it was never collected. When we were clearing out yesterday, it dropped out of a periodical.' He handed me a white envelope with distinctive red and blue airmail stripes around the edge; it was addressed to Miss V. Spencer, c/o South Africa House, Trafalgar Square, London, U.K. There was no sender's name and address, but it was postmarked December 20th 1981 from Richard's Bay – a small town in South Africa, close to the Mozambique border. 'Go ahead,' he said. 'It's unclaimed. You're her mother, you can have it. See what it says.' It was from your father, Johan Barnard.

"Now I have to tell you that he was on the run at the time. He had escaped from house arrest. The police wanted to silence political opposition, you see, and your father was an outspoken opponent of the government. They kept a watch on his house all the time, which is why it was such a surprise to find he had escaped. Anyway, in this letter to your mother, he told her that he was making his way to Europe. He couldn't tell her how, in case the letter fell into the wrong hands; but he told her that she should stick to their Plan B. I knew then that she was with him and my intuition told me that they were in London. There were a lot of South African émigrés there, you see. So our next step was to search for Johan Barnard as well. Once again, call it intuition, I asked the private detective to check marriage licenses. That's when we cracked it. We discovered that they had married in a registry office in Southwark, just a week earlier. Their address was written on the marriage certificate. Without stopping to think, I caught a taxi to the address in Tooley Street; it was only when I got there that I hesitated and felt nervous."

Fran got up and paced around, kicking at stones in the path. "So my parents were married. Why didn't they come and get me?"

"I suppose because they'd already given you up," I said.

"No, that's not true. They had six months to change their minds."

I scratched my head and sighed. "I don't know the answer to that. All I know is that when I knocked on the door, your mother told me to get out of her life. She never wanted to see me again. I never had the chance to ask her anything. She slammed the door in my face." The memory of that painful moment was one that I tried not to think about. It hurt just as much now as it did all those years ago.

"She gave you up as well then," Fran said heavily. In that moment I felt that my granddaughter saw me more as an ally, and not so much as an adversary."Did you ever see her again? Did you try?"

"I went back the next day, but there was no answer when I knocked. It was a dingy building that smelled of uncollected garbage; I shudder to think of it. A few days later, I tried again to see her. I left a note under the door with the address and phone number where I was staying, but she never contacted me. I went one more time to try and see her, but the neighbour told me that they had moved."

"What did you do then?"

"What could I do?" I shrugged. "I paid the investigator a retainer fee to find her again and keep a watch on where she was. It felt terrible doing that behind her back, but I needed to know that she was alive and safe at least. Then I came home and waited."

"Waited for what?"

I shrugged. "Waited for her to change her mind; waited for Tom to change his mind; waited for the world to change; I don't know. The life went out of me. My family had fallen apart. I can't expect you to understand it, Fran. We were pulled apart by something much stronger than what had pulled us together."

Fran sat staring at the ground in front of her. It was such a long journey she had made to discover her roots; was she now wishing she hadn't? "So... did you hear anything more from her or the detective?"

"Every month I got an update from him, but never a word from her. Then after four years, in 1986, the detective informed me that Johan had left England. Just after that, I picked up the newspaper one day and read the headline: 'Man on run for four years killed in Durban explosion.' It was Johan Barnard."

Fran gasped. "What? My father is dead?" Tears sprang from her eyes and she paled, as if she might faint. I automatically reached out to her, but she turned her head.

"I'm so sorry Fran." Seeing her body wilt, I wished that I could ease the shock for her. After a few moments of silence I said, "There was no explanation given about the explosion, but he was in a car when it happened. They were cruel times." I bit my bottom lip, wanting to comfort her, but not sure what to do.

She continued looking away from me and I could see the tension in her shoulders. After a while she blew her nose and whispered,

"Please carry on."

I continued with the story she wanted to hear. "Your mother came back to South Africa after that. I didn't know where to begin looking for her – South Africa is a big place – so I hired a detective in Cape Town, another in Johannesburg, and still another in Durban. I figured one of them would find her and I was right; she went to Cape Town. But still she never made contact. I knew she was renting a room in Rondebosch. This time I didn't want to have the door slammed in my face again, so I didn't rush there. The detective who found her was able to tell me where she worked and what car she drove – a very old Ford. I followed her from a safe distance when she drove to work and watched where she parked; she was working as a waitress in the mall at Cavendish Square. Then I orchestrated bumping into her one day in the parking garage; she was wearing dark glasses and a hooded sweatshirt, so I couldn't see her face very well. She hesitated for a moment and her hands were shaking. My heart was pounding as I tried to speak to her, but she turned on her heel and thrust me aside. 'Don't say anything. You don't exist for me any longer.' She drove away and I've never seen her again."

I didn't tell Fran my reactions, but I remembered them well. My anger was seasoned with hurt as I drove away, vowing never to make contact again. And I didn't. I had nothing left to live for. Sometimes my solace was a bottle of wine, and other times it was a bottle of pills. The only person who knew my dark secrets was Goodness, the Zulu woman who helped me in the house. She was a faithful friend and never told anyone, especially not Tom. When she found me almost comatose in the mornings, she would tell me that I was going to die if I didn't stop it.

Fran was frowning as I sat lost in my thoughts again. She interrupted them suddenly. "What did you just say?" Her voice jolted me out of my unhappy memories and I was taken aback. "You said you've never seen her again. You said it in the present tense. Why didn't you say that in the past tense?"

I stared at her and swallowed.

"Tell me,' she said, shaking my shoulders. "Is she alive? Where is she?"

I nodded. "Yes, she's alive. She lives in Cape Town."

Her face registered shock and then she sprang up, strode a short distance away, staring at a spot on the ground. When she turned and looked up at last, her face had softened. Hope had replaced anger, and the shock of knowing her father had been murdered, seemed tempered by knowing her mother was still alive.

"I'm going to Cape Town," she said simply.

****

I agreed to meet her at Cape Town airport when her exams were over, in two week's time. Hope was a balm and Fran's anger seemed to abate when she learned that her mother was still alive. My fear was that Valerie would reject her daughter's advances, as she had shunned me. I expected nothing for myself, but prayed she would reach out to Fran. It seemed appropriate that I would not make contact with Valerie; she was unaware that I knew where she lived and my presence would probably antagonize her.

168

My granddaughter must never know about the letter that had arrived for Valerie a while back: Thank heavens it arrived when I was at the farm, and so it didn't fall into John's hands. My hands were shaking when it had arrived on my desk and I was tempted to open it. In the end I didn't. I wanted no wounds, so instead I returned it to sender. I couldn't imagine anyone writing to Valerie at the farm after all this time, but deep down I suspected it might be from her child.

I'm ashamed to admit that twenty years later I was still afraid of the consequences her liaison would reveal. The laws had changed in South Africa, but attitudes had not. I saw no happy outcome and didn't want the whole saga exposed. Yet suddenly everything had changed. Fran had entered my life and, like the beetle in my room, a window had opened for me.

GLYNNIS HAYWARD

Chapter 2

She was already there when I entered the arrivals hall at Cape Town airport. This time Fran was dressed in a white shirt and denim shorts. Her legs were long and lean, and her hair was pulled back in a pony tail, high on her head. People turned to look at the beauty greeting her grandmother; I felt proud.

"Hey," she said with a whistle. "Look at you! You've had your hair cut – you look fantastic. Whoa!"

I blushed. It was a long time since anybody had paid me a compliment and I'd gone to a lot of trouble in the past two weeks. I'd had my hair cut and highlighted; it was useful being a natural blond in my youth, as grey hair contrasted less obviously against it. With highlights, it all blended very well and I was pleased with the short cut that framed my face; it made me feel younger.

Fran put her arms out and as she hugged me, said, "You don't look old enough to be my grandmother. Are you sure you have all the facts right?"

"Enough about me," I replied. "How did your exams go?"

"They're gone!" she laughed. Then she turned to a young man standing close by and said, "This is a friend, Joe Richards."

I heard a familiar American accent as he stepped forward to shake my hand. "Hi, Mrs. Spencer," he said. A fine American boy, with good manners and a firm handshake; I should have been pleased. Instead I felt a pang of disappointment that I would have to share my granddaughter. It appeared, however, that they had merely travelled together and Joe would be staying elsewhere. It was a relief, as there wasn't room in the two bed roomed holiday flat I'd rented in Camp's Bay – and I wasn't sure how I would handle the prospect of them sharing a room. From the way he looked at her, I sensed that Joe was wishing he were more than a friend. We gave him a ride to a hostel in nearby Seapoint, and my suspicions were confirmed when he hugged her, saying, "See you soon. Let me know how things go."

Fran seemed a different person from the angry young woman of two weeks ago. She was light-hearted and talkative. "I love Cape Town," she said as we drove off. "I came here with my family in July. I'm glad this is where she lives; it's where I would live if I stayed in South Africa. It's even more beautiful now than it was in the dead of winter. It's so clear. There's no tablecloth on top of Table Mountain. And look at that chain of mountains; are those the Twelve Apostles?" She paused for a moment and then said, "You know, I haven't been calling you anything. What would you like me to call you?"

I looked at her and shrugged my shoulders. "What would you feel comfortable calling me?"

She whistled tunelessly as she thought about it. "I had a Grandma in California, my Dad's Mom, but she died a few years ago. I never knew my Mom's mother. I could call you Sharon; how about that?"

It sounded too generic; I wanted our relationship recognized. "What about calling me Gran?" I suggested – and held my breath.

She nodded her head with approval. "I like that. Gran it is. I like having a grandmother again – my real grandmother this time. We share the same genes – that's the kind of real I mean."

I closed my eyes tight and tried to bottle the feeling of happiness bubbling inside me. It was enough that I had found my granddaughter; I had no need to pursue my daughter any further. I wanted no more hurt.

The ocean sparkled alongside the road and excitement was like a third person in the car with us. Fran's exuberance was infectious; I was overjoyed to be with her, and she was beside herself that she was finally in the same city as her mother. I had ignored that aspect of the trip as I'd made preparations, but the inevitable was upon us. Fran could barely wait to dump our bags in the flat before heading out to solve the mystery of her life. She had a city map clutched in her hand and laid it out on a table in the scantily equipped kitchen. Beckoning me, she said, "Here we are in Camp's Bay," pointing to a spot she'd marked in green ink. "Rondebosch is over here on the other side of the city. I can take the freeways to get there. What is her address?"

I walked over to her and put my hand on her shoulder. "She's moved, Fran. She doesn't live in Rondebosch anymore. That was years ago. I'm sorry; I should have told you that – I didn't think to do so. It looks like you've been finding your route to get there. She's moved several times since that time I saw her at Cavendish, and her last known address is in Vredehoek." I examined the map and found the area for her, explaining, "I believe she's the supervisor for a block of flats there."

Fran grimaced as she started to figure out a new route from Camp's Bay to Vredehoek. I marvelled at her confidence, remembering how intimidated I'd been driving in Johannesburg when I didn't know my way around. To make matters worse, everyone seemed to be riding on the wrong side of the road; but Fran was unperturbed. I gave her the street address and she had it located in no time. "Are you coming with me?" she asked.

I shook my head. "No, it would be a bad idea. I'd love to be there to help you, but I don't think your mother would want to see me. I'm going to keep away. This is your quest, Fran; I'll go and buy some grocery supplies while you're gone."

She stood up and stared at me, puzzled. "Don't you want to see her? She's your daughter."

How simple it all seemed to Fran, despite knowing the whole story of our estrangement. "It's a two-way thing. Every time I've reached out to her, she made it very clear that she wanted nothing to do with me. I cannot reach out again. It's futile and painful," I replied. "I hope she treats you better, I'm sure she will. But be careful. You might get the same reception."

"I know. I've warned myself that she might not want me in her life for any number of reasons. It's a chance I'm willing to take, though." She smiled at me and added, "Don't look so worried. I'm prepared for anything, but I have to do this. I have to meet her." She took my hand and I walked with her to the car. Before getting in, she turned to me again and said, "Are you sure? I'd feel much better if you came with me. You could wait in the car." She hugged me. "Please?"

I couldn't say no. Behind the façade of bravery, I could see that she was nervous. And to tell the truth, I was nervous for her. She had to find her way, as well as find her mother. I wasn't sure how safe Vredehoek was either; years ago it was a rough area, but I'd been told that it had received quite a makeover and was now very acceptable. Reluctantly I agreed to come with her, on condition that I stayed out of sight when we got there.

Traffic was chaotic and I was thankful to be a passenger, not a driver. It wasn't yet rush hour, but the roads were choked with cars, buses and taxis. Traffic lights and stop streets seemed a free-for-all and every driver seemed to drive with a hand on the horn – or hooter as they called it here. With the map in hand, I helped Fran navigate; we negotiated our way across town on motorways and city streets, until we arrived in Vredehoek.

There were older cars in its narrow streets, which were lined with a mixture of old houses and low-rise buildings. With a little difficulty we eventually managed to find *Helderburg,* where Valerie was the supervisor. It was three storeys high, built of yellow ochre bricks with a red-tiled roof. Every flat had a small balcony, except those on the ground floor. All windows had burglar bars, and doors had sliding security gates in front of them. All balconies had bars across them for additional security. It looked like a prison for those inside, as well as being impenetrable from the outside.

We parked across the road and as she turned the engine off, Fran turned to me and said, "It looks very bleak." I nodded. Her face was pale and her hands were shaking; we both stared at the fortress-like building where her hopes were pinned. Eventually Fran turned to me and said, "I'm going to leave the key with you and you must lock the doors. You have my cell phone number; if you're nervous, call me. I'll come immediately – no matter what's happening in there. Okay?"

"Of course, dear," I said. "Don't worry about me. I'm fine. I'll be waiting here for you." I put an arm around her and wished I could hold onto her forever. She was so young and vulnerable.

Fran walked across the road and hesitated only a moment, before pressing the button at the double front doors. There was a speaker phone and I could see her talk into it. She waited a few moments and then the door opened. Automatically, I covered my face with my hands while peeping through my fingers; I didn't want to be seen. I couldn't see anyone else at the doors, but Fran disappeared inside. It was 3.20 p.m.

It was agony waiting, not knowing what was happening. I kept looking at my watch. The minutes ticked by and I could do nothing but stare, trying to keep my anxious thoughts in check. A few people walked by and stared at me, but most paid no attention to a stranger sitting in a parked car. I, however, kept my eyes glued to the block of flats where my daughter had made her home, feeling sadness seep into me. She was now just another stranger, as much as any of these passersby. Just before four o'clock, I finally saw the front door open. My heart seemed to stop as Fran emerged. Her demeanour gave no clue about what had happened in all this time; she strode purposefully to the car.

"Well?" I asked, as she climbed back into the driver's seat. My heart was pounding.

She shook her head and frowned. "No luck."

My heart sank. "What happened?" I asked with dread.

"I asked to speak to the supervisor and a voice said she wasn't in, but inquired what I wanted her for. I thought quickly and said I wanted to put my name down for a flat when it became vacant. The voice said I couldn't do that, so I replied that Valerie Barnard had told me I could. I was let in and went into her flat."

"Who let you in?" I asked anxiously.

Fran shrugged. "I don't know what her name was, but she was cleaning the flat. I had to wait while she put away all her cleaning things and finished vacuuming the carpet, before she would speak to me. Then she said Mrs. Barnard was at work and she'd be home much later. I don't know why she didn't tell me that immediately. I think she wanted me to see that she did a good job of cleaning." Suddenly Fran chuckled and said, "I asked where Mrs. Barnard worked, not expecting an answer, but the woman said, 'Cafesie – she works at Cafesie. She's the manager.' I asked how far away that was and the woman looked at me as if I were mad. 'It's just around the corner. Go down the road and turn left.'

So that's what we're going to do. We're going to drive to the corner and turn left."

I was very relieved to have Fran back in the car. Gingerly, I asked what the flat was like inside. As she started the car, Fran said, "Much like the outside of the building – very dreary. There were no pictures, or books, or anything other than some basic furniture. It was tiny – just one room with a kitchenette. It had a bed, a table and two chairs. No T.V."

We stopped at the intersection and peered down the road, not quite sure what we were looking for. "Should we park the car and walk?" I suggested. "It's like looking for a needle in a haystack."

"I don't understand it," Fran said. "She was emphatic that it was just at the corner and I couldn't miss it. I don't see anything other than all these little shops, a few burger joints and Kentucky Fried Chicken."

Suddenly we both started to laugh; we laughed until we cried. "KFC," Fran shrieked. "That's it!" We were still laughing as we parked the car and wiped the tears from our eyes. I suppose it was a nervous reaction to so much tension, but at length we controlled ourselves and tried to decide what to do next. Fran suggested, "Why don't we just go in and sit down? We can eat there. It's perfect."

"No, she'll recognize me. You go in and order some take away. I don't think you should tell her who you are, not while she's at work. But you can try and figure out who she is and satisfy your curiosity a tiny bit."

"That's not going to help at all," she said. Fran tilted her head and looked at me. I was beginning to recognize the signs; she wanted me to accompany her and was going to try and persuade me to agree. I stopped her in her tracks. "No, Fran, please don't ask me to go in with you. It would ruin everything."

There was glint in her eyes. "I have an idea, Gran. Look at that shop over there." I glanced over my shoulder and saw it was a fabric store; it also displayed saris and burkas. "We can get you a veil and one of those things!" Before I could argue, she leapt from the car and entered the store, emerging five minutes later with a disguise for me. Despite my protestations, Fran coaxed me into complicity. "This might just work. You'll see her, but she won't know it's you. There's no downside," she argued.

It was difficult trying to put a burka on in the car. I felt foolish and complained as I struggled with the strange attire, "I needn't have had my hair done at great expense; and there's no way I'll be able to eat with all this fabric over my face. This is ridiculous, Fran."

She giggled nervously and said, "We'll get takeaway, but I need you there to spot my mother. I've never seen her – you have to come with me. Don't speak; I'll do all the ordering; just whisper to me when you see her."

Self conscious and awkward, I followed Fran into KFC. The smell of fried chicken was overpowering, but my granddaughter announced that she was suddenly hungry. "Would you mind if we ate here instead of getting takeaway?" she asked. There wasn't much I could say from behind the black fabric covering my face; I nodded in reply. She ordered a box of crispy wings and a young waiter pointed us to a booth, telling us he would bring our order when it was ready. His name, Weston, was displayed on his shirt. There was nobody I could see who resembled Valerie. I was beginning to sweat; it was hot under the heavy garb. We sat in a booth that afforded a good view of the whole room and I could feel my heart pounding in my chest. Somewhere in here was Valerie. There weren't that many people, so it was perplexing not to see her. Finally I whispered, "I can't find her. She must be in an office somewhere."

Fran sighed. At that moment, Weston arrived with our order. My granddaughter – ever resourceful – smiled at him and said, "Are you hiring here at the moment?"

He grinned and replied, "We like hiring girls with American accents. Maybe you come from Kentucky, hey!"

Fran was confused. "Kentucky?" she said in surprise.

Weston laughed and pointed to the logo. "I can hear your accent," he said, by way of explanation. Fran and I laughed politely, but then he looked more serious. "We are definitely hiring," he said. "You can speak to the manager when you've finished your meal. That's her behind the cash register."

We both looked in that direction. Weston followed our gaze and said, "She's the one wearing the red jacket." He smiled and said, "I can ask her to come here, if you like?"

"No," we both said hastily.

180

Weston nodded and grinned. "Enjoy your meal," he said as he walked away.

I was mesmerized. There was not anything about the manager that resembled Valerie. She looked much older and bore no likeness to my daughter. There were disfiguring scars on her left cheek; she wore her hair short and curly, but it was red. I was convinced it was not Valerie. As I watched Fran staring at the manager, I whispered, "That's not her."

Exasperated, Fran banged her fist on the table. Recovering her composure quickly, she said in hushed tones, "How the hell are we going to find her? Do you think there can be two managers? Maybe that cleaning person got the story wrong."

Just then another person walked up to the desk, apologizing for being late. We were sitting close enough to hear what was being said. "I missed my bus," she said. "I'm sorry M'am."

A voice that was very familiar, replied, "That's the second time this week, Lettie. One more time and you're fired. There are lots of people wanting your job, if you can't do it properly."

I felt myself go cold and the air went out of my lungs, like a punctured balloon. How many times had I heard those words said to an errant farm worker in just such a tone? There was no doubt in my mind who the manager was. She had learned from her father how to deal with troublesome employees; she was her father's daughter after all.

Fran saw me sink in my chair and said anxiously, "What's the matter? Are you feeling alright?"

I was crying. She couldn't see my face, but she heard my quiet sobs. I reached for her hand and said, "It's her – I recognize that voice. You've found her."

****

I ate nothing. I couldn't. My stomach was in a knot and I longed to get out of the burka. Fran however, stared at Valerie unflinchingly as she ate her chicken wings. It seemed as if her curiosity would never be quenched. But I couldn't bear to look. We didn't speak the whole time we were there. Weston kept coming by to check on us and eventually asked Fran if she would like to meet the manager. She looked at me but could see nothing except my eyes, which stared back at her blankly.

"She's not busy right now, but she will be later on. If you want, you can come to the kitchen," he suggested.

"What time do you close?" Fran asked.

"Eight o'clock. You don't want to wait that long, do you?" he asked.

Weston was clearly eager for Fran to join the staff at KFC. I was equally eager to get out of the hot garment and I nudged her with my elbow. "Please let's go now," I whispered.

"I'll come back at eight o'clock," Fran said, taking my hand.

"I'll tell her you're coming back to speak to her."

We watched as Valerie moved around to the side shelves, checking on the silverware that had been placed there. She moved without grace; there was no vestige of the ballet dancer left in her gait; she walked with a slight limp. It pained me to see her. We walked out the restaurant and when we climbed in the car, I pulled off the heavy clothing and stared out the window in silence. As we began to drive away, I was shivering; it was shock from seeing my daughter again. I would never have recognized her if it hadn't been for hearing her voice. All I wanted to do was cry in private.

It was three hours until closing time at KFC and I didn't want to go back with her, but I didn't want her going there on her own either. As if reading my thoughts, she said, "Have you had enough for one day?" I nodded, but couldn't bring myself to say anything. "I'm going to take you back to Camp's Bay and then I'll call Joe. He knows all about my search, Gran. He'll come back with me tonight. I can't wait until tomorrow. Will you be all right?"

It was useless to argue. I didn't want to return and I knew nothing would stop her now. As we drove she said, "I can't believe I'm going to speak to my mother today. It doesn't seem real." Her face was flushed. When I said nothing, Fran said, "You're very quiet. It must have been sad for you to see her and not be able to say anything – especially after all this time. Didn't you want to run up and grab her?"

I couldn't answer. Instead tears rolled down my cheeks. "She's not the girl I once knew," I murmured, unable to hide my despair. We drove in silence back to the flat. I heard Fran call Joe and then she came to sit with me on the balcony, where I was staring out to sea. "It's going to be a beautiful sunset," she said. She watched me for a long time and then, in her usual direct manner, said, "So what's bothering you, Gran? Is it because I'm excited about what lies ahead with my mother, and you're regretting what you've lost with your daughter?"

"In a way," I agreed, choking back my tears. "I would never have recognized her, Fran. It looks like life has washed her up like some flotsam on a beach. It's tragic. She doesn't look happy. What a waste of a life. What a waste of three lives; her father's and mine, as well as hers. We loved her so much."

Fran sighed. "You weren't happy either, two weeks ago. Remember? Things change... I don't know what she was like before, but I accept her as she is now. Would you have been less upset if she still looked beautiful and didn't work at KFC, in a bright red jacket? You speak of love in the past tense. Don't you love her still?"

I was surprised by the audacity of the question and stared at her. I was about to reprimand her when she raised her eyebrows and said, "You're a snob, Gran."

How could I expect this young woman to understand what might have been? The world had been Valerie's for the asking, but it had come down to this miserable existence. I was annoyed at Fran's presumptuous statement and told her so. "You've been in my company for precisely two days, Francesca; I don't expect you to make judgments about me. It's not about snobbery, it's about standards."

She stood up and took a deep breath, before turning to face me sternly. "It was those standards that caused the whole problem twenty years ago. If you still stick to them, then I shouldn't be calling you Gran, and you shouldn't be acknowledging me, and life hasn't taught you anything. You have no idea what her life has been like and why she's ended up where she is now. For all we know, she's doing the best she can to keep body and soul together. You're judging totally by appearances; you, of all people. You are her mother, whether you like it or not. Are you condemning her because she's working in a fast food joint and doesn't live in a fancy neighbourhood? Have some pity... Do you think she hasn't suffered as well?" My granddaughter turned on her heel and walked away.

Staring over the balcony and out to sea, misery returned to haunt me. When I saw Fran's car drive away, all the pain that had been building up, came pouring out and I howled like a dog. I was angry with her, yet deep down I knew she was right. We had no idea what Valerie's life had been like – all I knew were her various addresses. Those told nothing of the life she was living and her broken dreams.

I remained motionless on the balcony until the sun was an orange ball sitting on top of the ocean, waiting to sink. As I watched the day's end and the round shape drop below the horizon, my thoughts of my broken family turned to Tom. We had started out so brightly, but the light had gone from our marriage and left us in a black, emotionless void. Every day became a struggle to keep up appearances of a perfect world, each with our part to play, but never connecting with one another. Despite our differences, I knew that he would have been equally devastated to see our beautiful Valerie as she was today; she was the one thing that we'd managed to do right – and then that one thing came to an end as well.

Darkness and depression crept over me like the night. I went inside and fell into bed. My hand reached for the pills that soothed such unbearable pain, allowing me to sink into welcome oblivion.

Chapter 3

I awoke to raucous seagull cries, all but drowning out the lapping waves. For a moment I was disorientated until I remembered the previous day's events – and the pills. It had been a painful struggle to stop the habit and I'd vowed never to use them unnecessarily again. Why had I succumbed so easily to temptation? I needed to discard the entire bottle, but couldn't quite bring myself to do that. The pills offered security.

I dressed and went into the kitchen very quietly. There wasn't a sound in the flat and I presumed that Fran was still asleep; I didn't want to disturb her. I was beginning to feel famished, since I hadn't eaten any dinner the night before – in fact I hadn't eaten since leaving Johannesburg. Was that only yesterday? I hadn't eaten the fried chicken yesterday at KFC and hunger overcame me now. I scribbled a note to Fran, telling her where I was going, and slipped downstairs to the corner shop to buy some supplies. The smell of coffee lured me to a café and as I sipped my morning caffeine, I began to regain my strength and resolve. Pride had warped my sensibilities and I was in danger of losing Fran, the only thing in the world that mattered to me now. Our argument was regrettable; I needed to consider her feelings and keep my reactions contained. Anxiety began to gnaw at me again; what had happened last night when she met Valerie?

With a few groceries purchased to keep us going, I walked back upstairs and let myself in. There was still no sound, so I quietly opened her bedroom door to check. She lay fast asleep, with her hair around her head like a halo. Nervous that she might wake and think I was spying, I closed the door and returned to my toast and marmalade. I was contemplating another slice when the door opened and Fran emerged, rubbing her red-rimmed eyes. After an awkward silence, I said, "Would you like some breakfast?"

She nodded and came over to me, putting her arms around my shoulders. "I'm sorry I was rude to you last night," she said.

Tears welled in my eyes. It was a forgotten sensation to receive an apology; I hugged her in return. "There was truth in what you said, Fran. I'm sorry too." Then I didn't mean to say it, but it slipped out; "I hardly know you, but I love you very much."

She responded by hugging me again, before standing back and looking at me with a slight frown. "When I came in last night, I wanted to apologize to you straight away and tell you what happened."

"Tell me now," I said.

"I'll tell you in a minute. I went into your room because your light was still on; I got the shock of my life. You looked like you'd had a heart attack. You were lying on the floor and didn't stir when I tried to rouse you. I was terrified, so I called Joe and he came over; he used to work as a paramedic at home. He felt your pulse and said you were alright; so we lifted you back into bed, covered you and turned the light out."

I felt myself go red and was about to say something, when she stopped me. "Joe said that you were drugged. What did you take, Gran?"

"I took some sleeping pills, Fran. I'm sorry that I gave you a fright, but there's nothing to worry about. Sometimes I have difficulty sleeping, that's all…"

"I don't want to argue again," she interrupted, "but I think you overdid it. I've only just found you; please don't leave me now."

Ashamed, and at a loss for words, I nodded and looked away. She began to giggle, not unkindly. "It's my generation that's supposed to do drugs; not yours."

Despite my discomfort, I smiled. Even though she hadn't said as much, she obviously cared about me. Turning to look at her, my voice was hoarse as I spoke. "Now could you tell me what happened last night when you met your mother?"

GLYNNIS HAYWARD

PART 4

VALERIE BARNARD

There is nothing like returning to a place that remains unchanged to find ways in which you yourself have altered.

– NELSON MANDELA

(*A Long Walk to Freedom*, 1994)

Chapter 1

Some days I wish I could scream, "Get the hell out of here and leave me alone!" The tenants don't think for themselves; they run to me with every hiccup in their lives, because I'm the supervisor. I didn't sign on for all their problems – I have enough of my own. My job description here is to look after maintenance of the building, not tenants. And this is only one of my jobs. The one consolation about having three jobs is that I seldom have time to reflect. The only time for thought is when I'm alone on the bus going to work, or sometimes in bed at night. That's when I brood about my lost child and dead husband.

Remembering Greta is even more painful than thinking about Johan. There's finality about death. But my daughter is out there somewhere – twenty years old by now. I have memories of life with Johan, but Greta was taken from my arms as a baby and I have nothing, except a photograph of a newborn. She was perfect and beautiful; I was only allowed to hold her for a few moments. I clutched her, trying to remember every detail, believing that I would return soon to claim her back. She felt so warm and soft, but that is the only memory I have of my daughter. My mother made sure of that.

I can never overcome the anger I feel towards that woman. Her interference ruined everything for me. She intercepted my letter to Johan, I know she did. Because of that, he had no way of knowing what had happened to me, or where I was. We could have made plans and kept our baby, had he known. I hate her as much as I hate my husband's murderers. Between them, they took away everything that was worthwhile in my life.

Now, every day of my life starts with a complaint from at least one tenant. Today's beginning was no different. Yet again I awoke to pounding on the door. It was Mrs. Retief, from Flat 6, telling me she had no hot water. I told her that I'd call a plumber, but she complained it wouldn't help her get the kids ready for school. I gave her two buckets of hot water from my flat and sent her on her way, with promises of a plumber before noon. She had hardly closed the door when the phone rang and it was Bobby Govender from Flat 2, getting home from his night shift. He'd lost his key again. I told him it was going to cost R100 to get a new one cut – and next time I would charge him twice that much, as a penalty. That all happened before 5 a.m. and I need to be at my first job by 6 a.m.

Babysitting thankless tenants is tedious, but the supervisor job provides me with a flat and helps me survive; neither of my other jobs pays much. Thank heavens for Noshile, who cleans my flat once a week in return for English lessons that I give her. I don't have it in me to clean.

The buses were on time today and I didn't have to wait long in the early morning half-light. I feel nervous at the bus stop, although nothing has ever happened there to make me feel that way. I get anxious because of all the other things that have happened to me. Perhaps that's what they call post traumatic stress syndrome. It's a little comforting to know that I'm not alone in my suffering, but it doesn't make it any better. Anxiety is my constant companion.

I found an empty seat on the crowded bus. A young mother sat opposite me with a small child next to her; I couldn't help staring at the little girl, who was about three years old and very talkative. Her curiosity was evident as she asked questions about everything, saying "What's that, Mama?" It made me want to cry. I have never been called mama; I'll never know a toddler's trusting love. Someone else has enjoyed that privilege with my child. I thought then that even if I were to meet Greta again, she would be an adult now. For many years I had little bits of information about her from my aunt in California, but Aunt Lorna died last year – and with her death went the last link to my child. As I watched the mother and child disembark, holding hands tightly, I wished they weren't leaving. Even though it hurt to watch them, I stared out the window until I could see them no longer. Then I sank back into my seat and wallowed in memories...

When Johan was killed, I rushed back from London for his funeral. It was a terrible mistake. Members of the special branch were there, supposedly undercover. It was obvious who they were, but I was too grief-stricken to care. There were only a handful of whites present; me, them, and some journalists. One of the journalists startled me; he looked eerily like my father, but older and wearing tinted glasses. I hadn't seen my father for years, but he never wore glasses and wasn't a journalist. It couldn't be him. When I walked past, the man put his head down to write something, so I didn't see his face too clearly. It gave me a strange turn though.

The little church in Cape Town was packed for the service. It was a memorial rather than a funeral. There was not much left of the two bodies after the explosion and fire. By the time I arrived, all the pews were full. I made my way up the center aisle to see if there were any spare seats. Roelof saw me and recognized me from photos; I was grateful that he came towards me and took my arm, guiding me to the family pew up front. It was the first time I had ever met them. Johan's father merely nodded his head in recognition, but his mother put her arms around me, just as Johan had once predicted. United by our grief, we were two women who loved the same man. She had a frail body, but tried to carry herself erect. Her white hair was wound neatly into a knot at the back of her head; her sunken cheeks and hollow eyes hinted that she was close to death herself. I never saw her again after that day. The only words we ever spoke to each other were identical: "He loved you very much." After the service, she was so weak that Roelof carried her to a wheel chair and the family left immediately, leaving me standing alone. I was not one of them.

That day brought home to me the gulf between the different worlds of South Africa. Everyone's eyes were on me; it was difficult to tell whether they felt hostility or curiosity, but I didn't feel their sympathy. Greta Barnard, the woman after whom I had named my child, was the only person in the whole church who embraced me; I was an outsider. When I wept, my tears were not only for my murdered husband, but for our lost child and my isolation. I didn't belong anywhere and I had nobody.

I knew I was being followed when I went back to my rented room that evening. I had only just sat down after bolting the door, when I heard glass breaking. Two plain clothed policemen stormed in and shouted at me in Afrikaans. I knew they were policemen, even though they weren't in uniform; I remembered seeing them at the funeral. Calling each other *"Boet"* or brother, they were so confident of their power that they made no attempt to disguise their identity.

I tried to run for the phone to call the police, but as I did so, I realized the futility of my efforts; these were the police. I was terrified as they grabbed me and began punching my face, cursing and telling me in broken English, that they had come to show me what happens to white girls who screw around with coloureds. I could feel blood running from my nose, and I was seeing flashing lights from the pummeling they gave me. As I screamed, they ripped off my clothes, threw me on the floor and started kicking my naked body. I can still hear them laughing as they lashed out at me with heavy boots and then they each lit up a cigarette.

After a few puffs, they began scorching me with the tips, starting with my face and moving down my body, then setting my hair alight with matches. To this day, the smell of burning hair makes my stomach heave. The flames were licking furiously around my face before they quelled them, by smothering my head with a jacket. They almost suffocated me, laughing at my cries of pain and fright. I thought I was going to die; I would have welcomed death. Finally one of them smirked and said, "Pity to waste a good Lucky Strike on a whore like you, but I'm going to teach you a lesson you'll never forget. Let me explain; if you ever have sex with a coloured again, we'll be here to show you what happens to trash like you. Let's show her *Boet*." I can't bear to remember what they did to me with that burning cigarette. Mercifully I fainted.

When I regained consciousness, they were gone, but my torn clothes lay in a wet pile next to me; I could smell that they had urinated on them. In agony, defiled and helpless, my heart filled with hatred. With no money for medical attention, my scars and limp remain a testament to their butchery; they fractured my left foot and my nose with their battering.

Once a month, until I moved away, I used to receive an envelope with a note. It simply read "REMEMBER," and was attached to an empty Lucky Strike packet. Every time I moved, it took a couple of months for the envelopes to start coming again, but they always knew where I was. For nearly a decade they kept tabs on me, even as laws began to change, until at last in 1994, their power was finally broken.

April 27th 1994: What a day that was; the first time many people in South Africa – and some in exile abroad – had ever voted. The long lines, snaking to polling booths, are a sight forever imprinted on my mind. I stood in line with old men and women who had walked ten miles, and waited overnight, to cast their votes; I stood shoulder to shoulder with South Africans of all races for the first time ever. There was exhilaration that day. The struggle was over and apartheid was consigned to the history books. There was camaraderie; we were free at last. If only Johan had been there to see it; it was everything he had fought for. I remembered so clearly his words the first day I met him in 1980. As I'd listened that day to Johan, the orator, I began to fall in love with Johan, the man. When he said how ultimately justice would prevail and that right would win over might, I believed him; everyone in that room believed him. He should have been there in 1994 to see it all come true.

There were many of us in those long lines who had lost someone in the struggle to end apartheid. For all of us, the victory was bittersweet. Some would find a measure of peace through the Truth and Reconciliation hearings, created by Archbishop Tutu. For me however, I would find no resolution that way; I didn't know who had planted the car bomb that killed my husband, and I didn't know who my attackers were. I knew the truth, but there could never be any reconciliation for me. Twelve years after his death, I still ached for Johan.

I should have returned to London after his memorial service, but I didn't have the resources to do so, nor any focus. Then, just after I was assaulted, a monthly deposit began arriving in my bank account. I suspected it was my father, as he was the only person who knew what my South African bank account was, but I never knew for sure. I read that he died last year, so it would explain why the payments stopped. It was Judas money, but it kept me in South Africa. I couldn't survive without it.

The decision to stay in London had been much simpler because, at that time, I was filled with hope for the future. When I left California and arrived at Heathrow after Greta was born, I made an impulsive decision not to return to the country of my birth. South Africa, and everyone in it, had contributed to my plight; I had been rejected by those who had given me life and so, in turn, I chose to reject them. When I disembarked at Heathrow, I collected my baggage, made my way through immigration, and headed for South Africa House. That's where I hoped to receive communication from Johan. It was a mad gambol. I'd never been to England before and had no plan, other than finding a bus to central London. As I stared out the window, I couldn't quite believe what I'd done. Every time I saw a black taxi or a red double-decker bus, I felt a shudder of excitement. When I arrived at Trafalgar Square and saw famous landmarks for the first time, it felt like I was on a giant Monopoly board. I was awestruck.

It was a moment of truth. South Africa House was behind me; once I went in there and requested my mail, everything would be decided. If there were letters from Johan, my future was with him. If there weren't, I wasn't sure what my future would be. Paralyzed with anxiety, I sat rigid for some minutes, delaying the moment of truth. As long as I sat there, I could hold onto my dreams. I was prolonging the moment. Finally, with resignation, I turned and made my way into South Africa House.

It was an impressive building and, despite my anger, I felt a twinge of regret when I saw the flag and heard familiar accents. Where you come from is deeply embedded in you, especially when you don't know where you are going. In trepidation I approached the front desk and my voice sounded high-pitched as I requested mail. Another girl was waiting for her mail as well; we stood silently, side by side, as the clerk went to check for us. Eventually she turned to me and said, "Been here long?"

I shook my head. "Just arrived," I replied.

"Got somewhere to stay?"

"Not yet."

"There's a bulletin board around the corner with listings. Lots of South Africans stay in Earl's Court – Aussies and Kiwis too. You'll be alright there." I nodded and made a mental note of what she'd said. If Johan hadn't made contact, I'd make my way to Earl's Court. Further conversation stopped as the clerk arrived with two letters, one for each of us.

My hands were shaking as I saw Johan's familiar writing. The postmark was Stockholm, February 23rd 1982; it was just over three weeks since he had posted the letter on the other side of the North Sea. I burst into tears and raced outside to find a private place where I could read it. With fumbling hands, I ripped open the envelope and sank onto my suitcase. I still have that letter and reread it most days. It sits in a locked drawer beside my bed, and after all these years, I know the words by heart:

Darling Valerie,

I did it! I got away. What a relief – except that I don't know where you are. I pray you remember our plan B and get yourself to S.A. House in London.

Ever since I discovered that you're pregnant, I've been going crazy not knowing where you are. I went to your flat to try and see you after I was banned. I used Roelie's postman outfit to escape – the genuine postman agreed to stick around inside my place for an extra half hour, giving me time to get away undetected. I walked right by the special branch as I made my way on foot to your flat. God – what a shock to open the door and find your father there instead! I thought I'd met my end. He got a hell of a fright when he looked up and saw me, and I can tell you, I was ready to bolt. But instead of calling the police, he laid into me verbally. Man, I hate to think what he said to you because what he said to me wasn't pretty. He told me very graphically what he does to bulls on his farm, and made it clear that I would receive the same treatment if he ever

201

saw me again – and to keep away from you. He said I'd done enough damage, getting you pregnant. I had no idea until then what had happened to you.

There was no point going back home; I'd already escaped. It made sense to keep going. I didn't want to be caught trying to get back into my place – especially if your father had alerted the police. I knew we were in deep shit and I was helpless not knowing where you were, or how I could find you. I had to make a break for it and head for the border. There were road blocks set up and police watching the border posts; suffice it to say that your Johan made a very passable Johanna! I borrowed some of your clothes when your Dad left. He said he'd be back in thirty minutes to pack up your stuff and empty the flat; I needed to be out of his sight by then. I was afraid he was calling the police, so I moved really fast. Your clothes were too small, but I took your dark glasses, some loose tops which I wore with jeans I'd left at your place, and a hat. I also thought quickly and grabbed your razor! It felt good having something of yours with me; made you feel closer.

Your Dad wouldn't tell me where you were and I was lucky he didn't call the police immediately. Maybe he did, but I was long gone by then. I reckon he wanted to protect your reputation – and his own. I said that I would marry you if I could. Jesus, I thought he'd explode.

But you see, I asked his permission! So now I can ask you... Will you marry me, Valerie? I love you. I want to spend the rest of my life with you. Since we've been apart, everything has become clear... Nothing is more important to me than being with you. I'll give up everything else, but not you. I don't have much to offer; we won't be able to return to South Africa, but we can make our lives together somewhere else. I'm really sorry for all the pain I've caused you.

Please contact me if get this letter and I'll find you, wherever you are. I can't show my face in South Africa House because I'm still persona non grata there, so the best thing is for you to call this number; 011 44 207 129783. It's a safe house and I'll get the message from them. I'm in Stockholm at the moment, but I'm making my way to England. Whatever you've decided to do about the pregnancy, I'll support you 100%. I'm sorry you've had to endure all this on your own. I love you so much.

All my love,
Johan

It was an answer to a prayer; I clutched the letter, sobbing with relief and joy. People stared at me, but I ignored them, throwing my arms out wide and shouting, "I'm getting married."

****

The Strand is an artery into Trafalgar Square. There was a bank nearby and I ran inside to get change from a teller, who looked at me strangely when I asked how to use a public phone. Rather drily, he replied, "You dial the number and put your money in!" I giggled at the expression on his face. Everything suddenly seemed funny as I raced out to find a red phone booth. My hands were shaking as I held the paper in one, tried to dial with the other, while wedging the receiver between my shoulder and chin. As I put the letter back in my pocket, I could feel my heart beating in time with the deep, strange ring. Eventually an African voice answered, saying, "*Yebo.*"

"I… I'm trying to reach Johan Barnard. Is he there?" I stammered.

"Who is this?"

"It's… it's a friend of his. My name is Valerie Spencer."

"Valerie? Yes, yes. Just wait a minute. I'll get him."

I had to put another coin into the box before I heard his voice. "Valerie?"

My whole body started to shake, and I began to cry so much that I couldn't speak. Johan said simply, "Where are you? Tell me where you are and I'll come and get you."

"Johan," I gasped. "I can't believe it's really you."

"Where are you, Valerie? Are you in London?"

"Yes," I finally managed to reply.

"Thank God. I've been so afraid, not knowing where the hell you are. Oh my God, I can't believe you're here. I love you so much; I've been out of my mind with worry. Thank God you remembered plan B! I know I'm a worthless liability who has caused you nothing but trouble, but I love you. Will you marry me, Valerie?"

My voice returned. "Yes, yes, yes. I haven't stopped smiling since I read your letter."

"Except to cry," he laughed. "I am going to make up for everything; I'm coming to get you now, my future wife. Give me a landmark near you." I looked around and noted a little church. It was stuck in the middle of a busy street, surrounded by traffic going all the way around it. I asked a passerby what it was called and could relay to Johan that it was St. Mary le Strand.

"Wait outside that church and don't move. I'll be with you in about half an hour."

I made my way there, sitting down on a bench to wait and watch. Despite the trauma of the previous week, and the exhaustion of a guilt-ridden ten hour flight, adrenalin had kicked in and I felt alert and excited. The photo of our baby girl was in my pocket with Johan's letter, and I looked at her again for the hundredth time. "I'm going to get you back, Greta," I said, staring at her face. "We're coming to get you. Your Dad's coming to find me now. You belong to us, not them."

When I saw him across the road, I almost exploded with joy. He was leaner than when I'd seen him last, and his dark, wavy hair was longer. It suited him; he looked more handsome than ever and his smile broke into a laugh when he saw me. After bounding through slow-moving traffic to reach me, he picked me up and swung me around. When he put me down, we hugged and kissed, oblivious of cars honking noisily. Never before had we embraced in public; all my cares were forgotten as I closed my eyes and relished the sensation.

I have no idea how long it took us to get back to the safe house on Old Kent Road – time meant nothing, as we walked hand in hand to the bus stop. It seemed like a dream, climbing onto a bus and sitting next to each other. We had nothing to hide any longer. We didn't speak much; where do you start when so much has happened to each of you? We just kept looking at one another, until exhaustion overcame me and I put my head on his shoulder. In no time I was fast asleep, waking only when he gently nudged me and said, "This is our stop."

The house was an old Victorian in serious disrepair, but it offered a roof over our heads – a particularly welcome advantage by now, as it was raining and the sky was grey. Garbage cans lining the street, looked like they'd never been emptied; children were playing amongst them, while women stood in doorways shouting at their offspring to come inside.

We quickly made our way to the bedroom he'd been allotted and as he closed the door, Johan pulled me into his arms again. I felt safe for the first time in nine months as he held me tight. I think we both felt so full of emotion that we could find no words to express our feelings. They weren't necessary; we fell onto the small, concave bed and all the anguish of the past months was forgotten. We were together again and that was all that mattered.

But my body, still raw from childbirth just over a week before, ached. Although I tried to suppress my cries, they escaped spontaneously. When he realized I was in pain, Johan was distraught. It was then that I told him about Greta, left behind in California. I'll never forget the look on his face as he listened. "Oh my God," he exclaimed. "You had our baby a week ago?" He had tears in his eyes as he said, "And you called her Greta?" The corners of his mouth lifted in a smile. I nodded.

Just as quickly, the smile disappeared and he stiffened. "Why didn't you tell me before?" He sat up in bed and held his head in his hands. My heart was thudding loudly; his sudden reaction unnerved me. He shook his head vigorously, as if he had just awoken, and then turned to me. "We should have held off for six weeks. You're vulnerable to infection, Valerie; your insides have been through hell. We should not have had sex." Now he was the doctor-in-training, concerned about me as a patient. "When I saw you at the church without a baby, I presumed that you had terminated the pregnancy and I didn't want to mention it – not until you did."

"I'll be alright," I said.

"You've had so much to deal with – I don't want you ever to suffer again." He cradled me in his arms and whispered, "Just as soon as we can, we'll fetch our daughter, our little Greta."

Suddenly I was overcome. "Why didn't you ever write?" I asked. "Everything would have been so much easier if you'd communicated with me in California. I wouldn't have given Greta up for adoption – I would have brought her with me. I didn't know what else to do."

"How could I write? I had no idea where you were."

"But I wrote to you and gave you my aunt's address. I sent a letter to Peter, like you said I should. That was Plan A."

He shook his head and said, "The special branch was probably checking his letter box as well. The bastards! Their reach has no limits. They probably read it. It's just as well you didn't go back to South Africa – they would probably have picked you up at Jan Smuts Airport." It was a sobering and chilling thought.

We decided to call Peter Naidoo with our good news, without giving names or details in case his phone was tapped. The conversation was short, but he was relieved, saying that an envelope had arrived some time ago, presumably from me. It contained nothing but a blank sheet of paper and my photo. After that, he'd heard nothing more. He didn't know where either of us was. We still couldn't tell him – but it was enough for him to know we were safe.

It was then that I knew, without doubt, that my mother had intercepted the letter when I'd left it unopened for a few moments. The special branch wouldn't have bothered to put a blank piece of paper in an envelope; they would just have destroyed it. I would never forgive her.

****

As the bus neared Groote Schuur Hospital, an ambulance siren cut through my thoughts. Brought abruptly back to the present, I stumbled to the door, trying to keep my balance as the bus braked to a stop. Now my work day began in earnest; a morning shift in the hospital kitchen, followed by an afternoon shift managing a fast food restaurant in Vredehoek.

I'd taken so many privileges for granted in the past, with no concern about money. That had changed terribly.

Working in the hospital kitchen is hard work, but there are no problems and the time goes by quickly. However, there are always staffing troubles at KFC. I felt a knot of dread as I made my way to Vredehoek for my afternoon job, and once again, Lettie didn't show up. It seemed to be one of those days when everything that can go wrong, will go wrong. I had to cover for her at the cash register, which prevented me getting into the kitchen to supervise. Weston was hopping around and getting on my nerves, telling me about a pretty girl who wanted a job. The air-conditioning wasn't working and my uniform was hot. I felt sorry for a woman who came in wearing a burka; she must have felt hotter than I did.

Eventually Lettie arrived and I was mad at her; it's no excuse to say you missed the bus. Dammit, I have to catch buses all day and I make sure I'm there on time. I know she has a baby to take care of at home, so I suppose that's why I always end up cutting her slack. She has a hard life. It was a relief when eight o'clock rolled around and I could head home with a box of chicken wings for dinner. As I came out the door, a young couple approached me and I turned to say, "I'm sorry, we're closed."

The woman smiled and said, "I know that. I've been waiting for closing time because I wanted to speak to you. Are you Valerie?"

On my guard, I nodded. She had an American accent. "What do you want?" I asked.

"I have a message for you from Lorna Scott," she said.

I stopped dead in my tracks and froze, while looking more

intently at the young woman; she was pretty and smiled sweetly at me. Her companion hung back and said nothing. I studied her long, dark hair and beautiful eyes, wondering – just for a moment – if this could possibly be Greta. She would be about the same age. My mind was playing tricks with me and I needed to stop such fanciful ideas. I frowned as I replied, "But Lorna is dead."

It was a great sadness to me when my aunt had written to say that she was dying of cancer and hadn't long to live. If I'd had enough money, I would've flown to see her in her last months, but that was way beyond my means. Not only was Aunt Lorna the only member of my family who had shown me kindness in my troubles, she was the only link I had with my daughter. But could this be Greta? Did I dare get my hopes up?

"I'm Fran Walker, and this is Joe," the woman said, putting out her hand to me. I reached to shake it, but instead she took mine in both of hers and held it tightly. "I know that Lorna is dead. I'm so sorry. I'm a friend of her daughter, Addie. Can we talk?" she said.

I nodded, feeling disappointment like a kick in the stomach. This wasn't Greta. The three of us walked to my flat in silence; they politely kept pace with me as I limped up the hill – my damaged foot always felt tired at the end of the day. I ushered them in the front door, thankful that Noshile had cleaned in the morning, and gestured for them to sit in the two chairs. I was unused to having visitors. Joe looked around and asked if he could go out on my balcony, as he wasn't feeling well. He looked perfectly fine to me; I supposed he was making an excuse to get out of the way so that this young woman could deliver her message.

We sat down and once again she smiled sweetly, before removing an envelope from her pocket and passing it to me with a trembling hand. I frowned and held it without opening it, sensing it was something weighty. I was tired. I knew that the message from Aunt Lorna would be something about my child, and I wanted to read it on my own. It would probably be the last contact I'd ever have, so I wanted to savour the moment alone. The woman didn't move. "Aren't you going to open it?" she asked.

My eyes filled with tears and I looked away. "I'm not sure I can bear it," I replied.

"Please," she urged, "open it."

My fingers felt as if they didn't belong to me as I responded dumbly, fumbling with the envelope. I sensed her eyes watching me intently as I read the piece of paper. My eyes opened wide; it was a copy of Greta's birth certificate. My heart suddenly began to pound and my head jerked up to look at her again. "Where did you get this?" I demanded.

She handed me another piece of paper and replied, "Same place I got this."

I grabbed the second paper from her. It was another birth certificate; this one was for Fran Walker. My hands were shaking. I didn't dare to hope there was any connection between the two pieces of paper. When I examined them carefully, the names were different, but all the details of time and place were the same.

"That's the amended birth certificate issued when I was adopted," she said simply.

I dropped the papers as I steadied myself and looked at her. "Greta?" I said. "You're Greta?"

Once again she smiled and nodded. "I *was* Greta. I'm Fran now." There were tears pouring down her face.

I was dumbstruck. We stared at one another for what seemed an eternity, neither of us saying a word. It was incredible. At last, in a whisper, I said, "You're my daughter."

Once those words were uttered, the flood gates opened. I wept as I moved to put my arms around her and I'll never forget the warmth that rippled through me as we stood in the center of the room, holding onto each other. We were laughing and crying simultaneously.

After a while, I drew back and took her face in my hands to study it. I had to look up at her, as my head only reached her shoulders. This stranger was my child. I gazed at her through teary eyes, trying to absorb the news.

I wanted that moment to last forever. She had her father's eyes and eyebrows; it was like glimpsing Johan once more. It was hard to understand what she was saying as she sobbed, but it sounded like, "I was afraid you might not want me again."

Squeezing back my tears, I hugged her more tightly than ever. "I've always wanted you. I wanted you the day you were born. I wanted you *before* you were born. The worst thing I ever did was give you away and I've always wanted you back. Oh Greta, if only you knew how much I've longed to hold you. Aunt Lorna was my only contact; she sent me word about what you were doing. Oh my goodness, how beautiful you are. You smile like your father, and you have his eyes. I wish he were alive to see you." Twenty years of pain came flooding out as we clung to each other.

After some time I needed to sit once more. She helped me to a chair and then sat cross-legged on the floor in front of me. She cleared her throat and said, "I know about my father, and I understand why you gave me up when I was born, but I don't understand why you didn't come back to get me after you were married? Why?"

I didn't stop to think how much she knew about us. As I watched the anguished expression on her face, I understood the pain of rejection that had troubled her life. It was the same way I had felt when my parents pushed me out of the way. I wished I could make her understand and I told her so.

She nodded and replied, "Why don't you try?"

Chapter 2

My daughter sat on the floor and looked around the room, as I opened the box of chicken pieces I'd brought home. "I'll tell you as we eat," I replied, wishing that the first sustenance I would ever offer her was better than left-over Kentucky Fried Chicken. I felt an urge to feed her, to do something that would demonstrate my concern for her. She interrupted my thoughts saying, "You don't have any photos anywhere. Do you have any pictures of my father?" Even though her voice was raspy from crying, it sounded like music to me.

Putting the food down on a table, I was shaking as I crossed to a drawer and struggled to unlock it. I cleared away my pictures every week when Noshile came to clean; it made it easier for her to dust, I told myself. But really, I preferred my life to remain private. The last thing in the world I wanted was questions from anybody. I removed the pictures that were tucked away with Johan's precious letter, and held them out to her. "Look at these," I said. There was a photo taken of us on our wedding day, another of Johan when he graduated from medical school in England, and the third picture was of a newborn baby. "These are the loves in my life."

"Is this me?" she asked.

I nodded. It made me happy to see her smile as she studied the pictures of her father and asked, "What was he like?"

I couldn't stop staring at her. "It's hard to put him into words. He was funny, brave, and an amazing singer – rock and roll stuff, nothing classical. He loved music and dancing. We'd often dance in my flat before we were married – it was the only place where we could dance! We couldn't do it in public." I felt myself smiling as I remembered those happy times. "He made me laugh. Maybe that's why I fell in love with him. There was something about him that made light of things, even though he took them very seriously. Do you know what I mean?"

She nodded. "What else can you tell me about him?"

"What else? He was good-looking and clever. He was a doctor with plans to specialize as a pediatrician, because he loved children. And he would have been a wonderful father, I'm sure."

A knock on the door interrupted us and Joe emerged from the balcony, looking apprehensive. I offered him some chicken, but he shook his head, telling Greta that he would catch a taxi back; she should keep the car. I saw the grateful look on her face and my heart warmed to him. He was considerate and I felt like a mother suddenly; I cared about my daughter and wanted her to be safe and happy. It felt good.

After Joe left us, I turned to her and said, "Will it embarrass you if I take my wig off, Greta? It gets so hot."

She looked startled. "No," she stammered with a frown. "Why do you wear one?"

"I'll tell you in a minute," I said, going into the bathroom. As I looked in the mirror, I tried to see myself as my daughter would be seeing me. It was a long time since I'd bothered to scrutinize myself and I didn't like what I saw. The red wig was a poor choice, but it was cheap – you get what you pay for, no doubt. My reflection looked even worse when I removed the wig, revealing thick scars in my crown where no hair had grown back after those brutes had finished with me. In addition to that, there were many places where I was bald from hair loss – caused by stress, I was told. I'd cut the rest of my hair to an inch short so that it would be easier under a wig, but I was no Sinead O'Connor – my scalp was not an attractive sight.

She tried to hide her shock when she saw me, but I saw her fleeting reaction. "This is why I wear a wig," I said. "It's not how I would like to look, but it's the way it is. I have a disease called alopecia areata, which causes these bald spots. The scars, however, are a permanent reminder from the old regime about what happened if you broke the rules."

She paled and her eyes widened in shock. "Somebody did that to you on purpose?" she asked.

I nodded. "And much more that I'd rather not talk about. Thank God I spared you the ordeal of growing up here and suffering at their hands."

My daughter stood up slowly and put her arms around me. "I

217

had no idea how much you'd suffered... I'm so sorry." I wanted to say that she'd only seen the tip of the iceberg, but I refrained from doing so. If she chose to know more, she would ask. The choice was hers to make.

The warmth of her embrace was great comfort. As she held me, I whispered, "It's been tough, but I've survived." She drew away and stared at me. There was sympathy in her expression, but I was conscious of my bald head and meager dwelling. "My life wasn't always like this, Greta." I looked around and felt a need to explain. "I had a privileged upbringing, but that went away when..."

"When you got pregnant?" she finished my sentence for me.

I nodded. "My parents couldn't accept what had happened. It wasn't just that I was unmarried, you see. Your father was not acceptable to them because of the colour of his skin. It was as simple - and as complicated - as that.

"Although he hated me, your grandfather helped by sending me money; it came anonymously, but I'm sure it was him. It kept me going; otherwise I might not have survived. I suppose I should be grateful for small mercies. He had plenty of money to spare. He's dead now and he went to his grave without acknowledging how wrong he was." I shook my head and looked at my daughter once more. "I can't quite believe this is really you and that this is actually happening. I'm scared I'm going to wake and find it was another dream."

I wanted to hold her close to me again, so that I could feel her presence, not just look at her; but I was nervous to overwhelm her. Although she was my daughter, she was still a stranger. I steeled myself not to obey my impulse and said simply, "Here, Greta, our chicken is getting cold."

She shook her head. "I ate earlier." After a moment's hesitation, she added quickly, "Please will you call me Fran? I know that's not what you named me, but that's how I've been known all my life. I can't change."

"Of course, of course," I answered. "I understand. It's just that I've always thought of you as Greta and I had no idea what your name had become. Aunt Lorna never told me – she said that she didn't know. I wasn't sure whether to believe her or not, but that's why you've always been Greta to me. It's a pretty name – Francesca, I noticed on your adoption certificate."

She smiled with relief. "I thought you might be hurt or angry."

I took her hand and said, "I gave up my rights, I know that. But now please will you tell me about yourself. I want to hear all about you – I didn't get many details from my aunt. Did you have a happy childhood? And I want to know how you found me? We have twenty years to catch up. I still can't believe this is happening."

She smiled again. By now, our tears had finally stopped. "You have to go first. Tell me why you never came back to get me after you got married." I hesitated and she repeated, "Why?"

My daughter was doggedly determined, that was obvious. She

hadn't come this far to talk about herself; she wanted answers to questions and she wanted them immediately. There would be no chit-chat as we got to know one another, so I nodded and said, "Yes, Fran. I do have to tell you, you're quite right. I'll start at the beginning." It was such a long story though, that I wondered for a moment where the beginning was. Then I considered that the point of the story was about my daughter, so her birth seemed the logical place to start.

"After you were born, I couldn't bring myself to return to South Africa. Instead, I hoped to find your father in England. It wasn't a random idea, because we'd made a contingency plan to do so. To cut a long story short, our plan worked; he was there, in London. We got married, intending to fetch you as soon as we had enough money; we had six months to do it before the adoption became final.

"But nothing was ever easy for us, I'm afraid, except falling in love. About a week after I arrived in London, I started running a high fever. Fortunately your father was a medical student and knew what to do when I started to hemorrhage. He rushed me to hospital, and thanks to the generous National Health Service in England, I received medical attention immediately. We'll never know what caused it, whether there was retained placenta after you were born, or some other cause, but I almost died. If it had happened two weeks earlier I might have welcomed death, but not then. I had your father by my side once more, and we wanted to reclaim you. That was the focus of my life and I had everything to live for." Looking at Fran intently I said, "You can't imagine how I cried, longing for you. I'd only seen you for a few minutes, but you'd been part of me for nine months. I felt as if I'd lost a part of myself."

My daughter's eyes were moist and I thought I felt her squeezing my hand slightly. She needed to know how much I loved her; I had to tell her. "You meant the world to me. You still do. The only thing that kept my sanity all these years was the belief that you were safe and happy. But I never stopped loving you."

This time she definitely squeezed my hand and said, "I *was* happy, but I always wondered about you. So I suppose I wasn't altogether happy." They were poignant words from my daughter.

I made an effort to call her by her new name. "I hate to think of that, Fran. Did you feel different from your friends? Did they know you were adopted?"

She shook her head. "No, I never told anyone, until I met Joe. He knows, but I didn't want anyone else to know. It wasn't their business." She looked away for a moment and then said, "What happened next?"

She was not going to let me change the subject. "Your father managed to find a flat for us; it was a grim council flat that he managed to rent through his ANC connections, don't ask me how. Although it was dark and dingy, we didn't care. It was our sanctuary. As soon as I was a bit stronger, we got married. Here, this is a picture of us taken that day, May 4th 1982." I looked at our young faces, so full of hope for the future, and remembered how happy we'd been. It didn't last long.

Fran hardly stirred. It was cathartic for me to tell her what I had shared with nobody else. "What I didn't know was that your father had reluctantly committed to help with an attack in South Africa." I saw my daughter recoil and I looked away. "Despite vowing that he wanted to be with me and have nothing more to do with the troubles back home, he felt obliged to keep his commitment to the ANC. He'd got a lot of help while he was penniless and on the run. And of course, they also helped us to settle in London. But he truly believed he would only be gone for a fortnight, maximum. After that, we planned to save every penny so that we could get to America and claim you.

"A few weeks after our wedding, he left for Zambia. I had no way of communicating with him while he was gone. He would be slipping in and out of South Africa incognito and couldn't communicate from there. He was nervous before he left; he tossed and turned at night, and he was up early in the mornings, pacing the small flat in Tooley Street. After his departure, I was miserable, scanning the papers every day to see whether 'it' had happened. He hadn't given me any details, other than to say 'it' was going to be big. I waited for two weeks and there was no news. I waited another two weeks, and in desperation I called the number I had for a safe house. After a few times asking there about Johan, a Jamaican accent told me not to call again as there wasn't anybody there by that name. It was no longer a safe house.

"The money he'd left me was getting low and I had to find work. I was feeling stronger and got a job waitressing in an Italian café – the owner was happy to ignore my status. I had no work permit, you see. He paid me nothing, but the tips were good and I managed to make enough to survive. God, I got a fright when my mother came knocking on our door one day, just after we were

222

married. It freaked me out. I wouldn't speak to her – I can't remember what I said, but I didn't want her in my life. I don't know how she had found me, but I wanted nothing to do with her."

"Why?" asked Fran.

I was surprised by her sudden interjection and rolled my eyes in response. "Oh God, you don't want to know. In her estimation, your father was hardly a human being because he was 'coloured.' That's all she could see. My parents were crippled by their prejudices. They couldn't see that I loved him and that he was a good human being. To them he was a coloured and as such, not fit to be part of their family.

"Well, if they couldn't accept him, they weren't going to have me either – or my child. I didn't answer the door when she came again, and I told the neighbours to tell her that I'd moved."

Fran shook her head. "But if she came looking for you, surely she loved you?"

"She did a terrible thing. I wrote a letter to your father, telling him I was pregnant and where I was going. She intercepted that letter..." I felt myself begin to shake with rage all over again. Trying to control myself, I added hastily, "Her interference was wicked. I don't ever want to talk about her."

It was difficult to hide the irritation in my voice, but I said nothing more on the subject and continued with the story. "I was sick with worry about Johan, and anxious to get to California for you, but I was barely making enough to pay the rent and feed myself. I phoned Aunt Lorna to tell her that I was married, and that I had changed my mind about the adoption. I told her I wanted to keep you."

"What did she say?" asked Fran.

"Oh God, it broke my heart. There were only about seven weeks left before the six month window was up, and I had no money. When I told her, she said, 'There's your answer. Be sensible. You have nothing, your husband has gone off – you don't know where he is, and you can't go back to South Africa with your child. What are you thinking? Your baby is well-loved here in California. She's happy and healthy. Her life will be good. You have nothing at all to offer her.'

"When I put the phone down, I wanted to die. Everything she'd said was true. I had no idea where your father was, or when he would return – if he would return, in fact. Who knew what had happened? He could have been dead. There was nothing I could do. September came and went and I knew I'd lost you forever."

I dropped my head in my hands and felt again the despair that seeped through me that day. When I looked up, Fran was still staring at me, but she reached out and touched my hand. "That's why we didn't come to get you. That's why you're Fran Walker, not Greta Barnard." I sobbed as I said these last words.

I cried for a long time. All the while Fran said nothing and I was almost unaware of her as I relived my grief. When I finally quieted, I looked up to see her sitting at the table with her head in her hands, pressing fingers over her ears to block out the sound of my misery. The pain of my loss was unbearable now that I had allowed it to be spoken. For so long I had kept my secret deeply suppressed – as a result, the only emotion I'd felt was anger.

Despite my relief to see him, I was angry with Johan when he returned to London in October 1982, a month too late for our deadline. I was angry with my parents too, and Aunt Lorna. And then a few years later, maddest of all with the thugs who killed Johan and assaulted me.

At length Fran said, "What happened to my father? Did he come back?"

I nodded. "Eventually… When he got to Zambia, he discovered that the weapons and ammunition they needed, hadn't arrived. Even though he was there for almost six weeks before infiltrating South Africa, he couldn't contact me because they were deep in the bush. They had to keep moving. South African forces made raids to try and eradicate what they called, 'terrorist camps.' Once they went through Zimbabwe and over the border into South Africa, there was even less chance of communication with me. They were always on guard because of informers as they made their way to Pretoria. That's where they planned to blow up a post office, two police stations and the Voortrekker Monument – all targets that were strong symbols of the hated Nationalist government."

Fran swallowed hard. "It must have been dangerous. Was he afraid?"

"I'm sure he was. He was a wanted man. If he'd been caught, he would have gone straight to Robben Island. Actually, that's not true; the police might have hanged him. He had some narrow escapes, but he never slept in the same place two nights running. At one point he and his comrades got rides in hearses – inside coffins! Once they got to Pretoria, it took some weeks for them to scope out their targets without being noticed. Their big worry was how to hide their explosives. Somehow they managed that. One time they had to move in a hurry because someone warned them the police were coming – they hijacked a van and got away just in time with their explosives." I stopped to get a sip of water as my throat was getting dry; I wasn't used to talking so much. "They ditched the vehicle fairly quickly and buried their stuff in a grove of trees. That made it easier for them to move more freely."

"Did they... blow up their targets?"

I could see Fran was having a hard time with this knowledge. I understood completely, because it mirrored my reaction when Johan told me about it on his return. It was when he died that I changed my opinion. You had to fight fire with fire. If I could lay my hands on the perpetrators who ended his life so violently, I would take pleasure in bayoneting them.

"Yes, they had partial success," I replied. "They blew up two police stations, but they weren't able to get their other targets."

"Did they kill anybody?" she asked.

I looked away and shrugged.

Fran got up and walked out onto the balcony, staring up into the night sky. I suspect it all sounded terrifying to her, with memories of 9/11 fresh in her mind. How could I expect her to understand what the times were like? I wanted her to know that her father was a good man, but I feared, from the look on her face, that she didn't see it that way. I went outside and stood next to her. "If you'd known your father, you would've been proud of him. He was compassionate, but it was war, Fran. He was a soldier and he was doing what soldiers do. The discrimination suffered by anyone who wasn't white in those days, was humiliating and crippling. The law dictated where you could live, where you could go to school, what you would learn in school, what job you could have, how little you would be paid for your work. They also dictated whom you could not marry. We couldn't go to movies together, because we had to go to different theatres. We couldn't ride on a bus together, or sit on a bench together. It was insane and cruel, and made everybody who wasn't white, a second class citizen. I'd lived a very privileged 'white' life, but your father had suffered these harsh restrictions. When you've been humiliated all your life, there comes a time when you realize that talking achieves nothing. That's when you resort to stronger means in order to achieve your aim."

"Nelson Mandela didn't ascribe to violence." She looked at me with something like accusation in her eyes.

"He spent almost a quarter century behind bars; he couldn't act from there. It might have been different if he'd been free."

Biting her bottom lip, she looked at me and said, "So what happened after my father got back to London?"

227

It was getting cool outside and I was shivering. "Let's go back in," I said. When we we'd closed the balcony door, I continued. "Your father was able to finish his medical degree in England, thanks to education funds from the ANC. It was some time before my status changed to get a work permit, so I continued waitressing illegally. I took cooking classes and, once my permit was issued, I started working in the kitchen instead of waitressing. I enjoyed it and kept myself so busy that I didn't have time to think about my unhappiness. That's what I've done ever since; I've kept busy. It eases the pain."

She frowned. "But I don't understand. Why did my father return to South Africa? I thought you said he was committed to help them only once. Did he change his mind?"

It took me a moment to understand her question. "No, he was adamant he would never plant explosives again. He said that he would only help the cause by serving as a doctor – saving life, not ending it. He had nightmares about those months when he returned to plant bombs, crying out in his sleep and groaning. That happened often and he would wake up sobbing. No, he never did that again. When he went back to South Africa in 1986, it was for personal reasons. His mother was dying of cancer and he wanted to see her one more time."

"Was he still a wanted person?"

"Of course. He went back the same way he'd escaped the first time; he went over the border from Mozambique and was making his way to Cape Town. But he walked into a trap. They were sure he'd come back to see his mother. No doubt they'd been tapping her phone and looking at her post. He never got to see her. He reached Durban and managed to borrow a car from a friend to drive the rest of the way – hitchhiking was too risky. But the police knew he was there. He and his friend got into the car next morning and it was all over in a second. They perished when it exploded – the police had rigged a bomb. He didn't even get out of Durban."

There were tears pouring down Fran's face once more.

"At least he didn't suffer. They could have tortured him; that would have been worse. They would have shown no mercy. I had a premonition when we said goodbye. He looked at me as if he knew it too, but neither of us spoke of our fears. God, I wish I'd stopped him from going." I crumpled, sobbing as the heartache overcame me again. It felt as intense as if Johan's death was yesterday.

Between sobs, I heard Fran whisper, "I can't bear it. This is terrible."

I should have stopped then, but I continued with agonizing details that came out in bursts. "You can imagine how his body, oh my God, was burnt and blown into pieces of charred flesh and bone. There was nothing left to bury. One moment he was there and the next moment he was gone. There was nothing left of him. His life was over in one massive explosion." My chest felt like it was going to burst with physical pain. "In an instant, I was a penniless widow. Everything and everyone I had ever loved was gone. Oh my God, I can't talk about it anymore tonight, Fran…"

When I think back on that moment, I realize that Fran had gone very quiet. Ashen-faced, she stood up and left without uttering another word. At the front door she turned and stared at me, before slamming it and running away. I could hear her sobs all the way downstairs. It was a terrible moment of self-realization for me. Rapt in my own grief, I hadn't considered her shock or pain. She would never know the father she'd been seeking.

Stumbling as I tried to rush to the balcony, I wanted to call out to her, but my voice disappeared in my chest. I opened my mouth, but no words would come out. Instead, I stared silently as she disappeared into the darkness.

The day that had started so badly before dawn, had taken me to great heights for a few brief moments in time. Now it left me at my lowest ebb ever.

Chapter 3

Seeing my daughter climb into a car and drive away, filled me
with confused emotions. My initial joy was replaced by something
awkward and unexpected: resentment. I had given her up
because I could offer her nothing except my love, but when I saw
that rental car, it was as if I'd received a body blow. I was twenty
years older than her, yet I hadn't driven a car in years because I
couldn't afford one – not after an old second hand car that I once
owned, broke down. I didn't have enough money to repair it. I
couldn't even pay rent and ate leftover Kentucky fried chicken to
keep body and soul together. Yet here was this young woman, a
student with wealth and opportunities I could only dream of,
driving around in a hired car. How did she have funds to be in
South Africa, travelling the world with her boyfriend?

Why did I not feel happy for her? This wasn't just anybody. This
was my daughter after all. She wasn't just another wealthy
westerner, I told myself; it was the same little being that I had
brought into the world. I should have felt pride and happiness,
instead of gnawing envy. I hated myself for feeling jealous, but I
couldn't help it. This confirmed the self doubts that had plagued
me on sleepless nights: I wasn't fit to be a mother. My regrets
were oddly tempered by relief sometimes, that my failure at such
an important job had never been proven. My mother turned out to
be a dismal role model. Her love of "respectability" was greater
than any feelings she had for me, so what hope was there for me

to succeed? I feared that I would have turned out the same way. My parents' love for me had very strict conditions. Once I'd strayed from their tacit condition of falling in love with a white man, our ties to each other fell apart. No variation to the colour code would ever meet with their approval.

It suddenly struck me that Fran had parked the car right outside my flat, even though she and Joe had met me at KFC. How did she know where to find me? How did she know where I lived? My mind raced, thinking of possible ways she had traced me and I regretted not finding out. If only she hadn't been so insistent on hearing why we never fetched her, we would have spoken more about her. She had walked out of my life now and who knew if she would ever come back? She'd found her birth parents – well, one of them – and I supposed it couldn't have been a great comfort to her. I had no way of contacting her and cursed myself for not getting her cell phone number, at least. A wail of frustration escaped me as I collapsed onto my bed, overwhelmed with emptiness worse than anything I'd ever experienced before.

 When I rode to work on the bus next day, it seemed strange that everything looked the same as the day before. There were regular daily commuters scurrying to work, waiting for buses or waving down taxis. There was noisy traffic fighting for space on the roads and newspaper boys at stop streets, waving daily papers at passing drivers. There were flower sellers with buckets of bright blooms, and street vendors with wooden giraffes. Cape Town was going about its daily business much the same as always. But for me, life had changed overnight. It would never be the same again.

****

My morning was spent waiting for the afternoon, so that I could get to KFC where Fran might find me again. My afternoon was spent watching the door of KFC, praying that she would come back. She didn't. By eight o'clock, when I walked home, despair was weighing me down. I let myself into the flat and could concentrate on nothing, hoping the doorbell would ring. My hopes soared when it did and I raced to answer, only to find the tenant from Flat 7 complaining about the noise from Flat 8. I dealt with that and then ate a piece of yesterday's cold chicken. At about ten o'clock, I gave up hope and went to bed.

The next day I told myself that I was being a fool. As I sat on the bus, I reminded myself that I had given her up and now she had given me up. She had no obligation to have anything more to do with me; she'd satisfied her curiosity and that was probably enough for her. The thought crossed my mind that if I had lived in better circumstances, perhaps she would've been eager to establish a relationship, but I still had nothing to offer her twenty years later. She had the world at her feet, as well as another mother who had clearly done her proud. That thought made my heart ache. I was one of life's losers. Without doubt, the best thing I had ever done in my life was give her up. She was better off without me. I repeated the mantra silently, over and over, "She's better off without you."

For a moment, I dared to remember my sudden twinges of concern about her well-being the night before last; how relieved I'd been that Joe had left her the car to drive home and how good it had felt to connect with her. I quickly chided myself not to confuse maternal responsibility with a few concerns about her safety. She had already made it twenty years without my protection – it was too little and too late. "Just face it, Valerie," I told myself, "You're not her mother; you're a stranger to her. She has your DNA and nothing else. You don't know the first thing about her and you need to forget the encounter. If it hadn't happened, you would've carried on exactly as you have been doing, without entertaining any false hopes. You're nothing to her but the owner of a womb that bore her. Forget the whole thing."

I'd had to lecture myself on previous occasions to overcome difficulties and I'd come to appreciate my own counsel. It was too painful to live with hope that was unlikely to come true. Resolutely, I disembarked from the bus on that second day and tried to put thoughts of my daughter aside. The moment her words or face crept onto my mental screen, I shut them out by thinking about something else. The day was so busy that it wasn't difficult to do this while I was at work, but when I lay down to sleep that night, my dreams were of my daughter; as a baby, as a young girl that I could only imagine, and as the young woman I had recently seen. I couldn't protect myself when all barriers were down and my subconscious took command. I wanted my daughter back. I wanted a second chance to prove myself to her – and I wanted to prove something to myself as well.

I awoke exhausted. "This has to stop," I told myself. "Get a grip on yourself. Maybe she'll come back, maybe she won't. There's nothing you can do about it now." I looked at my reflection in the mirror as I climbed out the shower, staring long and hard – as if at a stranger. I had lost interest in appearances after Johan died. I wanted to wear a scarred face because it mirrored all the misery I felt inside. I had no desire to look attractive any longer; I didn't care. All of a sudden, as I stared at myself, I realized that I did care very much. If my daughter came back, I didn't want her to be ashamed of me.

My thoughts were interrupted by the phone ringing. Looking at my watch, I saw that it was just after five o'clock. If it was Bobby Govender who'd lost his key again, I would explode. Maybe it was another hawker trying to sell stolen avocados, when the 'No Hawkers' sign was very clear to see. Angrily I picked up the phone and said gruffly, "Yes?"

An American accent replied, "Can I give you a ride to work?"

I began to shake. "Fran," I gasped, "Is that you? What are you doing here at this hour?"

"I picked up some breakfast for us. Can I come up?"

My hands were trembling as I pressed the button and opened the door for her. Speechless, my mouth opened and shut as I swallowed hard. She looked at me and smiled hesitantly. "Are you feeling better?" she asked softly, placing take-away food on the small table that was still full of yesterday's leftovers. "I should have called first, but I figured you'd be up and about."

I nodded silently, afraid to say anything in case I messed up again, and trying hard to hold my tears in check. I lost that battle fairly quickly. Fran came to me with her arms outstretched. My arms found their way around her waist without hesitation. With my face buried in her chest, I felt like a child as I whispered, "Thank you, Fran. Thank you for everything."

PART 5

FRANCESCA AGAIN

Living is being born slowly. It would be a little too easy if
we could borrow ready-made souls.

- *ANTOINE DE SAINT-EXUPÉRY,*
Flight to Arras, 1942

Chapter 1

I was almost blinded by tears as I drove away. Worse was to come; by the time I reached the corner, I had to stop because I felt ill. I only just managed to get the car door open before starting to retch. I'd promised Addie that I would let her know immediately I met my mother, but what was I going to say? "Guess what? I found her and she's pathetic." The last person I wanted to speak to was Addie.

As I'd watched the realization dawn on Valerie that I was her daughter, tears had welled in my eyes. That moment was everything I'd ever hoped for – I always lived with fear that she wouldn't want to acknowledge me. It had been like a miracle to hear her say she'd always wanted me. But after that I became confused. It was shocking to learn about my father. It was all so violent. My mother was trying to say that he was a good man, yet he was planting bombs. She wouldn't admit it, but he must have killed people. That made him a murderer. And then to hear how he died, it made me want to be sick there and then. And she kept on about it, like she wanted me to suffer.

It was hard to stomach the trauma of it all, and I felt disillusioned and angry. What an anticlimax. She was a mess. Her life was dismal. Perhaps I had expected some magical understanding between us that could only be explained as love; something that time and distance couldn't break. Instead, I found her self-absorbed, weighed down by the pain that life had brought her. Her life was screwed up and I didn't want to fix it for her. It was obvious that this wasn't going to be any fairy tale; this 'once upon a time story' would not have a 'happy ever after' ending. That's what I'd always wanted, but it was madness. There wasn't a wicked witch who'd cast an evil spell – certainly not my grandmother, whom I'd always cast in that role. The simple truth was this: my mother had given me away and the umbilical cord hadn't kept us bound together. She was her and I was me. I wished it could have been otherwise, but it wasn't.

Oh God, can I ever forget that first moment in KFC, when Gran acknowledged it was my mother we were looking at? My heart was pounding so loudly, it sounded like a drum in my ears. I longed to run and announce who I was, but I couldn't. Instead I stared at her, trying to absorb that this woman was actually my mother. This was finally her – I had found her.

I didn't register the dreariness surrounding her, because I was so excited. Reality seemed suspended. It was only afterwards, when I'd heard her explanations, that it began to sink in how pathetic she was. The phone call to her aunt all those years ago should have been decisive, but when she called to say that she'd changed her mind about giving me up for adoption, she was so whimpish. She was full of excuses and blamed everybody but herself. It was her mother's fault, Aunt Lorna's fault, and it was also my father to blame, but it was never her own fault. And then, no matter how she tried to justify the facts, my father was a killer. I couldn't get my head around that. This wasn't the fairy tale that had been my dream since childhood.

I drove with tears pouring down my cheeks, not knowing what to do or where to go. I couldn't bear the thought of my grandmother gloating, nor did I want her sympathy. What I wanted more than anything was my Mom, Grace. I wanted the familiar comfort of her arms around me, assuring me of her love. I wanted to pour my heart out and tell her what I'd been doing, what I had discovered. I wanted to apologize for my clandestine search. Why had I been so secretive? I had made weekly calls home without saying what I was doing. Did I think that Grace would be hurt? Or did I think that perhaps, when I found my birth mother, I would love her more and therefore I wanted to keep it all from Grace? I had been crazy not to trust my mother with the facts, but then she had been secretive as well. Was she also afraid of something? Why had she never spoken about my adoption, other than once when Billy was born? Perhaps this is just the thing that she was afraid of: I would go in search of my birth mother and leave her.

I drove to Joe's lodgings and called him on his cell phone from the car park. It was a comfort to hear his voice and know that he was at hand. "I'll be right there," he assured me. It was a dark night and I looked around nervously, making sure that all the doors were locked. The parking lot was deserted of people, but full of cars. I kept watch to make sure that nobody appeared unexpectedly. There were too many horror stories to feel safe. I was still shocked by Lauren Marlowe's recent abduction and shuddered involuntarily, thinking of her ordeal. As soon as Joe climbed in the car, I poured out the story Valerie had told. He said nothing, but sat listening and watching me. When I finished talking, he said quietly, "So what do you want to do now?"

I swallowed hard and looked out the window at the stars. They seemed closer here than in California. "I want to go home."

"Home? To California?" he said. I nodded. "Fran, you've come half way around the world for lots of things, not just to find your birth mother. Well, I presume you came for more than that, didn't you?" I said nothing and he continued, "Why don't you phone your Mom?"

"Which one?"

"Whichever one you want," he said with a laugh. "Phone your mother in California. Tell her what you've just told me."

"Are you crazy?" I retorted.

"No, I'm perfectly serious. You've been chasing after a pipe dream most of your life, I think." He reached out and held my hands. "You're disappointed now. Don't be. From what you've told me, Valerie is a brave person who has lived in difficult times and places. We can't imagine what it was like for her, because we've never lived in that sort of society. Apartheid was evil, and your parents were both victims of the system. For that matter, so were you. But think of the magnanimity of your adoptive parents. They love you, Fran. Call them."

He had a calming influence on me and I held his hand tightly as we walked into the hostel. He lay on his bed while I texted my Mom to call me. Almost immediately, my phone rang. I heard her voice exclaiming, "Fran, are you OK? What's the matter?"

"I just wanted to speak to you, Mom. Did my texting wake you? I'm sorry, I didn't check to see what the time was."

"It's fine, Fran. It's lovely to hear your voice. What's going on?"

"Oh Mom," I began, "I don't know where to start. I've been so stupid – you see I've been looking for my, um, my…" I couldn't continue and started to sob. Joe came over and put his arms around me.

"I know what you've been doing, Fran. That's OK. I would have done the same thing if I were you, darling. Have you found them yet?"

I sobbed even harder and heard my mother say, "I was afraid that it would be painful for you, Fran. Do you want to talk about it?"

I told her everything, from the very beginning of the search until half an hour ago, when I left Valerie's flat. She said nothing, but as I told the story, the load seemed to lift. By the end, I was dry-eyed and calm again, and finished by saying, "I'm sorry that I didn't tell you about all this earlier."

"You don't have to apologize, Fran. I understand how difficult it's been for you to understand why she gave you up, and so it's good that you have the facts now. Don't judge her harshly. You haven't walked in her shoes. Remember that. Hindsight is a wonderful thing, but people have to make their choices without it. They have to make the best decision they can, with what they have in their hands at the time. She did what she thought was best for you, not what was best for herself. She made the biggest sacrifice anyone could ever make, short of giving their own life. It must have been very difficult and painful for her."

"But what about my birth father," I said. "What do you think about that? He killed people. He was a terrorist."

"Maybe he did, maybe he didn't. But then as Valerie said, it was war. You could call him a terrorist or a freedom fighter, depending which side you were on. Dad went to fight in Vietnam. Perhaps he also killed. He probably did – that's what soldiers do. It's barbaric, but it's what they're required to do. Kill or be killed. You haven't walked in Johan's shoes either, Fran. You can't judge their actions back then by looking at them through your eyes now."

I looked over at Joe who was lying on the bed again, staring at the ceiling, with his arms behind his head. He was so strong and manly, but I couldn't imagine him ever holding a gun in his hand, pulling a trigger, or planting a bomb somewhere that was destined to kill passersby. He must have sensed me watching him, because he looked at me and smiled. My heart pounded suddenly.

"I suppose not," I said to my mother, smiling back at Joe. "I love you, Mom. I'm so relieved you understand," I said as we ended the call.

I went over to the bed where Joe was lying and sat down next to him. "You were right," I said. "You know me better than I know myself. I feel much better after talking to my Mom. Valerie and Sharon are strangers to me. It's such a weird feeling. I wanted to find my birth mother so badly, yet I don't know what I expected to achieve. I found her a bit irritating after a while, to be quite honest. Is that bad?" Joe smiled and shook his head. "It's a bit of an anticlimax. I feel sorry for her, but nothing much else." Reaching across to him, I took his hand. "You're a good friend, Joe. Thank you. You've helped me every step of the way, even when my car broke down. What would I do without you?"

We stared at each other and without another word, he reached up for me. I fell into his arms as he pulled me down on top of him. "Now that you've got that out of the way," he whispered in my ear, "forget about the past for a bit. I've been waiting patiently for a long time. I thought you'd never notice me here in the wings. I want to be much more than a friend to you." He began unbuttoning my shirt, as I ran my fingers through his hair.

****

It was much later that I drove back to Camp's Bay, feeling happier than I could have imagined. Joe had wanted me to stay the night with him, but I wanted to get back. I had spoken harshly to Gran and it was weighing on my mind. However, as I drove, I had the radio on and sang out loud. Life had never felt so good. Joe was right. It was time to forget the past and get on with my life in the present.

A light was on in my grandmother's room and I decided to go in and apologize immediately. What a sight met my eyes – she had passed out on the floor. Her mouth was hanging open and her eyes were closed; I thought she was dead. Thank God for Joe, who jumped in a taxi and came over to help me the moment I called. I was relieved that I wasn't dealing with a dead body. After we put her back in bed, we examined her pills. Joe assured me that she'd sleep it off, for her pulse was strong.

"What a family I found myself!" I exclaimed.

Joe lifted me up and carried me to my room. "I think I need to put you to bed too," he said. "Your grandmother won't hear a thing for hours."

Dawn was breaking when he finally left. We stood on the balcony and watched the soft morning light on the waves below us. It felt right standing there with his arms around me, watching the start of a new day. The air was fresh and the world was still quiet – the only sounds were waves breaking and seagulls cawing.

"Come away with me for a few days," he said, "just the two of us. Forget about all of this and let's go somewhere on our own."

It was exactly what I wanted to do. Although I had just found these two women, I couldn't face them for a while and wanted nothing more than to be with Joe. I nodded and smiled.

Chapter 2

There were tears in her eyes as I told Gran about the evening with my mother – her daughter. She stared at me silently for a long time, visibly shocked. At length, she walked to the balcony and stared out to sea, lost in thought. When she turned around, her face was wet with tears that she made no effort to stop.

"Poor Valerie," she said. "She's lost everything, hasn't she? I didn't realize how much she loved your father. I never gave him a chance. It's a strange thing Fran, to feel my heart warm when it's been cold for so long." She scratched her head and frowned, "That's just like Tom to be sending her money without telling me, but I'm glad he did it. Why didn't he tell me though? I would have supported him and admired him for it."

"Probably for the same reason you never told him you'd hired a private detective," I replied.

She looked away and grunted. "I'm going for a walk," she murmured. "I need to be alone to sort out my feelings."

I shrugged and went back to bed, still warm with the memory of Joe. It had been an exhausting twenty-four hours; I drifted off to sleep, happy and in love. I couldn't wait to be with him again. It seemed dream-like to awake some time later, hearing my cell phone ringing and his voice saying, "Hey you, are you still coming away with me? Let's go wine-tasting over in Franschoek."

"I'll pick you up in twenty minutes," I replied, jumping out of bed to shower and change. Gran still wasn't back. I felt a bit bad leaving her unannounced, but she obviously wanted to be on her own. I knew she wasn't prepared to drive a car in Cape Town, however, so I didn't feel guilty taking the car. I left her a note, explaining that I was going away for a couple of days 'to sort out my feelings' as well, but she could reach me on my cell phone. We both needed our space.

It was a relief, speeding over the mountains, to the wine country, leaving all my cares behind. The first winery had a bed and breakfast establishment adjacent to it in the Cape Dutch style, with its unique gables and shutters. There were vineyards as far as the eye could see, and craggy mountains rising behind us to Hellshoogte – the Heights of Hell. It looked more like paradise to me. The air was warm and fragrant with the scent of roses and heliotrope. We were fortunate there was a vacancy, which we reserved, before going on to explore the quaint town.

French Huguenots had settled here three hundred years ago, bringing their winemaking skills with them and starting the Cape wine industry. We spent our time sampling food and wine, and enjoying our new found delights in one another. For two days I didn't give either of my mothers a thought, although I did phone Gran to see if she was alright. She sounded a bit annoyed at first, but said she was fine and that John Spencer was flying in from Durban. He was keen to meet Valerie again. I wasn't sure Valerie would be receptive to meeting anybody just yet, however.

"I know," Gran replied when I said this. "I've told him that, but he is a dear person and he was very fond of Valerie. I think he just wants to be close to the scene." As we talked more, I could hear her voice soften. She said she was relieved to hear from me, understanding that I wanted to sort out my feelings. I didn't tell her that my feelings had never felt better.

We drank wine and ate, drank more wine, and enjoyed each other for two days. As we lay in bed on the second night, talking about this strange and beautiful country, I said to Joe, "Do you realize something? Twenty years ago, we would have been breaking the law; we could have gone to prison if we'd been caught. You've been having relations with a woman of colour."

"Oh my God, what colour are you?" he shrieked. He rolled over and stared at me, then pulled the blankets off the bed. "Let me see!" I giggled as he scrutinized my naked body. "And all this time I thought you just had a good tan." We were both laughing as he ran his hands over my body and said, "You're my most favorite colour, and I especially like these two dark circles right here." He kissed me and said, "You know, I was crazy about you from the start, but you kept heading off without giving me a thought, unless you had car problems. I'm not sure you deserve all the attention I've given you…"

"I'm sorry," I laughed.

"You aren't really," he said. "You've no idea what torment it was, living in the same house as you and waiting for your car to break down. I was tempted to tamper with the engine, just to get noticed."

I laughed again and said, "Well, I did notice you, but I didn't want to make the first move. Anyway, I've made up for it now, haven't I?"

Lying in each other's arms, he pulled me close, saying, "Not quite, but you're getting there. I love you, Fran. I love every part of you."

I hugged him tightly and said, "I love you, too." Long after I could hear he was asleep, I lay awake, giddy with love, conscious that I hadn't experienced anything in life to compare with the happiness I felt right then. Nothing could spoil it. I didn't care what anybody else might think; it felt right for me.

For just a moment I wondered what Grace Walker would think about the relationship; I don't think she would have approved of us sleeping together. But Valerie was not in a position to judge. When she got pregnant, my mother was about the same age as I was. With that thought, I froze. We had taken precautions; I'm sure that my birth parents did too. But accidents happen and even the pill is not 100% safe. It would be a catastrophe if I got pregnant right now. There was a sudden knot of anxiety in my stomach.

For an instant I could imagine Valerie's panic. My parents didn't want to have a baby at that time. Pregnancy spelled disaster for them. They had felt the same way about each other that Joe and I were feeling, but their love was forced to be a dark secret, hidden from the world – even their friends and family. Apartheid had made something beautiful into something sordid and forbidden. For the first time, I understood deeply what only my head had been able to comprehend before.

I slept fitfully and dreamed about my birth parents being chased by uniformed policemen. It was a recurring dream and no matter how many times I woke, I went back to sleep and dreamed the same thing again. A little after 4 o'clock, I knew what I had to do. Gently nudging Joe, I told him that I had to go and see my mother. He rubbed his eyes and shook his head. "What – now?" He looked at his watch and cursed. "You aren't serious, are you?" I nodded and as we got dressed without speaking, it was evident that he was annoyed. I attempted an explanation, but he muttered, "It's too early in the morning for me to deal with all of this." He slammed the car door when he threw our backpacks into the trunk. We drove in silence, watching the headlights on the road in front of us penetrating the darkness. Even at this hour, buses and taxis were making their way to Cape Town; the roads were getting busier as we neared the city. Stopping in Vredehoek to pick up breakfast, I said, "I'm taking some food to her and then I'm giving her a ride to work. Hope you don't mind." He shrugged and inhaled deeply, muttering something inaudible.

She was surprised to see me and her happiness convinced me that what I had done was right. It was an inconvenience for Joe and me, but it meant the world to her. When we returned to the car and she saw Joe, she smiled shyly and climbed into the back. Besides giving us directions to Groote Schuur, she said nothing. When I promised to see her again that evening, with dinner for two, she nodded.

****

After dropping her at work, we continued in silence to Joe's hostel. I stared out at the bustling city, without registering anything. Seeing Valerie again had thrown me back into her world and I realized the problems I now faced. I felt unwelcome responsibility towards her and my grandmother. It seemed unfair that I should have that responsibility when they had shown none towards me, but I couldn't simply walk out of their lives as quietly as I'd walked in. My thoughts were interrupted by Joe saying, "What's worrying you? You look really pissed off."

I sighed loudly. "Yes, I am. I wish we could go back to Franschoek and forget about these two women again, but I can't. I feel terrible saying this, but they're like a nagging toothache. It's weird. I've dreamed about meeting my mother since I was four years old, and now I wish I could just resume my life as it was before. She and her mother are both such victims. I feel as if I'm the adult and they're the badly behaved children. That's not what I was expecting." I sighed again and looked at him. "What am I going to do about them? How am I going to get them to meet? They're impossible. And by now, John Spencer will have arrived in Cape Town as well."

"Well, for God's sake, let him engineer the meeting. You don't have to be the saviour, you know. It's not all up to you."

Just then, a car swerved in front of us and Joe jammed on brakes. The car screeched to a halt and he opened his window shouting, "Christ Almighty! Try indicating, you ass hole." The driver of the car continued cutting across to the next lane and this time caused an accident. It was a fender bender and nothing serious, but it startled us both.

Joe shouted again at the bad driver, "You idiot, do you think you own the fucking road?" The guy behind us began honking for Joe to move on, shouting and waving his fist.

"Please, just drive on," I begged Joe, who was turning round and gesturing at the car behind us. I was appalled that he had suddenly erupted into rage over something so insignificant in the big picture. "Just forget it. It's not your problem," I said.

"It could have been my problem," he shouted. "I can't stand these morons who drive as if they were the only ones on the road."

"Well, you can't do anything about it and we weren't hit."

"Oh yes I can. I'll teach him a lesson," he replied, reaching for the door handle.

"Joe, this car is rented in my name. You shouldn't even be driving it. You're being as stupid as the other guy. Do you want to start a minor war, or what?" All the cars behind us were now honking. "If you want to stay here and argue, go ahead," I said, "but I'm leaving. Either get out the car, or drive on."

He glared at me. "Holy shit, Fran! Thanks for the support." He revved the car and we took off with a lurch, driving in silence until we arrived at the youth hostel where he was staying. Climbing out of the car and grabbing his bag from the trunk, he muttered, "See you around."

I walked around to the driver's seat and watched him stride away, unable to believe he was storming off over something so petty. I shouted after him, "Don't count on it." He didn't even turn around.

Chapter 3

With my head spinning, I needed a walk on the beach to calm myself. I suddenly thought of Josie and wished she were here, but I'd never even told her about being adopted. It was a secret I'd kept all my life until I shared it with Joe, and now I felt betrayed. I had trusted him with my most vulnerable, intimate self, yet he had trampled on it because of some stupid road rage.

Walking to the water's edge, I waded in the waves as they lapped around my feet. There were a few swimmers out already, and lots of joggers, but mostly I had the beach to myself. I could smell salt in the air, undiluted by sunscreen washing off well-oiled bodies. Soon crowds would begin to arrive and there would be no solitude. The lull of the waves would be broken by screams and shouts, but for now the beach was mine.

I walked the length of the bay, watching my footprints disappear as water washed over them. Apart from a slight indentation, it was as if nothing had been there only moments after I passed by. The transience was like so much else. Everything seems important in the moment, but in reality it leaves little impression on the world. My father had come and gone; what was left of all his efforts? There was no trace of him left behind, except me, and he had never known me. And now there was Joe. I didn't want him to be another disappearing print in my life and felt myself choking back tears.

I stopped and stared at the ocean, overcome with sadness. The water was mesmerizing and after a while I was lulled into a numbing trance. The waves crested and ran to shore; then they either flowed backwards into the next wave, becoming part of it, or they were pulled into the undertow. As I stared, it came to me that I was part of a bigger picture, like the waves. My father hadn't disappeared without a trace. He'd played a part in bringing about change in South Africa and that had made a difference. He had also loved my mother. Through that love, he had perpetuated himself by providing me with his genes. Even if it was just biology, he hadn't died without making his mark. He had made me. I was the ongoing flow.

****

My grandmother looked up when I opened the door and exclaimed, "Fran, I've missed you, dear. I'm very glad to see you again." Her smile was disarming and despite my previous grudges, I smiled back.

John Spencer had arrived the previous night and was making coffee. "You're just in time," he said. "Would you like some?"

We all sat at the kitchen table and it felt like there was a proverbial elephant in the room. We all stepped over it without mentioning it was there. We chatted about the weather and how beautiful Cape Town was, and where I had been. Then we sat in silence, sipping our coffee. Finally I blurted out, "I don't think she's ready to see either of you. She's very resentful and she's had a very hard life. You won't recognize her, John. Maybe Gran has told you; she's disfigured and she's lost a lot of hair, so she wears a wig. She doesn't walk very easily either. I suppose Gran has told you the whole story by now."

"I've told him that your father was coloured, if that's what you mean," said Gran.

Something inside me snapped. It was the way she said it that sounded so disparaging. "Yes, that's the whole story. That's what this was all about wasn't it? My father was a doctor and a good man, but his skin was like mine. I'm coloured too, in case you hadn't realized. Our skin's darker than yours and that made all the difference. Because my mother fell in love with this man, she had to leave the country to give birth to me. She gave up everything. And then she still lost her husband and I lost my parents – all because my father's skin was a bit too dark."

John looked embarrassed and my grandmother looked aghast. And I – I felt confused. What was I doing defending my birth mother whom, a few hours ago, I had found a burden of responsibility? The picture of a wave flowing back to become part of the next wave sprang to my mind, and I realized that I had to say this on my parents' behalf. They were embodied in me. I was their spokesperson. Like the wave, I could either disappear inconspicuously into a massive body of water, or I could regroup and come to shore once more. Unable to stop the flow of anger that was now unleashed, I continued, "And if you want to meet your daughter again, it's up to you to figure it out. You know where she lives and works, so don't ask me to help you. I'm done with all of this."

I hadn't noticed the clock before, but now I heard it and saw it on the kitchen wall. It ticked loudly, making the ensuing silence palpable. Nobody spoke a word. I glared at my coffee cup and felt my lower lip quiver, as I struggled with my emotions. The last few days had turned my life upside down. I'd found my mother, but lost any hope of finding my father. I'd fallen in love and given my heart, but now it seemed I'd lost my love. Try as I might to control myself, I felt tears running down my cheeks.

My grandmother's soft voice broke the silence. "Fran, dear, I wish things could be undone, but they can't. The past is what it is. We have to try and look forward. There have been many wrongs committed and yours are not the first tears that have flowed over this. All we can do is accept that and see our mistakes. I want to try and put things right while I still have time. I've wasted twenty years that I can never regain, but I don't want to die without making amends." She came over to put her hands on my shoulders. "I hope you can learn to forgive us and I hope you can learn to accept us. I'm truly sorry for all the pain you've felt."

I was now crying with wrenching sobs that made me gasp for air. I ran mutely to my room where I collapsed onto the bed, burying my head in the pillow to muffle my cries. How stupid I'd been to think that finding my birth parents would help me find myself. I didn't like what I'd found. My temper was out of control – as bad as Joe's recent explosion of anger. We were both irrational. I felt so miserable, however, that I didn't care. I suddenly went from feeling like the responsible adult, to a frustrated toddler. I don't know how long I lay there crying before I fell asleep. I woke to a tap on the door. It was my grandmother, who peered into the room and came towards me when she saw I was awake. "Your cell phone has been ringing, Fran." She handed it to me and went out quietly, closing the door behind her.

I looked at the list of recent calls and saw that it was my Mom, calling from California. Her calls showed up as 'out of area.' I texted her immediately and it was comforting to hear her voice on the other end when she called back. The distance seemed to fade and I could picture her in the kitchen, making a cup of tea before she went to bed.

"Hi, darling," she said. "Just wondered how things were going with you."

I swallowed hard before replying. "I'm OK, Mom. It's been a bit rough."

"I'm sure it has, Fran. I've been thinking about you so much and trying to imagine how you must be feeling. It's a very difficult situation you've found yourself in."

"I wish I hadn't started digging myself into this hole, Mom, because I can't walk away now. I didn't think it through. I thought I'd find her and we'd be friends. Well, that's not how it is. I didn't realize how much I resented being given away like a pair of uncomfortable shoes, and even though I understand why it happened, I can't get beyond being angry with her. I try to, but then I feel this weird duty to do something about her miserable existence and I feel angry again." I paused for a moment and said, "Mom, I remember being very rude to you once; I told you that it took more than feeding me to be a mother. I'm sorry I said that. I've always regretted it; I should have apologized before." I swallowed hard and added, "You're the best mother I could ever have wished for."

My Mom's voice choked as she said, "Thank you, Fran. That means a lot. And you're the best daughter I could have wished for. When you came into my life, all the heartache disappeared that I'd felt about not being able to get pregnant. One tiny cry tugged at my heart and I knew you were my child, my responsibility. You grew in my heart, if not in my belly. It was terrifying and exhilarating at the same time. I treasured every moment watching you grow, perhaps even more because I realized how precious life is. Having a baby should have been so easy, but it wasn't for me." She paused and I could hear Buster, Billy's dog, barking in the background. I could picture him wanting attention, wagging his tail with his tongue hanging out, and I smiled at the recollection. She continued, "I know there were always unanswered questions for you. Don't have regrets that you pursued this search. You needed to do it."

"It's not that I wasn't happy, Mom. I didn't want to leave you, but I wanted to find out where I came from. Billy never cared about his birth parents, did he?" I queried.

"No, but that's Billy. You would never have been satisfied until you'd got this squared away – and I daresay now that you know all the details, you've still got some squaring away to do. Nothing is ever simple."

"You can say that again."

"As I said the other day, don't stand in judgment of them. You haven't walked in their shoes."

"But I don't feel anything for her. It's so weird, Mom. I look at her and she's... well she's a stranger. I feel like I should feel something, but I don't. You know, I often got mad at you and said stuff I regret, but I knew you, and I knew I loved you, and... somehow, it was different... " I trailed off, unable to find the right words.

"You can't expect to love someone on demand, Fran," my Mom replied. "Don't beat yourself up. These things take time. Your birth mother and grandmother are women whom you may choose to continue seeing – or not. The more you see them, the more you'll understand them, and perhaps come to love them, but you can't hope for instant results. Relationships are built on more than genes. If you choose to walk away, that's alright. Be gentle with yourself and do what feels right. You'll know, and there's no right or wrong answer to this."

"Thanks Mom."

"Dad and I will support whatever you decide to do, but you will have to decide what that is."

It was a relief to hear her quiet, calm reason. It helped restore my own, and I suddenly felt compelled to add, "Mom, there's something else."

There was silence on the other end, as she waited for me to continue. "I've met someone. He's really cool – one of my roommates from Durban. I like him a lot."

"That's great, Fran."

"No it's not. We had a huge row over some stupid thing. I refuse to apologize because it wasn't my fault. But I don't know what to do."

"Are you asking my advice or just telling me?"

"Just telling you," I replied. "You'd really like him, Mom. He was only a friend until a few days ago, a really good friend, and then I realized that I felt a lot more than that. The fight was ridiculous..."

"Well you'll have to sort it out then, otherwise it sounds like I won't get the chance to see whether I like him or not." I laughed and agreed with her. "By the way, have you booked your ticket home yet? When do you start back at UCLA?" she added.

"I have to be there on January 5th. Yikes, time's gone so fast. I'd like to come home for a bit first, but there isn't much time. We're almost in December."

"Yes, one more day left of November, that's all. Will you be home for Christmas?" she asked.

I hesitated before replying, "I'm not sure, Mom."

She hesitated as well. The short silence was awkward before she said, "It's a wonderful opportunity for you being abroad. Make the most of it. Christmas will come again next year."

I was overcome with love for my mother. She hadn't quite disguised the excitement in her voice when she asked if I'd be home for Christmas, yet she was quick to encourage and support me, even if it was disappointing that I might not come home. "Thanks, Mom," I said, adding on a whim, "Any chance you would all come and spend Christmas here?"

"We were just there a few months ago." I heard my Mom's familiar laugh. "You have expensive ideas. Money doesn't grow on trees, darling," she said.

"You always used to say that to me when I was little. One day I saw a dollar bill lying on the ground, under a bush, and I thought, 'Aha! Money grows on bushes, not trees.' I was sure that the dollar had fallen out of that bush, like a ripe apple from a tree." We both giggled and it came over me then, that while I'd been searching for clues to my identity for so long, all the time this woman was the key to who I was. She might not have given birth to me, but she'd loved and nurtured me, and I felt better just talking to her. A dark cloud lifted and, as we said goodbye, I knew how lucky I was to have her in my life.

My thoughts were disturbed by voices getting louder and louder. I heard John saying, "I can't believe you could be so self-centered. You knew how close Val and I were. I was heartbroken when she disappeared and you led us to believe that she was dead. How could you know that she was alive and do nothing? How could you know that you had a grandchild somewhere and never say or do anything about it? Didn't you ever think Uncle Tom needed to know that his daughter was alive? Valerie was like a sister to me. If I had known the trouble she was in, I would have moved heaven and earth to help her. You should have told me."

I heard my grandmother reply, "It's all very well to say that with hindsight, John. They were different times and you know it. And by the way, it turns out your uncle did know that she was alive after all. He sent her money, but he didn't tell me either."

"It's madness the way you two behaved. Do you know how much Louise and I would love to have a child? I know she feels the same aching emptiness that I do. You had so much and you let it go away, without trying to hold onto it."

I could hear sobs and then my grandmother shouted hysterically. "You have no idea what I went through, so don't dare accuse me of letting everything slip away. I don't have to defend myself to you, but trust me, I tried to help my daughter and I despaired losing my husband. Valerie wouldn't have anything to do with me. There was nothing more I could do."

"But why didn't you tell me she was alive? You even knew where she was all this time, but you said nothing. I could have reached out to her, I know I could."

"If you think it's so easy, why don't you march over to Kentucky Fried Chicken right now and fix things up? I'm sure she'll drop everything and run into your arms, like Lazarus arisen from the dead."

"Maybe I will," he retorted and stormed out. I heard doors slamming.

It was unnerving that they were at one another's throats and I sat very still, hoping they would forget my presence in the flat. I emerged from my room only when there was no more sound, relieved to discover that Sharon and John Spencer had both gone out, presumably not together. I was thankful to be spared the immediate awkwardness of seeing them again. Everybody's tempers were frayed and a cooling off period was needed.

I made my way to Pick 'n Pay and purchased ready-cooked lasagna, salad and wine, as well as some lychees that were in season. I'd recently tasted them for the first time in Durban and couldn't get enough of the exotic fruit. The tough prickly skins disguised the juicy flesh; their sweetness was a well protected secret. Like much else in this place, it was strange how such delicacy could emerge from a hostile exterior.

Glynnis Hayward

Chapter 4

After parking the car, I decided to be bold and phone Joe before time dragged on and made communication even harder. Now that I had calmed down, I could see a clearer picture and felt that I had taken him for granted. He had been there for me whenever I needed him, and I didn't think twice about waking him early in the morning, insisting that I needed to see my birth mother. He must have felt really irritated, but didn't argue as he knew it was important to me. His road rage was deflected anger. He probably wanted to shout at me. In my heart, I knew that Joe was not a fiery person; his patience had been endless. But I felt nervous excitement as I dialed his number and waited for him to answer. It was frustrating to get his voice mail. I hoped he wasn't playing games by screening his calls and avoiding me.

I sat and stared at the window of Valerie's flat. There was a light on, so I knew she was home. I closed my eyes and willed myself to be positive, hoping for a happier reunion with her. As I reached across to grab parcels of food from the back seat, my cell phone rang shrilly. It was Joe calling back; a rush of relief made me smile and my hands were shaking, as I hit the answer button. "Joe?"

"Hi Babe, you called. I was driving and couldn't take your call. How're things?" he said.

"OK. Did you say that you're driving?"

"Yeah, I rented a car to get around this morning. I'm on my way to Storm's River." I felt a stab of disappointment, which my silence illuminated. "It wasn't fair to rely on you. You need your car to get yourself around. This was the obvious solution," he added.

I wasn't disappointed that he had hired a car. I was disappointed because he had gone away. "Are you going bungee jumping?" I asked. I'd heard about the place and knew there wasn't much else to do there.

"Mmm, some guys from my engineering class are camping there and I decided to meet up with them. The jump off the Storm's River Bridge is the longest commercial jump in the world. Did you know that?"

"Geez, Joe, that's a crazy thing to be doing. Have you ever tried bungee jumping before, or are you going to start with the most difficult?" I asked.

"Actually, I have done it up in Oregon with my brother and some friends. It's kind of cool – exhilarating. You should try it sometime. It was on my list of things to do in Africa. I also want to get to Zimbabwe and jump at Victoria Falls. They jump off the bridge there, over the Zambezi River."

"I don't know if I have the nerve to do it," I replied.

"Sure you have. The rush you get is almost as exciting as an orgasm. You'd love it."

I giggled and felt myself blushing. I longed to be with him again and wished I were there now. "How long are you going to be at Storm's River?" I asked. I was also wondering whether he was even coming back to Cape Town, but I didn't want to ask that question.

"Just a couple of days," he said.

There was a pregnant silence. At length I said, "What are your plans after that?"

He hesitated before answering and then said, "Well, if you're prepared to drive in a car with me again, I'll come back to Cape Town and we can figure something out together. But if not, I'll head up to Vic Falls."

"Joe, I'm sorry we had that fight," I replied. "I miss you. It seems like forever since I saw you and it was only this morning. I'll be waiting here in Cape Town. Please don't make it too long."

"Two days, Fran, that's all. I'll be back. I'm also sorry about the incident. I suppose it was a Y chromosome thing. Am I forgiven?"

"Forgiven for having a Y chromosome? I love your Y chromosome, but that outburst was a bit of a shock."

"Just face it, Fran. I'm a jack ass. What more can I say?"

I knew he felt as much relief as I did that our fight was over. A truce had been declared and when we ended the call, I felt happy. I could cope with everything else, knowing that in two days he would be coming back to me. I was still smiling as I rang the doorbell. Valerie must have seen me coming because the downstairs entry door opened as I approached, allowing me to climb the stairs to her front door. My thoughts were all of Joe as I stood there, wondering how I would survive two days without him, and praying he would survive the bungee jump. As I heard the door rattle I was startled back into reality, remembering what lay ahead of me.

I listened to the various locks and chains being released and finally the door opened. Valerie stood in front of me with a weak smile and it was evident she'd been crying. My heart sank. I couldn't face another evening of heartache. She said nothing, but stood aside to let me in. As I stepped into the room, I saw John Spencer seated in a chair. He also looked red-eyed as he greeted me. "Hello, Fran," he said.

I was at a loss for words and looked from one to the other of them. How much did my mother know? Did she know that her mother was just a few miles away, across town? The atmosphere in the room was tense and I longed to break free of this saga. I no longer felt it was my issue; it was theirs. I had moved on and I didn't have any inclination to become involved, so I smiled and said, "I've brought dinner. I'm sure there's enough for three."

John replied, "I was going to suggest that I take you both out to dinner."

Valerie looked panic-stricken. "No, no. Thank you, but no. Fran has been kind enough to bring dinner, we must eat here." She went about setting the small table and helping me warm the lasagna in the microwave. There wasn't a salad bowl and there were no wine glasses, but we used plastic tumblers and a cup for the wine, and a plastic container for the salad. She looked embarrassed, but made no apology. John remained silent as we busied ourselves, but rose to open and pour the wine. He then turned and lifted his cup, which he held at arm's length in front of himself. We watched expectantly as he cleared his throat. "I propose a toast to the future. May it be better than the past!" he said solemnly.

We raised our tumblers, echoing his toast, "To the future."

The scraping of forks on plates was the only sound for a while as we ate our dinner, but soon the atmosphere seemed to relax; perhaps the wine was a contributing factor. I was dying to know what my birth mother's reaction had been when she saw her cousin after such a long time, and whether he had been able to recognize her. She was still wearing her red wig, although it was clearly irritating her as she was continually scratching her head. I saw a finger surreptitiously slip underneath the wig at one point, when John's head was down. Breaking the silence, I said boldly, "So, are you pleased to see each other?"

They both looked at me with startled expressions, and then they looked at one another. I could see my mother's jaw twitching, considering her answer. John stared at her, blinking hard. "I know that I'm pleased," he said. "I can't speak for you, Val." His lower lip trembled and then he said, "Dammit, Valerie! Why didn't you call me for help? We were like brother and sister, growing up. No, that's not true; I wished we weren't related because I was madly in love with you. When I thought you were dead, I was wretched.

I'm shattered by this whole situation. I can't believe that your parents would withhold the truth from me; it's preposterous. To think they knew all along where you were, and never said so, is despicable. But I feel betrayed that you, of all people, would disappear out of my life without a word. Why didn't you trust me when you needed help?"

My mother looked down for a long time as he was speaking, and for some time afterwards. He continued staring at her and gulped his wine, before filling his glass again. Finally she looked up at him and said, "I'm sorry, John. I don't know what else I can say. I screwed up." She looked at me and said, "I want to look forward now. I want to hear about my daughter. That's what matters." She smiled and lifted her glass towards me. "I propose a toast to Fran. May you know only love and acceptance in your life." I smiled at her in return, and then she faced John once again. "Please don't ask why I acted as I did – I hardly know why myself. All I can say is that grief and anger, with a big dose of fear, inhibited all my sensibilities. I don't know what more I can say. If you loved me once, you can love me again – as a cousin. Please just accept the past and let it go; I am truly sorry that I hurt you, John. And to answer Fran's question, I was overjoyed to see you walk into KFC."

I began to see another dimension to my mother. She had suffered so much, yet it was evident that she deeply regretted the pain her cousin had endured, especially the part she had played in it. But suddenly she frowned and said, "What do you mean, my parents knew where I was?"

John looked at me and I shrugged my shoulders. I wasn't about to bail him out of the deep water he was in. He'd got himself there all alone. My mother looked from him to me and stared hard at me. "Have you met her?" she asked. I nodded.

"Oh my God," she exclaimed. "She found you. After all these years she went and found you. Is that what happened? Did she suddenly decide that she was old and lonely and a dark skin wasn't the worst thing in the world after all? Loneliness was worse than that. Is that what she decided? So she went out, and found my daughter, whom she'd rejected, to make herself feel better."

I stared back at her angrily. "You know, I'm beginning to regret that I ever stumbled into this hornet's nest. For your information, she didn't come and find me. I found her in the process of trying to find you. In fact, I found John first and he led me to your mother, my grandmother, because he cared about her. Maybe you're right; maybe she has learned a lesson after all these years, that loneliness is the worst thing in the world. The good thing is that she is trying to make amends for her ways. I don't get the feeling that you can do that. On the one hand you're saying you hope I only feel acceptance, and that John should leave the past behind, but on the other hand, you carry twenty years of baggage on your shoulders all the time. I think you're just living and re-living all the sadness you've felt, like you're stuck in a rut. I don't believe you know how to move forward. You're just staying in the same place all the time, with one foot pinned in the past and the other running small circles around it."

Her jaw was really twitching by the time I'd finished speaking, and her hands were shaking. John added to my outburst by

saying, "She's quite right, Valerie. Your daughter has inherited
the clear-thinking that you once had. I don't know what
happened to it in the past twenty years. For someone who prided
herself in her lack of prejudice, I've seldom seen more of it
steaming out of anybody. Give your mother a break."

"Stop it," she shouted. "I've said let's forget the past and I mean
it. But I can also tell you that I do not want to see my mother
again. So don't try to make that happen. If she's befriended Fran,
good luck to her. But don't expect me to forgive and forget." She
turned to me and said, "And Francesca, I would appreciate more
respect from you in future. Watch your tongue, young lady."

I stared at her in amazement. I was too shocked to be annoyed at
the reprimand. She had suddenly become a mother and I found
myself stammering an apology with downcast eyes.

"Now," she continued as if nothing had happened, "please tell me
about yourself. Tell me everything; tell me what makes you
happy." Her demeanor had changed and I saw the sweetness of
her expression as she gazed at me. "I claim little credit for the
person you've become, but that doesn't stop me loving you," she
added.

And so I began telling her about my life and she hung on every
word. It's difficult to tell somebody about yourself. You can't just
squeeze the contents of your life out like toothpaste from a tube.
She realized this, and continually prompted me with questions
that kept me talking. The delight on her face was evident when I
spoke about Los Gatos, the town where I'd grown up. She could
picture where I'd gone to school, where I'd played and where I'd

run races. She knew exactly where the high school was, down the road from the library, and she was excited that I had visited her aunt's old home. She asked about Addie and Mary and was interested to hear how they had helped me in my search to find her. I told her that I'd met Dr. Smith and that he remembered her. I wished that I had pictures to show her of my family and our home, but that might have been hard for her to see, so I suppose it was just as well I had none with me that night. She asked about my family though, and I saw sadness in her face as I described our lives together. I could feel the approaching moment, when I would have to refer to my parents, and I was anxious. What would I call them? I took a deep breath and went right ahead, calling them Mom and Dad. That's who they were and that's what I'd always called them, so there was no point in tip-toeing around that fact. Valerie didn't flinch and the moment passed. I was glad when it had.

I told her about my interest in South Africa since discovering my origins, and that I had studied Afrikaans. She laughed when I told her this and immediately spoke to me in that language, to test me. Then she said, "But surely you're not majoring in Afrikaans. What use would that be in America?"

"No, I just studied it for a year. I'm an English major. Another of the many who'll be trying to find a job soon, without much useful stuff to offer," I laughed.

"Oh, don't you believe it. Having a degree is so important – I regret that I never finished mine."

"You still can," I replied. She just smiled, then added, "Don't change the subject. We're talking about you. Tell me how Joe fits into the picture? When did you meet him?"

"Just a few months ago when I arrived in Durban; we live in the same house with some other students. We became good friends and then somehow, it became more than that. Who knows what will happen when we return to California. He's at Berkeley and I'll be back at UCLA. Hopefully it'll work; we won't be that far apart."

There was a lengthy silence when I talked about returning. John, who had sat very quietly listening to us talk, finally asked the question. "When do you go back, Fran?"

I looked from one to the other and said, "I'm not sure exactly, but I have to be back for classes in the first week of January."

I heard an intake of air from Valerie, as if she had been punched. "January? So soon? That's just a month away," she said.

I nodded. "Time has flown – I wish I'd found you sooner." I told about my wasted efforts to find Ixopo and they both smiled, especially when they heard about Joe coming to rescue me.

"Can I make a suggestion?" John asked. We turned and looked at him expectantly. "Why don't you both come and spend Christmas on the farm? Ask Joe as well, if you'd like Fran." Neither of us said a word and John hastily added, "Of course you need to think about it and you might have other plans. I haven't spoken to Louise about it, but I'm sure she would be happy to have you."

Valerie turned and looked at him. "John, you are very thoughtful and I would love to meet Louise. It's a very generous invitation, but there's one snag in it for me. I'm sure my mother will be invited as well, won't she?"

"We always spend Christmas together, Val. When they had the farm, we spent Christmas with your parents there – you know that. Now we're living on the farm since your father died last year, and we'll continue the tradition. We would love you to join us, but your mother will have to be there too. We're family. Sometimes family members don't see eye to eye, but one would hope that they make an effort to be civil."

"This is bigger than not seeing eye to eye, John."

"Well, you have a choice to make. Think about it carefully. Choices have far-reaching consequences sometimes, for better or worse." He got up and carried his plate to the sink. "I think I'm going to leave you two now. It's been a long day and I have a meeting tomorrow morning." Valerie got up and he put his arms around her. "It's been an amazing day, Val. I still can't get over it. I need to get back to the farm in two days time, but I hope we can see each other tomorrow."

"I have to be at work at 6 a.m. and I don't finish until 8 p.m. Maybe after that we could meet."

"That's a hell of a long day. Do you work at KFC all that time?" he asked.

She explained about the other job at the hospital and he looked at her with concern, before giving her another hug. "Maybe some changes are needed," he said softly, and then made for the door. He turned as he was leaving and added, "Dinner's on me tomorrow night. I'll see you here just after eight."

After he was gone, I rose and said I should also leave. She smiled and pulled the wig off her head, exclaiming, "Whew, what a relief to get that thing off!"

I felt less shock seeing her without it this time. "Why don't you leave it off all the time?" I asked. She looked at me in horror. "Honestly, it doesn't look so bad. It can't be comfortable having that wig on all day. Why don't you let your hair grow?"

"Fran, I have my pride still. I don't want to be seen walking around like this. It looks ugly; I only have to look in the mirror to see that for myself. It's sweet of you to say otherwise, but I'm not fooled."

"Can I give you an early Christmas present then? I'd like to buy you a decent wig that fits properly and looks good. You're not meant to be a redhead by the way, and definitely not maroon." She looked shocked. "Sorry," I said, "it's my right as your daughter to tell you. It looks bad. You look much better without that wig, but if you insist on wearing one, you need a decent one. I would like to give it to you. Let's go shopping tomorrow at lunchtime. I'll pick you up from Groote Schuur, we can look for a wig, and then I'll drop you off at KFC." She nodded in agreement and I continued to ask, "Have you seen a doctor about the condition?"

"Yes, I have. There are topical ointments, but I don't think they really help."

"Have you tried?"

She looked away and so I repeated the question. "No," she answered. "They're expensive, and not guaranteed to work. It's a waste of money."

I sighed and said, "Well, things might need to change there, too. Please will you at least try?" She turned and looked at me and was about to say something, but I cut her off by adding, "For my sake."

She put her arms around me. "I'll see you at 1 p.m. tomorrow Fran. Same place you dropped me off. Can you find it again?"

I nodded as I walked out the door. She was watching me when I crossed the road to my car, and I could see her waving when I was all the way down at the stop street. I waved back, then turned the corner and drove to Camp's Bay along the coast, feeling relief that I had found my birth mother; really found her. All my life I had needed to know who she was. I had needed her to care about me. It was more than wanting to know why she'd given me up. Once I had discovered all that, I wanted more. I needed her affection and recognition. I was like a 5,000 piece jig saw puzzle with everything put together except an integral portion at the center. I had no picture on a box to guide me and couldn't fit the missing pieces into the space properly, no matter how I tried. They were shapes that didn't fit. With those pieces missing, I couldn't tell what the picture was.

That changed tonight as my birth mother sat listening to me, asking questions about my life. It became clear that she cared about me very much. She valued who I was. The missing pieces had been put in place. The picture was complete at last and I felt whole.

Chapter 5

When I woke, I found my grandmother busy packing her suitcase as she drank her morning coffee. "I've decided to go back to Johannesburg, Fran," she said, stopping to look up at me. "I thought about it last night and realized that I've done all I can do to help you. You've found your mother and the rest is up to the two of you now. She won't want to see me, so it's better that I get out of the way. It's important for you to have time with her, without worrying about me."

"Whoa!" I exclaimed. "Wait a minute. What if I want you to be here? Doesn't that count?" I asked.

"That's kind of you dear, but you'll be much better off with me out of the way. I've made up my mind. I'm not saying goodbye, mind you, don't think that. I hope very much that we will see one another lots more; you'll have a hard time shaking me off. But I would appreciate it, in the meantime, if you could give me a ride to the airport. There's a flight at 12.30 that I want to catch."

I walked over to her and took both her hands in mine. They felt smooth and delicate, like the hands of a much younger woman. "Gran, please don't go. Not now," I said. "I have to go back to California soon, so let's not waste the little time we have left. And you never know, your daughter might change her mind. Wouldn't you want to be here if that happens? She knows you are here now. If she discovers that you've returned home without seeing her, you'll be closing the door. Don't you want to leave it ajar, even if you don't hang a big *welcome* sign outside?"

She squeezed my hands and sighed, "Darling Fran, I'm so tired."

I held her close and felt how tiny she was as she leaned against me. It wasn't right that she should feel so alone and I was ashamed of my previous irritation. "Well, that's another good reason why you should stay. Have a bit of a break here at the beach and forget about all this other stuff. You can have a good rest. But first we're going to buy a computer for you so that when I'm back at college, we can email each other every day. I'm going to teach you how to do that. What do you say about that?"

"I don't believe I'll ever be able to say no to you, Fran," she laughed. "If it wasn't that I loved you, I would find it infuriating!"

"Well, let me help you unpack your suitcase and let's go get some breakfast together."

We spent the morning quietly on the beach. Gran sat under a hired umbrella, while I swam and sunbathed. The water was cold, so I didn't stay in long. It was nearly as chilly as the ocean in Northern California, reminding me of days at the beach in Santa Cruz. I explained to Gran what I was going to do for my mother and she was enthusiastic. When we made our way back to the flat, we looked in the yellow pages for a wig shop. There were some near the hospital, catering for chemotherapy patients who had lost their hair. I wrote down the addresses and Gran gave me a blank, signed cheque to pay for a wig. "Be sure she doesn't see whose cheque it is though," she admonished me. "And be sure you get her the best wig you can. She needs to feel good about herself again and looking good will help." I smiled. My grandmother had recently discovered the same thing for herself, when she had her hair styled and highlighted. "And if there's time, go and buy some clothes for her," she continued, shaking her head as she recollected the sight of her daughter when last she'd seen her. "Buy her a few decent outfits, for heaven's sake." She opened up her wallet and took out a wad of cash. "Take this and spend it on her. Get something for yourself too."

"I can't take that much money from you, Gran."

"I can think of nothing I'd rather spend my money on, than this. And, if the truth be told, I have more money than I can spend. I can't take it with me you know – there are no pockets in shrouds, as they say." She pressed the cash into my hands. "Now get going, otherwise you'll be late. Don't worry about me. I'm going to have a nap while you're gone. I didn't sleep too well last night."

Valerie was waiting for me when I got to Groote Schuur and she announced that she was taking an extra long lunch to be with me. She didn't need to be at her next job until four o'clock. Her delight was apparent when we found an attractive wig with no difficulty at all. It was made from real human hair, styled with bangs (or as they called it here, a fringe) and the back and sides hung to chin length. She assured me that the light brown colour was the same as her natural hair colour, and when she put it on, she looked stunning. I watched as she stared at herself in the mirror, slowly turning her head from side to side, admiring the new look from every angle. A smile stole across her face. The broken nose seemed less noticeable, and cosmetics would hide the scars.

While an assistant described the washing instructions to her, I surreptitiously paid for the wig and announced that we were on our way to Cavendish Square, stopping only to buy lunch on the way. We ate it in the car. All the time I was driving, I noticed my mother looking at her reflection whenever she could. Gran was right; Valerie was feeling better about herself already.

Stuttaford's Department Store proved equally productive. My mother had a good figure that she'd kept hidden under shapeless garments, found at thrift shops and jumble sales. I became her personal shopper and carried loads of things to the fitting room. At one point, I caught a glimpse of scars on her chest, similar to the burn marks on her face. I quickly averted my eyes and said nothing. We worked our way through the pile of clothes and she emerged with jeans and shirts that fit perfectly, as well as dresses, skirts and a jacket. The shoe department was easier, as she could try on items seated right there.

Laden with parcels, we headed for the parking garage – or so Valerie thought. I had other ideas. We passed by the cosmetics department and an eager assistant sat Valerie on a stool to examine her face. She introduced herself as Mina, smiled at me and said, "Is this your Mom?" I nodded. "We are going to fix you up, madam," she said to Valerie, "and everybody will think you're sisters!" I watched with fascination as she plied my mother's face with cleansers, toners, crèmes and concealers, before applying eye make-up and lipstick. After twenty-five minutes, Mina stood back and handed my mother a hand mirror.

The surprise on her face brought tears to my eyes and made Mina laugh. She looked at me and said, "Your mother is beautiful, hey?"

Needless to say we had more parcels to carry, but this time we returned to the car. It was 3.30 p.m. There was time to get Valerie back to Vredehoek, drop off the purchases, and get her to work on time. She was flushed with excitement and laughed as I said, "Please throw that red wig away."

"No. I want to keep it as a reminder of how you came and changed everything," she said.

"The only reminder you need is to look in the mirror each day," I replied. "You look amazing. I don't think you should keep that red thing anywhere close. Throw it out or give it to a thrift store. If you keep holding onto the past, it'll suffocate you. You'll never be able to breathe fresh air. Let go of it, please."

She was silent as we drove, but when we arrived at her flat and offloaded the parcels, she turned to me and said, "Just wait a minute, Fran." Opening her bag, she removed the old wig and handed it to me. "I need to change for work, but please throw this in the trash outside as you leave."

I hugged her tightly and smiled. "See you tonight at eight."

Chapter 6

The flat appeared empty when I arrived back in Camp's Bay; my grandmother's door was closed. I didn't know whether she was still asleep or had gone out, so I took the opportunity to sit outside on the balcony and text both Joe and my mother, Grace. My Mom was anxious to know how things were working out and I reassured her that all was well. I, on the other hand, was anxious to know how Joe was, and find out whether he had survived jumping off bridges. Just as I finished sending the texts, I heard voices coming from my grandmother's bedroom. Listening carefully, I could discern her voice and the deeper tones of John Spencer.

"I think this is the only way it will work. If she believes the money is legally hers and it's in her bank account already, she'll have no choice but to accept it. She's so stubborn that if it were offered as a gift, she'd refuse it and continue to live in poverty," I heard him say.

"John, I want this to work. I'd give anything to have my daughter back in my life and I hope that will happen, but the least I can do is help her financially, so that she doesn't live this miserable existence any longer. It broke my heart when Fran told me what her life is like." I could hear some muffled noises and sounds of drawers opening and closing, then my grandmother continued to speak. "Tom apparently gave her money every month, anonymously. The bank must have some record of the account number that he deposited money into. Let's get it from them and transfer the money as soon as possible."

"It's not that easy. He made cash deposits and there's no record. But I have a plan, Aunt Sharon. All I need is your agreement to make the transaction out of your bank account into hers; I'll tell her that I need her account number as there is some money left to her by her father. I'm sure she'll object but I plan to say that it's legally hers and if she chooses not to take it, it will become the government's property. I think she'll decide to take it if she hears that. So it's really up to you to decide how much you want to give her."

"I want to give her half of my assets, John. I'll change my will when I get back to Johannesburg."

"Half your assets!" he exclaimed. "Are you sure, Aunt Sharon? That's an awful lot of money; you need to be able to support yourself for the rest of your days."

"Please do exactly what I said. I told you earlier, the farm is yours and I want no more payments from you – consider it paid in full. No, don't argue. That's my decision. And half of the rest of my assets are to go to Valerie immediately, with no strings attached. I'll take care of my will when I see my lawyer in January, but if you could take care of this transaction, I would be very grateful. I have my cheque book here and I'll make an initial payment of a hundred thousand rand until we've figured out the actual numbers. That should help her immediately. Oh, and John, please try and encourage her to give up the job at that chicken place."

I heard John Spencer laugh and say, "Aunt Sharon, you said no strings attached, didn't you?"

"That's not a string I'm attaching, it's a very strong suggestion, that's all. I can't believe that she enjoys working there, so why should she continue to do so if she doesn't have to?"

"I'll see what I can do," he said. "She'll need to reach that conclusion herself, though. We can't barge in and sort out her life for her."

"You can say that again – I've learned that lesson, John. I made a mess of things when I tried to sort it out for her before, didn't I?" I heard their voices fade and then the door closed as the two of them departed.

I closed my eyes, lifting my head so that I could feel the warmth of the sun on my face, and I smiled. It wasn't so long ago that I had chastised my adoptive mother Grace, saying she couldn't buy motherhood – or words to that effect. She had replied that it took more than the act of giving birth to be a mother. As I sat listening to Sharon Spencer, I realized what a complex task it was to be a mother. Perhaps I was lucky I had two of them.

****

I was waiting for Valerie when she closed the door of KFC and we hurried back to her flat, like a pair of teenage girls going to their first co-ed party. She was stunning with the new wig and facial make-over. But when she pulled off the work uniform and pulled on a pair of new jeans with a black shirt, the result was mind-blowing. She stared at herself in the mirror in disbelief, still not used to the new image, and I felt myself bursting with pride that my mother looked so good. "Wait. There's something else," she said hurriedly, turning to a drawer next to her bed and pulling out a small box. In it was a strand of pearls; she held it in her hands as she stared at them. Finally she looked up and asked me to put them around her neck. When I'd done this, she turned to me and said, "One day I want you to have these. Your father gave them to me after he qualified as a doctor, on the third anniversary of your birth. I haven't worn them since he died, but I think he would want me to do so now."

I could feel tears spring to my eyes. She was staring in the mirror, not at herself but at the pearls. "I loved him so much," she whispered.

My eyes were riveted to her. She was the most beautiful woman imaginable. It wasn't so much what she looked like, but there was an unexpected aura of sweetness about her. Along with the whole physical transformation that had taken place, her face had softened with a gentle expression that seemed to indicate there was an emotional change taking place. She turned to me and put out her arms. "Thank you for finding me, Greta." She hugged me tightly, and then apologized quickly when I stiffened. "I'm sorry, that just slipped out. I meant Fran." I said nothing, just hugged her even tighter in response.

The moment was interrupted by a loud buzzing. It was the entry intercom and John Spencer's voice announced he was waiting to be let in. I stood back and watched to see his face when he entered the room and saw Valerie; I couldn't have imagined a better response. He stopped in his tracks and stared with his mouth agape. "Holy Smoke!" he exclaimed, scratching his head. "Am I dreaming?"

My mother smiled. For a moment they looked frozen in time, staring at one another without another word, recalling years gone by I supposed. At length, he closed the door behind him and hugged her. I could hear sobs, but it was difficult to know whose they were. Feeling as if I were intruding in a very private moment, I walked out onto the balcony, peering through the burglar bars at the street below. When I turned and looked at them inside, sitting side by side and deep in conversation, it seemed best to leave them alone a while longer. Perhaps John was discussing the financial issues with her that he had promised to take care of for my grandmother. He was doing a lot of talking and she was listening intently. Sometimes she frowned, and other times she nodded her head. Finally, I saw her bury her face in her hands. When she looked up at him, I thought I saw her lips form the words 'thank you.' Shortly afterwards, they called me in to join them.

"We have a dinner reservation we're about to be late for," John announced. "We're going to my favorite eating place in Cape Town, the Cape Malay Restaurant in Constantia. There's lots to celebrate tonight, and I'm a lucky son of a gun with two beautiful women to accompany me; one on each arm."

I was intrigued by Cape Malay food as it was unlike anything I'd ever tasted. While colourful and spicy, it was mild and sweet. I wanted to try everything and ended up ordering a taster's menu, which enabled me to do just that. Valerie smiled at my enthusiasm and said it was my Barnard blood coming out.

"Did my father eat stuff like this?" I asked.

"Not every day, but he loved it when he could get someone to cook it for him. I was never very good, but I tried. We used to cook together sometimes, but it wasn't easy getting the ingredients we needed in London. Fortunately, his mother used to send food parcels." She paused, playing with her fork, before looking at me sharply. "Fran, there is someone I think you ought to meet."

I stopped chewing and looked at her expectantly. She was still staring at me thoughtfully and so I swallowed and said, "Who?"

"Your grandfather," she said simply. I was taken aback. I hadn't considered that there were relations on my father's side to meet. I knew that his mother had died and that my mother had little to do with his family.

"He's an old man whom I haven't seen for years. Johan's parents never knew that we had a child. There was no point in telling them. The old man might not have cared for me over the years, but I think it would mean a lot for him to meet you, his son's daughter. Will you come with me to meet him?"

I nodded eagerly. "Of course, I'd love to," I said. "Where does he live?"

"Near Stellenbosch, in a little place called Pniel. If you blink, you almost miss it. He used to live in Cape Town at Mitchell Plains, but some years ago, after his wife died, he moved back to this town where he was born. It's strange how we often like to return to our roots, isn't it? "

"When can we go? Do you ever get time off work?" I asked.

She glanced quickly at her cousin and smiled. He reached across and took her hand; I saw him squeeze it. She looked down shyly and then said, "I'm going to have lots more time. I'm quitting the job at KFC tomorrow, and soon I'll give up the hospital job too."

John beamed and said, "Thank God. Valerie, I'm so glad you've reached that decision."

She turned to me and said, "I discovered tonight that I have an inheritance coming to me. It has changed my life as much as this new wig," she laughed. "There are two things I've wanted for a long time, but I haven't been able to afford the time to even dream about them. I want to have plastic surgery to repair some of the damage that was done to my face, and I'm going to have physical therapy to strengthen my leg. It might be too late after all this time to fix things completely, but I'm going to try."

"Those are two very important things," said John.

She smiled and said, "Actually, I was only thinking of that as one thing, under the category of getting my body back. The other thing comes under the category of getting my life back. I've wanted to finish my degree and study further, and now I'm going to do that too. Ever since I started working in the food business, I've wanted to become a dietician. Then I can get the job I really want at the hospital, not cooking breakfasts and lunches in the hot kitchen every day for a pittance. And I don't think I'll ever eat chicken again!" She raised her glass and said, "Thanks to both of you."

"Don't thank me for the inheritance," John laughed. "I'm still alive as far I know." He drank to her toast and then said, "How long will the studying take?"

"If I start full time in March, with the credits I already have, I can finish by the end of next year."

John nodded. "Actually, here's another option for you to consider. I told you that Louise and I are building a health spa on the farm. Well, I've discussed it with her and we were wondering whether you would join us in the venture, to oversee the diet part of things; the food and menus. No cooking, I promise. There'll be others to do that. Spas are very popular as tourism increases. We have a website going and already we've had lots of interest, even bookings for next year when we open. There's loads of room as you know, and we can build you your own separate cottage, or you can just have one wing of the house – whichever you prefer."

My mother paused as she considered this proposal. "That's very tempting," she said, "can I think about it? I want to complete my studies though – can you wait a year for me to join you?"

"Sure," he said. "In fact that will work perfectly. Think about it."

I felt a huge load lifted off my shoulders. My birth mother had found her way again and she was going to be alright. I smiled at her and then decided very impulsively to try and resolve the thing that had been troubling me. "Can I ask *you* to do something now?" I asked.

She frowned slightly and looked wary, but I bulldozed on relentlessly. "If you're prepared to go and see your father-in-law again, please will you come and see your mother?"

Her eyes narrowed and she looked away, shaking her head. "I told you not to ask me that," she said. Then angrily she blurted out, "I've told you, that woman intercepted a letter I wrote to your father. She was oh-so cunning, replacing my letter with blank paper so that I wouldn't know when I posted it. That act of hers caused every tragic thing that happened afterwards. She's to blame for all my misery."

There was silence for a few moments, before John spoke. His voice was solemn. "Valerie, I think you need to face up to some facts. Your mother was not the one who got pregnant; she was not the one who made the apartheid laws; she was not responsible for Johan being an activist and she was not responsible for his death. In fact quite the contrary, she was the one you turned to for help, and help is what she gave you. You seem to forget the situation you were in and what the consequences would have been. Your mother saved your hide and she tried for years to reach out to you, but you were the one who rejected her. You broke her heart. She isn't a young woman any longer and if you don't come to your senses, you might never have the opportunity to make amends. For God's sake, swallow your stubborn pride. If you believe she opened your letter and made a switch, why don't you at least ask her? You can't know for certain it was her. Perhaps it was the police who intercepted it, or someone else. I agree with Fran. If you can find it in your heart to see Johan's father again, I can't see why you won't agree to put this matter right between you and your mother. She loves you, Valerie."

I nodded. "She does, Mom."

Valerie turned and looked at me. Instead of frowning as I expected her to do, she was staring at me with her mouth open. "What did you just say?" she said.

"I said she loves you."

"No, repeat exactly what you said, please."

I looked puzzled and shook my head. "I don't know what you mean?"

"Your exact words were – *She does, Mom.* That's the first time in my entire life that I've been called Mom."

I blushed and felt confused, suddenly overcome with embarrassment. She was still watching me. I shrugged and said, "Well, I guess you can't deny biology, can you?" Just as she began to smile, I continued my line of argument. "I rest my case. I'm sure your mother would like to be called Mom again too."

The smile froze on her lips and slowly faded. "You don't give up, do you?"

I heard John laugh quietly, before saying, "She takes after her mother. It's definitely biology."

She looked hurt as she spun on me and said, "Did you say that on purpose to trap me?"

I shook my head. "No, I didn't even realize what I'd said. I wouldn't do that." I felt indignant that she would suspect I had ulterior motives and was tempted to retort that if she wanted to continue screwing up her life, she was free to do so without always finding someone else to blame. Suddenly she put her knife and fork down with a clatter and glared at us.

"I'll agree to think about it," she announced.

"Really?" I shouted rather too loudly for the small restaurant we were in. "Will you see her tomorrow?" People turned and looked at us, but I didn't care. I was relieved that I hadn't had another outburst I would have regretted later.

"Fran, I said I'll think about it. You're asking a lot of me," she replied with a determined set to her jaw. "I still have to hand in my notice. Give me a few days to get things sorted out at work. I've got a lot on my plate."

Just at that moment, a waiter arrived with a platter of fish dishes. There was an array of exotic sounding preparations; snoek pâté, kabeljou, kingklip and pickled fish. The waiter beamed with pride as he announced what each dish was, and we all got busy helping ourselves to food. The business of Valerie and Sharon was pushed aside, remaining unresolved.

Chapter 7

My grandmother looked slightly surprised when I told her that I would be meeting my grandfather that afternoon. She disguised it quickly, but I saw a fleeting change in her expression before she swallowed hard and said, "I'm sure he will be as happy to meet you as I have been." She got up quickly and busied herself, looking in a drawer for something that she never found. Finally she turned and looked at me with teary eyes. I knew that she wasn't concerned about sharing me with him; she had realized that Valerie would be visiting the old man, but not her own mother.

"Gran," I said gently, "have patience. We've come this far, we're almost there. Don't give up. I have a feeling you'll be seeing her soon." I put my arms around her and added, "I wasn't going to tell you this, but I think I must warn you. She believes that you intercepted a letter she wrote to my father before she left for California. If you did, you have some answering to do. She says that is what she can never forgive." I hugged her again and turned away. "I'm not asking any questions and I don't want to know whether it's true…"

My voice trailed off before I took a deep breath and turned to look at her once more. "There's something else, though. I can't help wondering whether you interfered with a letter that I sent to my mother, some time back. I sent it to the farm, but it came back, saying she was no longer at that address. Did you do that, Gran? Did you send it back?"

My grandmother's face crumpled and she looked away. Silence hung heavily between us and my eyes smarted. Neither of us could look at one another until I said, "I'm glad you didn't say she was deceased. I probably would never have come to South Africa if you had." And then I added, "But I still find it hard to believe that you didn't want to meet your grandchild."

A terrible moan came from her, disproportionate to the size of her small body. She dropped her head in her hands, as her shoulders began to shake. "I'm so sorry, Fran," she whispered.

****

My mother walked out of KFC for the last time without the red jacket and less of a limp. I watched her climb the hill; by the time she reached the top, the uneven walk was barely discernible. She smiled when she saw me and said, "It's done. I handed in my notice with immediate effect. They weren't happy, but they'll survive. Tons of people are looking for jobs. And I'm very happy, so that balances the equation on the happiness score."

"Well I'm happy too," I added.

It wasn't long before she'd changed into jeans and a T shirt and we headed to Stellenbosch. Just a few days ago, I was there with Joe. Only one more day and he'd be back. I decided there and then that I would go to Victoria Falls with him. Life was becoming simpler, despite the fact that there were still hurdles to jump.

When we arrived in Stellenbosch, I parked the car outside the towering Dutch Reformed Church, the first one built in the area in 1679. My mother left to get directions, and I walked around the church and gardens. It gave me a chill to think that my ancestors might well have worshipped here, looking up at these same stained glass windows. I wished I knew more about them. Had they been slaves, had some woman, one of my forbears, been taken advantage of by a slave owner? Was that my ancestry? I would probably never find out, but sensing I had come back to a place of my ancestors, I knelt in a pew and bowed my head. There, with my eyes closed, I felt at peace in this strange society. I belonged to it.

We drove to the top of Hellshoogte, overlooking the vines of the Drakenstein Valley to the Groot Drakenstein Mountain opposite. The play of light and shade on the rocky crags was dramatic and I knew that the little village of Pniel lay there in the valley, on the way to Franschoek. I had been past here with Joe, without realizing that my grandfather was nearby. I remembered reading that the community had been founded for freed slaves by a missionary in the nineteenth century. Perhaps that answered my question: I was descended from slaves.

We followed a dirt road and stopped outside a white cottage, with a covered verandah outside the front door. An old man sat in a rocking chair, dozing in the warmth of the afternoon sun. Barefoot children, otherwise clad in school uniforms, played outside in the street. They looked at us curiously, smiling and laughing as they spoke in Afrikaans to one another. It was a very different dialect from the Afrikaans I had learned at UCLA and I could barely understand them. They were kicking a ball around in a dusty, makeshift game of soccer and lost interest in us when we climbed the steps to approach the old man.

We stood quietly for a moment and watched before waking him. His hair was white and close-cropped and his skin was the colour of a peanut shell, with the same sun-dried, wrinkled surface. He had a short-cropped white moustache and his mouth was slightly open, emitting gentle snores as he slept. Neatly dressed in a homemade blue sweater, he had a crocheted rug over his legs and woollen slippers on his feet. As we stood watching him, he stirred and opened his eyes. After a moment he turned his head towards us and frowned. He was blind, but despite the unseeing opaqueness of his gaze, he sensed our presence.

My mother stepped forward and said, "It's Valerie here, Johan's wife. I've brought someone to meet you." She took his hands and held them in hers.

His wavery voice said, "Valerie? After all these years?"

"Yes."

"How long has Johan been dead?" he asked.

"Fifteen years," she replied.

"Who is this you are bringing here? Some new husband?"

"No, I have never remarried." I could see the hurt on her face, but she swallowed hard and said, "I'm bringing Johan's child to meet you. You have a granddaughter. Johan and I had a daughter."

He sat bolt upright in his chair. "What kind of nonsense are you telling me now? Am I such an old man that my mind is playing tricks with me?"

"No. We never told you because she was born before we were married. She was adopted by someone else as a new born baby."

"*Magtig!*" (Almighty) he exclaimed involuntarily in Afrikaans. "What in heaven? He rubbed his knees and shook his head. "Suddenly I'm nearly in my grave and I have a granddaughter? Where has she been all these years when I could have seen her, before my eyes stopped doing their job?"

"She was living in America. That was where she was born in 1982, and where she was adopted. She came looking for us and now she has found me. I brought her to see you."

He put his hands out blindly and I moved forward to take them in mine. I knelt down on the concrete floor in front of him and his hands held my head gently. As his fingers played through my hair, I said, "I'm Fran, your granddaughter." Then with tears in my eyes, I repeated it in Afrikaans, "*Ek is Fran, jou kleindogter.*"

He gave a slight grunt. "And where did you learn to speak my language?" he asked.

I laughed and said, "I learned especially for you." I took his hand and kissed it.

"*Magtig,*" he said again and began to cry. "How I would love to see you, but I will just have to listen and make a picture in my

303

mind. You never knew your father, but at least you will know *his* father before he dies. God has given me a great gift. *Magtig.*"

And so I sat and told him about my life and he listened with a smile on his face. He laughed when I told him that I liked to run, and said that he had been a fast runner in his day. "You wouldn't think so to see me now, but I was faster than anybody around. We ran barefoot in those days. We used to train by running up the mountain and down into Stellenbosch."

"That's a long way," I said in admiration.

"*Ja,* well then we turned around and came back again," he laughed. "They used to call me *Boesman,* because I could run endlessly like a Bushman hunting and tracking an animal."

We chatted easily and I described how I had come looking for my parents. I told him how I'd found my mother and talked about her hard life. We were interrupted suddenly by a middle-aged woman, who came out the door and looked at us suspiciously. "What's going on here? Who are these people?" she asked angrily in Afrikaans.

My grandfather beckoned to her and said, "It's alright, Kristina. This is family. It's my granddaughter, Johan's girl."

Kristina threw her hands to her face and began to wail. It was difficult to tell whether it was joy or sorrow, but it was loud and full of emotion. She looked at me finally and sobbed. "I knew that he wasn't totally dead. I knew that he had left something for us that we didn't get." She dropped down on the floor next to me and said, "Poor child, where were you?"

My grandfather replied for me. "In America, Kristina. Now can you get us some coffee, please?"

I smiled as he shook his head. "She's an old friend who looks after me now, but she wants to know everything. What does she mean 'he isn't altogether dead?' What does she think? That you can be a little bit dead? This isn't her business anyway. This is time for you and me."

We laughed and chatted and forgot that my mother was there. She sat listening to us, without interrupting. I wondered for a moment what was going through her head. Suddenly the old man stopped and said, "Is your mother still here?"

"I'm here," she replied quietly.

"I just want to tell you that I'm sorry, Valerie. I'm sorry for us both. We loved that boy of mine. He was a good man. He was so clever. It made poor Roelie jealous that Johan got everything he wanted; he didn't realize how hard his brother worked for things. I can't complain about Roelie though, because he has looked after me in my old age. But I think now he will be jealous again when he hears that Johan had a child. He and his wife are as barren as the Karoo.

"Johan died so young and he had so much promise. It was a tragedy. But I can tell your life has been hard too. We were angry with you because we thought you had taken him away from us. Now I know that... it wasn't your fault." At a loss for words in

English, he had to speak intermittently in his native Afrikaans. "It was worse for you. You lost everything, not just Johan. I know now that you didn't take him, he gave himself to you and you had his child. And then you lost his child. This country was bad; there was no place for love like yours."

I turned and looked at my mother. She stared at the old man with tears in her eyes, as she said, "I'm sorry for you too, It's hard to lose a child, I know that."

"But now we have Fran," he said. "*Magtig*. If only my wife had lived to meet you. *Ag*, she was the sweetest woman. My little wife, she was a brave one. She understood that it was hard to marry without your parents' blessings. She was a Muslim, you see. Her parents never forgave her for marrying a Christian, and they never spoke to her again. What sort of love is that? How can you be like that and not care about your child? Not even once did they contact her, not once. If they had tried, she would have been so happy. She was a good daughter, as well as a good wife and mother. She went to visit them once when Johan was born, but they slammed the door in her face. She cried for days.

"But she always told me it was hard for Johan and Valerie. She was right. I was too proud. I know she used to send parcels and things when you lived in London. I was so angry that I told her she was wasting her time. She ignored me and just used to say that love always wins."

My mother was clearly moved. "I didn't know all that," she said. "Johan loved his mother very much. That was why he came back to South Africa when he heard she was ill. The Special Branch knew he would return and they were waiting. He was making his way to Cape Town, to see her, when they killed him."

The old man covered his face in his hands and wept. It was hard to see his pain and I felt powerless to ease it. Time had clearly not dulled it. At length he put a teary hand on my bare shoulder and patted me gently. "But we have you," he said. "God has given me this chance before I die. My wife was right; love always wins, that's what she said. I can hear her now, 'Say sorry and forgive and just love without questions.' Thank you, God, for bringing this child to me. I love you both and no more questions," he said, facing in the direction of my mother, all the while patting my shoulder. "It's never too late for love. Learn this lesson, otherwise your soul will dry up like *biltong* and you'll sit in your old age with so many regrets that your heart will break." He sighed and, with a choking voice, whispered, "Forgive me, Valerie. You are my son's wife and I should have helped you. You are my daughter, you are family."

We were interrupted as Kristina pushed open the door and emerged with a big tray, carrying china cups and saucers, a coffee pot, milk, sugar and a plate of plaited pastries that glistened with sticky wetness. She'd removed her scarf, replacing it with a large, black hat to which she'd added a bright flower. Smiling brightly, she said, "Sorry about just now. I didn't know who you were." Placing the tray on a table, she giggled nervously and pointed to the pastries. "They're *koeksusters*. My friend makes them." She smiled again and served the coffee and pastries, before returning inside. Her hand was held firmly to her hat, preventing it from slipping when the wide brim bumped against the wall.

"I suppose she's got her hat on," remarked the old man. "That's her hat for church, but whenever I have visitors, she likes to wear it." He chuckled and said, "Sometimes it's not so bad being blind." My mother and I laughed spontaneously at his dry humor and he looked pleased with himself. "She has a good heart old Kristina, but not much up here," he added, tapping his head.

It seemed impolite not to try the strange-looking *koeksusters*. Nothing could have prepared me for the taste. The first bite exploded with syrupy sweetness in my mouth and was surprisingly delicious, despite its odd appearance. The coffee, too, was strong, tasty and aromatic. Nobody in Pniel worried about calories or caffeine, it would seem.

The tray, set with good china, seemed a world apart from the dusty street outside. I was curious to see the inside of the house and had the opportunity to explore when I asked to use the bathroom. The interior was small; there was a living room adjacent to the kitchen, with a bedroom and bathroom leading off the kitchen. Someone slept in the living room, and I presumed that my grandfather slept in the bedroom. Everything was clean, comfortable and tidy, but the furniture was sparse, with no carpets on the concrete floor. Kristina was leaning over the bottom half of the stable door in the kitchen, talking to another woman who was taking washing off a line. She turned to me and said, "Do you like the *koeksusters*?"

I nodded and said, "Yes, thanks. They were great."

She turned and repeated this to the other woman, who clapped her hands and laughed. I noticed that both women were missing their front teeth. I could hear them conversing loudly while I was in the bathroom, and they were still talking when I emerged a few minutes later. Kristina explained that the woman was her friend who had made the pastries, adding that she was the best baker in Pniel. I thanked her again and waved, leaving them to continue their discussion about my origins, and the fact that I liked *koeksusters*. This seemed all the proof necessary for them that I had returned to my roots.

We said goodbye to the old man with promises to come again soon. He held my hands firmly, then lifted them to his face and kissed them. He didn't speak anymore, but took a pipe from his top pocket and lit it. As we walked away, he began to rock in his chair, sucking hard on the pipe.

My mother and I hardly spoke at all, each of us deep in thought as we drove back over Hellshoogte and headed home. Once out of the traffic of Stellenbosch, however, I ventured to ask whether my father was Muslim or Christian. "He wasn't either," my mother responded. "He was a spiritual man, and ethical, but I never knew him go to a church or a mosque. And he never talked about religion at all. I think I understand why, after listening to his father this afternoon."

"But his father sounded very religious. He kept talking about the Almighty."

"Mm," my mother murmured. "It sounded to me like he's had a grudge against his God for a long time. I think he might only have settled his differences when you walked into his life this afternoon."

"That's a big responsibility put on me."

"No, not really. He asks nothing of you. But you know, where there is life there is hope. You are life and you've given him hope, Fran. He's a wise old man and a humble one. And he's big enough to see when he was wrong. That's not always an easy thing to do."

My grandfather had said much that went to the heart of my mother's issues with her mother. I wondered whether she was thinking the same thing, as we continued in silence. She appeared deep in thought. My question was answered as I dropped her off in Vredehoek. Just before I drove away, she turned to me and said, "Fran, will you bring your grandmother here tomorrow morning for tea?"

I was stunned and my head spun around to look at her. We stared at one another for a few seconds, without saying a word. At length, I nodded.

"I'll see you at eleven o' clock, then."

I nodded again and felt a chill run down my spine.

Chapter 8

I awoke early the next morning when my phone rang. It was Joe. "Hi there," he greeted me. "Wake up sleepy head."

"Joe," I murmured, as my brain tried to register. I looked at the clock and saw it was only 6.45 a.m. "Why are you calling me so early? Is something wrong?"

"No, I'm heading off to George with the guys and I wanted to call you before we leave."

"George? That's north from where you are. You're going in the wrong direction for Cape Town," I said with alarm.

"Yeah, I know. There's been a change of plan that I want to run by you."

"What?"

"We've decided it's too far to drive to Vic Falls from here and everyone would rather fly. So we're heading to George airport. It's closer than Cape Town and we can get lots of flights from there to Johannesburg. But here's the thing. I've run out of money. So after this, I'm going to pack up and go home. Are you going to get to Vic Falls? Can you meet me in Johannesburg today?"

"No, I definitely cannot meet you there today! I've got important stuff going on here. You were supposed to be coming back to Cape Town today."

"I know, sorry about that. How soon can you get away?"

"Day after tomorrow at the earliest, maybe even the day after that."

"Well, I might not be able to stay at Vic Falls that long. I need to get home for Christmas."

"You're going home for Christmas?" I was stunned.

"I have to. I told you, my money's running out."

"We've had an invitation to go to the farm in Ixopo for Christmas. That wouldn't cost you anything and you'd get the money back when you sell your car. We could just use my car."

He laughed. "Fran, the trip to Vic Falls will use the money from my car! How else do you think I can manage?"

"Well still, Christmas in Ixopo would be free."

"We can discuss it later, but if you want to see Vic Falls, you'd better plan to get there fast."

"Oh forget it," I muttered. I didn't bother to hide my disappointment. "I can't hurry what I'm doing. I'll just see you back in Durban. The Victoria Falls will still be there for a while."

312

He ignored my barb. "I can't wait to see you again, Fran," he said. "See you in Durban."

The line went dead and I sat holding the phone in my hand, feeling close to tears.

****

My thoughts of all this were banished as I drove my grandmother to the momentous meeting with her daughter, my biological mother. Gran had been shocked into silence when I announced Valerie's invitation. She stared at me and visibly paled, before grabbing hold of a chair and sinking into it. I was afraid she would faint; the blood looked like it was draining from her face. As I ran and steadied her, she continued staring at me in silence. Finally, she wordlessly resigned herself to her fate, like a lamb to the slaughter, and agreed to go.

She was a long time getting dressed. When she emerged from her room, her face looked drawn and for the first time I noticed two deep furroughs that turned her mouth down. She had been wearing a dark blue skirt and a white blouse. Around her neck she wore a string of pearls. She touched them briefly and said to me apologetically, "I know I shouldn't wear these before noon, but I'm wearing them for luck. My mother gave them to me when I got married." Other than that, she showed no emotion.

We drove in silence all the way, but as I parked the car outside Valerie's flat, Gran said very softly, "Please come in with me, Fran." She clutched my arm nervously.

I put my hand on hers to reassure her. "Of course," I replied. "I'm going to be with you all the time."

I knew we were being watched as we approached. Sure enough, my mother opened the bottom door before we even had a chance to press the buzzer. Likewise, the front door opened as we neared it, and she stood there in denims and a white blouse, with pearls around her neck. Was this a good omen? The silence seemed long and protracted as they stared at each other. At length, Valerie stood aside and said, "Please come in."

I followed my Gran with my arm gently behind her, supporting her. As soon as the door closed, she said, "Valerie, I'm sorry. I did a terrible thing. I have no excuse other than I thought it was for the best. There was a letter, all those years ago; I had no right to do it, but I removed it from the envelope before you posted it. I should have trusted you – I'm sorry. Please forgive me. I know that you've suffered. We all suffered."

I could see her swallow hard and then she began to search in her bag for a tissue. I led her to a chair and said, "Sit down, Gran."

My mother watched silently, but I saw that she was fingering her pearls as if they were rosary beads. Her face was like steel. Finally, she said in a hoarse whisper, "Why? Why did you do such a thing?"

Gran blew her nose softly. "It was an impossible situation, Valerie, and all my concerns were for you. I never met Fran's father and knew nothing about him. All I knew was that you were pregnant. You couldn't have the baby in South Africa and remain in the country. You were in grave danger of being sent to prison if anyone found out. You know that dreadful *Immorality Act* would have sent you straight there. All I could think was that I needed to protect my child. I did it to protect you, Valerie. I didn't want anyone to trace you."

"You didn't want Johan to trace me."

My grandmother nodded. "Yes. I wanted to protect you."

"Protect me from the man I loved? The man whose child I was going to have?"

Gran nodded again. "You never trusted me enough to introduce the man you loved. If I had known all the circumstances, I might have been less afraid for you. I would have done everything to help you both start a life abroad, I know I would have. You could both have moved to the United States and had your baby there. But you never gave me the opportunity to support you. I could only try to protect you from disaster."

Valerie sat down in the other chair and stared at her mother with a steely gaze. Finally she said, "Are you trying to tell me that you would have accepted Johan?"

"If you loved him and he loved you, then I would have," Gran answered.

"Really? You would have accepted a coloured son-in-law into your comfortable, respectable, white home? You would just have opened your arms to him?"

"If you had introduced us and I had got to know him, yes. If you'd given me the chance...." Gran's voice trailed off.

My mother continued staring at her. "I don't believe you," she said finally. "You say this now that he's dead, believing that your word can never be tested. It's revisionist history on your part. You and Dad couldn't accept it, you know that."

Gran sighed. "I can't speak for your father, Valerie; I can only speak for myself. If you don't believe me, there is nothing I can do about that. The love I have for you is such that I would have moved heaven and earth to help you. I did the best I could in the circumstances. I've tried to reach out to you, but you always turned me away – until now. I don't know what more I can say, but I'm thankful that you've given me the opportunity to see you again and apologize. I have never stopped loving you."

My mother was visibly moved and as I studied her face, a strange look came over her. "Come with me to visit Johan's father then," she said sharply, showing no emotion. "Can you bring yourself to visit a coloured man, in his coloured home? Will your white skin be able to stand that?"

I cringed at my mother's words and immediately felt a desire to defend my grandmother. She had shown me only love and kindness, even though I would be defined 'coloured' by the old system. I had never been classified by anything in my life and I resented my mother's obsession with this race issue. It felt as if she was stuck in the past, without noticing that South Africa had changed, along with people's attitudes. However, I refrained from expressing my views, for I was on the sideline of something that was strictly between them. I needed to stay out of it. There were scores to be settled and they were being played out before my eyes.

Gran frowned. I knew my mother was testing her. The tension in the room grew as they stared at each other, each one aware of the weight the answer would carry. I got up and put the kettle on to make tea, unable to stand the strain. Would my grandmother agree to visit an old coloured man, with whom she shared a granddaughter? Accepting me had been easy for her, but would she accept my ancestry as well? I knew exactly why my mother was testing her and I prayed silently that good sense would prevail.

I heard her clear her throat and when I looked around, I saw her swallow hard. "We have a great common bond. Yes, of course I'll visit him," she said.

****

I stood silently, watching the tableau of these three people with whom I shared genetic history. Oupa sat blindly in his chair, rocking and nodding his head; my grandmother stood stiffly aside; my mother, with her usual defiant tilt of the head, made introductions. For a moment they all seemed frozen in time, as if each was thinking of the terrible road they had travelled to this place. Then suddenly my grandmother relaxed her stance and moved towards the old man seated in front of her.

"I'm afraid I don't speak Afrikaans," she said, "but I believe you can speak English."

He turned his head towards her and nodded again. "Yes," he said gruffly.

My mother watched her mother with narrowed eyes. Gran took Oupa's hand and said, "What a strange world we lived in. We have a wonderful granddaughter, yet we've never met her until now. And we've never met each other."

"*Ja*," he agreed. "*Mevrou*" (Mrs.) Spencer, I think we can blame apartheid only so much. We must also blame ourselves." He put his other hand on top of hers and patted it. "I know I was mad at my son and your daughter. I didn't know that they had a child; I didn't know how much they loved each other. I just thought to myself – how can they do this thing? I thought they were bloody stupid and defiant. That's what I always thought – they wanted to break the rules to prove a point, and it went and got my boy killed."

"They were bad rules," Gran said softly. "I'm very sorry about your son. We're not meant to outlive our children; that's a hard thing to accept."

"It was so hard," he said. "My boy... he died and I didn't tell him I still loved him, even though I hated him leaving our country. I was so angry and then it was too late. I lost him. They killed him.

"I'm ashamed because I hated Valerie for that. For a long time I hated her because she was white." He lowered his head. "But I suppose at least they didn't kill her because she was white," he said at length. "At least they didn't do that. Her white skin saved her."

"I understand your feelings, Mr. Barnard," Gran replied. "I came to this country as a foreigner and I was shocked by the strange system. But there wasn't much I could do to change it, so I simply lived with the system. Maybe I lacked moral fibre, maybe we all lacked it. Those who tried to do something, got into trouble with the police. Our children were very brave – and they were right. We were the ones who were wrong. I was wrong to sit comfortably in my white world and ignore the hardships of everyone else."

"Apartheid made good people bad, just because they did nothing. But I know it was hard for you too. Those bastards made life difficult for white people too."

"That's exactly it. Our silence made us just as bad as the system. And they certainly made Valerie's life difficult," Gran acknowledged. "She had to give up her baby, our granddaughter. Those laws meant mother and child couldn't live together, because one was white and the other wasn't."

He shook his head. *"Ja,* it was bloody cruel."

Suddenly I couldn't stop myself and blurted out, "They did much more to her than that. It wasn't just that she gave me up. They physically tortured her for loving my father. They did terrible things to her."

My grandparents spun around and stared at me, as my mother remonstrated, "No, Fran. I told you that in confidence. How can you break a confidence?"

Very calmly I replied, "I won't say more than that. You can choose to tell the whole story or not. But I've seen the scars. You are brave and I'm proud of you. The police tried to break your spirit by breaking your body. You didn't get off easily just because you are white. The regime made you pay dearly for breaking their rules."

My grandmother gasped and dropped Oupa's hands, running to her daughter's side. Without hesitation she put her arms around Valerie, cradling her like a child. My mother didn't resist. She buried her head in her mother's shoulder and whispered something. Gran held her even closer and softly kissed her daughter's head.

I gazed at them in wonder, feeling a smile spread across my face even as tears welled in my eyes. A picture sprang to mind of my mother Grace, sitting me on her lap, predicting that one day I would understand what 'happy tears' were. This afternoon she was right.

Chapter 9

I sank into my seat on the flight back to Durban, closed my eyes, and thought how different everything was since I'd arrived in South Africa, six months ago. My quest was over. I'd found my biological family and understood their stories. My grandmother had transformed from somebody whose life was merely a journey to the grave, into a bright, positive force. My biological mother had finally allowed herself to let go of her miserable past, and move forward with hope. And then there was Oupa; I hadn't expected to meet him, but he had been the catalyst that sparked the reconciliation with his confession about prejudice and remorse. He had bared his soul to us with touching honesty. All four of us had finally come to terms with the past.

I was on my way to see Joe and I felt giddy once again. It was time to pack up our belongings in Durban, before travelling back to San Francisco together. The pleasure of seeing him made me forget my disappointment about Victoria Falls and our earlier argument. I couldn't stay mad with him.

He refused the offer of Christmas in Ixopo; he wanted to get home. I decided that it would be a good time for me to leave as well. I had a longing to be home again and, despite the fact that I hadn't seen all I wanted of South Africa in the past six months, I vowed to return. This continent had worked its way into my soul. Perhaps I might live and work here for a while, doing volunteer work with the Peace Corps, or Habitat for Humanity. My contribution at the Durban orphanage had been regrettably small, as I'd been pre-occupied with my own agenda. It made me determined to return and do a better job. Maybe Joe would return as well.

My stay in Durban was quick. Lizzie and Brett had already gone and I left ahead of Joe. I wanted to say goodbye to my mother and grandmother in Johannesburg. They appeared to have reached an understanding, learning to forgive as they spent time together. I was relieved that they both wished to do so, at last.

Gran's home seemed a different place from the one I had visited earlier. It was hard to pinpoint the difference until it dawned on me that there was music in the house, and there were parcels and newspapers strewn across the couch. People were living here. My mother was singing *The Long and Winding Road,* along with the Beatles, and Gran's mouth was turned up in a smile. There was life in the place.

Lunch was a variety of Cape Malay dishes. My mother made no comment, but was appreciative when I remarked how much I enjoyed the food. The significance of this meal did not go unnoticed; it was the first she had ever cooked for me, and she had chosen to honour my father's heritage. My grandmother's contribution was a bowl of her signature white roses on the table. The scent filled the room and forever afterwards, when I smell roses, my thoughts return to that moment.

I dreaded breaking the news about my imminent departure to them and waited until lunch was over. However, when I explained that I would be returning to California for Christmas, their disappointment was tempered with understanding. Valerie took my hand and said, "Come and sit with me a moment. I want to tell you something that I've been thinking about a lot." My grandmother smiled as she left the room quietly, leaving us alone.

When we were settled on the couch, my mother put her hands on my shoulders and looked at me. "You can never have enough people who love you, Fran. I loved you for nine months before you were born, and I never stopped loving you. I know it's not a competition about who loves you most, but I do win the prize for loving you the longest." She laughed and looked down for a second. When she looked up she was smiling with tears in her eyes. It was sunshine and rain. "Hardly a day went by that I didn't think of you," she continued. "Your birthdays were the hardest, remembering that another year had gone by without you. But the Walkers loved you just as much as I did, of that I'm sure.

"What I want to say is this; you need never feel that you have to choose one mother over the other. You don't. You're the lucky one with two mothers who love you, and you can love us both in return. I hope I'm not being presumptuous when I harbour hopes that you will come to love me in time.

"We lost twenty years of our lives together, but we have the rest of our lives to catch up. You must go back to your life, I know that. You see, we have found each other and this is just the beginning of a story, not the end." She looked down at her hands, to regain her composure. I remained silent, too choked up to speak.

"Thank you for coming to find me, and thank you for rescuing me from myself!" she said at length. "I'm very proud of you – and I know your father would have been too." She squeezed my hands and looked intently at me. "I'm sorry you won't be with us for Christmas, but I understand that you have to go. Now that we have found each other again, saying goodbye is not forever – it's just until we meet again."

I burst into tears. She had put into words what had been bothering me, except that I wasn't able to express it. As she encircled me in her arms, I felt my anguish ebbing away. I was at peace. When I stopped crying, we sat holding hands for a while, saying nothing. I imagine she was thinking much the same as I was, wondering what it would have been like if things had been different and I had grown up with her.

That maternal embrace felt good and I knew that there would have been a lot of love from her. But I had received plenty of love from Grace Walker – despite venting a lot of anger on her. I had spent my life thus far, trapped in a cage of my own making. I had created a labyrinth of questions that prevented me seeing further, because I always returned to the same point; who was I?

Now, free of those limiting constraints, I was at peace. I understood that I was a product of everything that had gone into my making, and I was happy being me. My life was not only the sum total of my choices, it was the sum total of all my parents' choices, too. I had grown up oblivious of racial prejudice, loved, supported, and educated in fine institutions. I was Francesca Walker from California, with South African roots.

My eyes turned to the oil painting that my grandmother had shown me on the first day I'd met her. From across the room, the paint strokes blended harmoniously and I could see the picture clearly. It all made sense.

PART 6

GRACE

No, I didn't give you
the gift of life....
Life gave me the gift of you.

- AUTHOR UNKNOWN

Chapter 1

I longed for Fran's return from the moment we left her behind in Durban. She seemed so vulnerable. I longed to scoop her up and hold her close, but I knew I had to step back and let my daughter spread her wings.

Life is strange. When I first knew that I would never be able to have children, I resisted adoption. I worried that I wouldn't be able to love a child enough if I hadn't borne it myself. How wrong I was. I loved Fran from the first moment I held her, but I often worried that she might not love me enough. That's why I wanted to keep holding onto her when we left her in South Africa; I knew she was looking for that other mother and I was afraid she might not come back to me.

Robert and I drove to San Francisco airport in a rainstorm. After the long, dry summer, early winter storms are enthralling in California. Mother Nature flexes her muscle, unleashing heavy downpours and plummeting temperatures. But, while much else goes dormant, the hills revive. They turn green almost overnight as they take on new life. It was fitting that Fran was returning in the rain.

We were surprised when she called from Johannesburg and announced she would be home for Christmas. I'd resigned myself to her staying in South Africa for the holiday, especially once she'd found her birth mother. It was that terrible fear that plagued me always: she would find her biological parents and I would lose her. It was irrational, as many fears are, but it has been my nightmare since the day we told her that she was adopted. I remember that day well. We brought Billy home and explained to Fran that she had also been adopted by us when she was a baby. I told her that we were lucky because we *chose* her and Billy. She seemed to accept that explanation, but occasionally she would ask odd questions about 'the woman who had babies and gave them to us.'

I suppose I didn't really explain too well, but what do you say to a four year old? I couldn't tell her of the anguish we experienced as I suffered one miscarriage after another; I couldn't tell her of the humiliating infertility counselling we'd endured – all to no avail; I couldn't tell her of the despair when I finally realized that I would never have a baby of my own – my body had let me down; I couldn't tell her how long it took me to accept that realization, before I could contemplate adopting someone else's baby. It was so final, like admitting defeat. I was angry; I couldn't bear to see a pregnant woman, or a baby, as it reminded me of my own loss. I felt cheated.

But I could tell her of the joy on the day she arrived in our lives. She was the prettiest baby, born with a full head of dark hair that soon fell out. She settled into our lives happily and brought us great joy as she grew up, although I have always felt anxious about Fran. Billy was uncomplicated and accepting, but she was different. From a young age she had dark moods; it was difficult to deal with them. There were moments when, I'm ashamed to admit, I wondered why I had taken her on. I wouldn't really have had it otherwise, but there were times when I resented bearing the brunt of her moodiness. Yet through it all, I felt overwhelming love and responsibility for her. She was my daughter.

For the first six months of her life we lived in dread that her birth mother would return and claim her; we'd heard that it happened. I thought about her birth parents and wondered how they were coping. Our joy was their sorrow. I knew very little about them except that they were unmarried and came from South Africa. There were some American relations, which is how Fran came to be born here. I felt somewhat reassured, because her biological parents were so far away that it would be difficult for them to reclaim their daughter. But a phone call would be all it needed to take our baby girl away again. I couldn't bear the thought.

When Billy arrived, I was much more confident, having been through the experience once before. And Billy didn't spend much time thinking about things, he was too busy *doing* things. Fran was a thinker and I wasn't ever sure what was going on in her head. I remember once when we were in the park; Billy was a baby and Fran was playing nearby, when she suddenly ran to me, sobbing. She said something about a woman taking her away. I couldn't understand it, but she clung to me desperately. For days she didn't leave my side. I don't know what frightened her, as nothing untoward happened other than there was a woman looking for her dog. I think my little girl had some issues going on about strangers. All I could do was keep her close to me.

I remember also when Fran had her first period. I cursed myself for not having prepared her. She was afraid that she was sick. It was negligent of me not telling her about such things, but I've always been a procrastinator. It was about then that she no longer wanted me to call her Frannie because it was a baby name. I wanted to say that it was a term of endearment, but she was embarrassed and it was easier just to call her Fran. Those adolescent years had their moments. Once she flew into a rage and told me that it took more to be a mother than simply feeding her. That really frightened me, even though I stood my ground. It was undeserved criticism; I had done my best for her at all times and it struck me that being a mother is often painful. You're expected to be resilient enough to endure ingratitude, as if mothers are not supposed to get hurt feelings. I suppose mothers have to learn to listen to the sentiment rather than the words. I knew it wasn't meant as warfare, but a way of voicing her frustrations.

I was touched that she remembered too. She apologized on the phone when she was in South Africa. That meant a lot. But had she found me lacking at the time? Was she desperate to find her biological mother because she thought I was inadequate? I felt sorry for her, knowing how she agonized over it all. She didn't say anything and I never found an opening to talk to her about it. She kept everything bottled up inside, which is why she was moody. Sometimes the turmoil was overwhelming. I had to remind myself about that, and realize that my own experience growing up was different. I never had to question my origins; the parents who raised me were the ones who had given birth to me. These were uncharted waters for both Fran and me, and we simply had to do the best we could.

I remember the moment she asked for her birth certificate. Her rage was frightening that our names were on it, rather than her birth parents'. Robert dealt with that situation well. She seemed

332

appeased when he told her the little we knew about them, but I was sure that we hadn't heard the end of it. Strangely, she never spoke about it again and there seemed to be a fence that went up between us. I didn't ask questions because I respected her privacy.

It took me some time to get used to her being away from home when she went to college. I missed her and worried about her, but we spoke often on the phone and I drove down to Los Angeles every couple of months to see her. I remember wanting to feel her close and going into her bedroom at home. All I felt was her absence. Maybe I was unsure of her love for me, afraid that I had lost her. I desperately wanted her back again.

I suspected she was on a quest to find her biological parents, and when she announced that she wanted to study abroad in South Africa during her junior year, I knew I was right. My heart was very heavy, filled with dread for myself and for her. What if her discovery was painful? There had to be good reasons why she had been given up for adoption, and those reasons might be better left unknown. You have to be careful what you wish for. I didn't know how far she'd got in her search, but I sensed the result would be inevitable. Fran is a very determined young woman.

Was determination an inherent characteristic, or had she learned it from us? She could be determined to the point of stubborn at times. We weren't like that, and Billy wasn't either. Maybe her biological parents were responsible for that trait. There were moments when I had irrational fears that perhaps some illness had been passed on to her that might manifest in later years, like schizophrenia. There was no basis for my fear, but that didn't stop it manifesting itself. When she had temper tantrums that were probably quite normal, I immediately had a nagging concern that perhaps one of her parents was a psychopath. The unknown always lurked in the background, waiting to pounce. I'm not surprised that she needed to find out more, because I felt the same uncertainty, except I also felt threatened by the possibility that they would take her away from us. And there were other concerns for her. What would have happened if she'd found them and they'd been criminals, or drug addicts? It turned out my fears were justified, because the father's associations with terrorism clearly unnerved her. I was thankful that she finally spoke to me about these things on the phone. My reassurance seemed to help her. I wished I could have been there with her, but I suppose it was something she needed to do on her own.

When she told me that she had met Valerie Spencer, I was consumed with jealousy. Never in my life had I felt such tumultuous feelings. I had done the real work of motherhood, raising a decent human being, and suddenly this woman was moving into my space, without any contribution other than being pregnant for nine months and giving birth. Did she think that was enough to make you a mother? I was irate and wanted to shout out about the injustice of it. Fortunately, common sense and natural reserve made me bite my tongue. If I had expressed my real feelings, I'm sure Fran would have been unable to cope with additional stress. She was teetering on the edge herself; I needed to be her anchor.

I think that I provided a safe haven for her and consequently she told me about the young man she'd met. Fran is a beautiful girl, very exotic, and there has never been a shortage of male admirers. She'd never met anyone who made her heart skip a beat for more than a couple of days, though. I seemed to spend a lot of time taking phone messages when she lost interest in suitors. But when she spoke about Joe on the phone, he seemed to have something about him that kept her coming back. I wondered how long it would be before I met him, or if he'd last.

My rambling thoughts were interrupted by Robert. "Did I tell you that Josie called the other day, before we knew when Fran was coming home?"

"No, you didn't mention it. What did she want?"

"She said she hadn't heard from Fran for ages and wondered if everything was alright. She asked when Fran was coming home and I said she might be staying in South Africa for Christmas, with family. There was an awkward silence for a moment before she said, 'I didn't know you had family there.' I told her that it was Fran's biological mother. She was stunned; she had no idea that Fran was adopted. Isn't that amazing? Those two were as thick as thieves, yet Fran never told her. It was a secret she kept all to herself."

I watched rain bouncing off the window as I thought about this information. It made sense and I wasn't at all surprised. "Don't you see that Fran couldn't speak about it to anybody, not even us? It was too close to her heart to let anyone trample on it."

Robert glanced at me and smiled. "Are you sure you didn't give birth to her yourself, Grace? You two think alike at times." Then he added, "You even look a bit alike, with your dark hair and long legs. She could be your daughter. "

"She *is* my daughter," I said. Laughing, I added, "Poor Fran, they say that people grow to look like their dogs after a while. Well, she's grown to look like me instead!"

"I don't know whether you're fishing for compliments or not, but I would say she'd be happy to look like you. I'm very pleased, anyway."

His words were an antidote to a thought that had plagued me; what did her birth mother look like? I'd stared at many women in South Africa who looked the appropriate age, wondering if they could be "her." It was crazy, but I couldn't help myself.

Robert had also been lost in thought, but he suddenly began speaking again. "I hope Fran can get on with her life now that she's found this woman, and also that she knows about her biological father's death. I feel as if she's been marking time for too long."

"You say that with such feeling and authority. How long have you known that she was looking for them?"

"A few years back I discovered some notes she'd left on my desk by mistake. It was just after she'd asked for her birth certificate. She'd been doing some searches online."

"Why didn't you tell me?"

"I didn't want to upset you, Grace. I felt bad enough myself."

I reached over and touched his arm. "We are a pair of fools, aren't we?" I said. "There we were, worrying about the same things, and not saying a word to one another. And not speaking to Fran about it either."

"Hindsight is a wonderful thing. The bottom line was that we were both afraid she would want to be with them when she found them. We didn't trust her, or ourselves, enough," he said.

"I suppose so, but now she's coming back. We can't be too bad after all," I laughed.

"Maybe she'll find us very dull after all the excitement she's had, especially with this boyfriend." We looked at one another and I shrugged.

"My hope is that she's found peace of mind. You and I had unspoken fears, but she had unspoken questions, lots of them. She had to go and find the answers. Now she's found what she was looking for, for better or worse. She knows how she fits into the scheme of things and how we fit into her life as well. We'll just have to hope for the best."

Robert nodded thoughtfully and then said, "I guess it gets back to the old nature/nurture question. She's found her natural mother and her genetic roots, but let's pray that the nurture we provided has given her roots here."

"Time will tell," I murmured.

****

There was plenty of time to park the car and make our way to the Arrivals Hall. Here we positioned ourselves in a good spot to see Fran on the CCTV screen the moment she exited immigration. She would enter a long passage and we'd be able to see her on the screen before she emerged into Arrivals. I didn't know how I could get through the next few minutes. Her plane had arrived, according to the information board, but passengers were still going through customs. We waited patiently, catching our breath every time another person appeared on the screen. The area was congested and, amidst the chaos, it didn't seem possible any more passengers could be left to disembark.

Suddenly she appeared on the screen and I shrieked; there she was, looking tired but happy. Overwhelmed with love and pride in that instant of seeing her again, I felt privileged to be the woman who had raised her. She was glowing as she walked with a good-looking young man, who looked equally tired and happy. The way they walked next to each other made it evident that they were a couple. Suddenly he put his arm around her and said something. She turned to him and as we watched, they dropped their bags to embrace.

They obviously thought they were alone in the passage, unaware they were being watched on camera by everyone in the Arrivals Hall. I felt myself blushing as they kissed passionately. People around us noticed and began to laugh. Robert cleared his throat and we turned to look at one another. He smiled and his eye brows shot up; I shrugged. Just then another late straggler entered the passage behind them and Fran quickly drew apart from her young man. They stood smiling at one another a moment longer, before retrieving their bags and proceeding to the exit.

I watched the screen until they emerged through the double doors, feeling as if I was about to explode with excitement. Oblivious of anyone else, I rushed forward, calling her name above the buzz of surrounding voices. Fran stumbled over her suitcase as she ran to meet me.

Clinging to each other, we hugged wordlessly until at length she murmured, "It's good to be home."

There was nothing I could say that could express my emotions when she said that. With tears in my eyes, I smiled as I remembered a small girl, sitting on my lap, asking about sunshine and rain. So many years had passed since those days and here she was in my embrace once more; she had found her way back to me. When we drew apart, her face was moist too. As she wiped her eyes, she smiled at me and whispered - so softly that I strained to hear, "They're happy tears, Mom.

GLYNNIS HAYWARD

THE END

GLYNNIS HAYWARD

Glynnis Hayward is an award-winning essayist and novelist. Born in South Africa, she was educated there and in Zimbabwe. After graduating from the University of Natal (later renamed KwaZulu-Natal), she taught English in her native South Africa, as well as in London and California. She now lives in the San Francisco Bay Area.

Other novels by Glynnis Hayward:

A TELLING TIME

A SIGNIFICANT TEST OF BLOOD

(You can read about Lauren Marlowe's abduction
and assault, her work and her love affair, in
A SIGNIFICANT TEST OF BLOOD.)

Lightning Source UK Ltd.
Milton Keynes UK
UKOW04f1354290913

218127UK00001B/34/P